R

IN THE FIELD

An addictive crime mystery full of twists

ROY LEWIS

Arnold Landon Mysteries Book 11

Originally published as
Angel of Death

JOFFE BOOKS

Revised edition 2021
Joffe Books, London
www.joffebooks.com

First published in Great Britain in 1995
as *Angel of Death*

ISBN: 978-1-80405-050-7

NOTE TO THE READER

Please note this book is set in the 1990s in England, a time before mobile phones and ubiquitous CCTV, and when social attitudes were very different.

PROLOGUE

The last breath whispered raggedly from his chest as lines of dawn light sent shafts of gold across the lowering, cloud-shrouded hills.

The ceremonies had already been discussed with the shamans for some days, ever since Volcas had been brought back to the camp with the dark blood bubbling in his mouth. It had been a great victory, on the mountain above the lake, but the final outcome had been devastating.

In the days before the expedition, the shamans had told Volcas it would be a magnificent triumph. They had sung their songs to the gods and reiterated what every warrior already knew — the soul did not perish after death but merely passed from one body to another. War and death were one. Battle was the warrior's way to attain the underworld, but death did not mean he lost his foothold in the terrestrial world — his soul passed to another warrior deemed worthy to receive it. And all who died in this coming battle would be loved by the war gods.

So they had marched and ridden out with exultation, and among the trees, on the dark hills above the lake, they had found their enemies. Volcas had led the charge with his great bronze boar shield and his flailing axe. They followed him as though he were a god himself, and perhaps he was that day for the enemy had fallen before him like ripe corn as he had swept his way down the hill, roaring in blood lust, up to the gates of the enemy encampment.

The slaughter had been great. Many slaves had been taken, there had been a wild wailing of women, and the fires had blazed to the heavens when they had entered the village and sacked it.

For two days they had remained there, eating, drinking, using the women, selecting the strong for slaves, slaughtering the young and infirm. They dug a great pit to celebrate the victory, and into it they piled a vast array of weapons, ritually broken — spears, shields, swords, axes, helmets — a tribute to the gods. Into the pit, Volcas had cast his own sword and his helmet, the boar crest, his talismanic war symbol. He had proclaimed himself as a great chieftain, and he saluted the gods for their support.

A shaft of evening sunlight had glowed on the darkening hill beyond them, as though in recognition of the dead.

But who could know what the gods intended? Who could ever know?

On the third day, careless, exhausted, and laden with booty and slaves, they began their march back across the hills, homeward. As they approached the treeline where they had fought the final stages of their great battle the noise of their approach caused great flocks of ravens to fly upwards, their harsh cries tearing raggedly at the sky.

And in the undergrowth, a man who had for two days lain with a spear lodged along his left rib finally felt the surge of hate and power that enabled him to draw it out completely.

The blood coursed over his naked torso down to his left hip but oddly there was little pain; he had slept a drugged sleep except for the intervals when his eyes had opened to see the ravens pecking away at the bodies of his comrades. He was the son of a chieftain and he knew he would not die like this, alone, without honour, life seeping away under the trees. He had been destined to die like a warrior, not from a stray, surprise spear-thrust in the darkness before he could lift his own sword.

The ravens had called him, woken him, told him of the approach of Volcas's horde.

They were shape-shifters, the ravens: they could assume the body of men and goddesses, they brought war and destruction and had the power of prophecy. Perhaps, if the shamans had asked them, they would have foretold of this disaster at the hands of Volcas. But perhaps they were telling the wounded prince something now, as they sang their violent songs in his head till he rose, dizzy and weak, to his feet.

Their raucous battle cries were in his ears when he stood, braced against the tree, and the strength seeped back into his body at the sound. His left arm was useless but the spear that had stretched him on his face was now in his right hand, the long wooden haft clamped fiercely under his armpit.

The screams of the circling ravens were mingled now with the tramp of feet, men moving up the hill, the jingling of bridles and the clang of swords, backed by a low, murmurous hum, the sound of mourning women, pinioned slaves.

Seconds later the warriors came into the trees.

For them the battle was over. There were still spoils to be picked up on the battlefield and as they came on some of the semi-naked men stopped, turned aside, picking up a sword here, a shield there.

Volcas did not.

He rode forward, at the head of his men, a burly, black-haired, black-visaged figure astride a stocky pony. He came on and he saw the man with the spear under the trees. For one long moment he stared. His eyes were a piercing blue, a long white scar marked his left cheek and part of his chin had been severed in a long-ago battle. Perhaps when he saw the man with the spear he shivered to recognize his own destiny and death; perhaps the screaming ravens had sent their message to him also. It made no difference. He was a warrior and a chieftain, and to die in battle was a cleansing of his soul. The hesitation was momentary only. Without a word he kicked his heels into the pony's sides and charged.

The young warrior under the trees waited as the pony thundered forward. Then, as Volcas raised his great axe and brought it down, swinging in a deathly arc, he leaned forward, spearhead upright, slipping the blade under the bronze boar shield, into the exposed armpit, locking the haft end against the ground as the driving charge of the pony thrust Volcas onto the point.

The warrior prince never saw what he had accomplished. The whirling axe cut deep into his neck, half severing his head. The spear haft broke and the pony careered onwards into the trees. Mortally wounded, Volcas slipped and fell from his mount, the spearhead deep in his chest.

When his men came up to him, the blood was pouring from their chieftain's side, and that night it began to bubble darkly from his mouth.

* * *

It could be no ordinary ceremony, the shamans had decreed.

For a poor man it was customary to make a small boat, place the corpse in it, and carry it down the hill for it to be burned on the lakeside, or on the marshy flank of the hill. For a man such as Volcas, there was so much more to do.

First, there was the matter of his wealth. It was to be divided into three parts: one part for his family, one part to provide for the clothing in which he would be laid to rest and for the ceremonies and rituals that the gods demanded, and one part for the fermented drink that they would all partake of on the Last Day.

Then there was the last shelter.

They had begun its construction when it was clear that Volcas's violent life was coming to an end. They had thrown up the birch walls quickly and roofed them with larch. Under the shadow of the roof, men had dug the wide, deep grave that would receive the corpse and its companions on their voyage to the underworld.

It was the oldest of the shamans, fur-hooded and bent, who had then taken on the task of gathering the slave women and the slaves into Volcas's hut.

Though the night was dark there was a strange, intermittent glow in the sky, and a keening wind whined among the tall trees at the edge of the encampment. They had sat on their haunches in the darkness, silent, swaying slightly under the influence of the strong drink provided them until the shaman, in his reedy voice, had begun the incantations that called up the gods from the deep pits and the high hills, from the winds and tempests and dark, dread depths of the forest, from lake and glen, from lair of boar and stag and bull.

When his voice died away there was only the silence; even the wind was still in the trees.

He used his magic to conjure up splinters of fire and the sudden shards of light threw long, flickering shadows against the walls of the great hut. The shaman dropped a powdery substance into the flames beneath his hand and a sweet, heavy incense flooded the hut, deadening the senses, lulling the brain, yet making the images of the gods clearer in their minds as the shaman chanted his mystic words. He called the names of the Great Ones, conjuring up their presence from the howling darkness of the past, bringing them into the hut of Volcas so they could see that what was being done was right and proper for the great warrior they would soon be receiving among them in the underworld. The shivering light danced crazily on the walls and the trembling slaves saw crest and tusk and antler, and heard the shuddering grunt of the bull.

When the last silence fell, it seemed endless. The slaves — men and women — waited, swaying slightly, half drugged by the incense, eyes wide and staring yet almost sightless in the presence of the ancient gods.

The silence was finally broken by the shaman's thin, cracked tones.

'Who will die with Volcas?'

The words seemed to shimmer, hang like bright drifting threads in the air about them, shifting slightly under the breath of the Great Ones as everyone waited, hardly daring to move or breathe.

'Who will die with Volcas?' the shaman repeated.

Now the words changed their shape, and were no longer drifting threads of gold: the sharp fingers of flame under the shaman's hand showed them the raised dorsal bristles of the boar shadowed on the hut walls; the broad brow of the great-horned bull lowered at them beyond the fur-hooded head of the shaman; the serpent slithered around the edge of the hut, raising its ram-horned head; and over all the twin-headed eagle stretched its powerful beaks and spread wide the wings that covered its prey. The gods were here, and demanding an answer; the gods waited, the doom of their power heavy and breathless in the room as the flames flickered high again, rising under the ministrations of the shaman's withered hands.

He cried out again.

'*Who will die with Volcas?*'

The question stretched endlessly in the darkness. It suffocated them, filled their throats with agony until someone must speak. It was a woman.

It was always a woman.

'I will.'

The flame reared at the words, reaching up almost to the roof of the hut, and they all started back, seeing their bodies shining redly in the glow, hearing the rush of wind as the eagle, satisfied, took to flight on powerful pinions. They heard the wild snort of the bull god and the rumbling thunder of the boar hooves and the ram-horned snake seemed to curl in the flames, writhe, fall back, fading with the dying firelight.

It had been said.

Now it would be done.

There was no retreat from the agreement; there was no desire to retreat. The shaman went to the door of the great hut with the proclamation and then, among the flickering torches, the selection was made. Two female slaves to guard the appointed one wherever she went, to feed her, serve her the fermented drink, watch over her, dress her, wash her feet with their hands. Then a swift selection of her companions: two male slaves, powerful and young, to be bound and kept in a separate hut, for the gods loved the count of three.

When sunlight poured on the hill it was the second day and they began to get everything ready for the dead man, to cut out his clothes, to wash his body, to arrange his armour and select those things that he would take with him on his journey to the underworld and the gods. They laid him on the birch poles above the grave pit and already his body was black from the coldness of the air under the roof. They brought bread and onions and herbs and placed them about the body. The fattest pig was slaughtered, and the great leg of pork was placed at his left hand.

The slave woman and her attendants kept to the small hut at the edge of the tall trees. The attendants were silent, but the slave woman drank heavily from the death bowl, and the fermented liquid gave her great happiness and she sang every day, joyfully, rocking on her heels to the rhythms of her youth. She rocked and she sang and she waited as the dawns came and the evenings died, until the fifth day.

On that day the village was silent.

The shamans had gone into the hills in the early morning, deep into the shadow line of the trees, and there had been rumbles of thunder in the air. The heavy clouds hung low but there were distant flashes of lightning as the shamans communicated with the boar and the bull, the snake and the eagle, and conjured up with their magic the One who was to come. The afternoon was still and expectant, prescient with the coming, the encampment almost stunned in its fearful anticipation. The dark clouds that piled up beyond the mountains were rent and split by strange glowings and distant, heavenly fires.

They brought fruit to the slave girl, and sweet-smelling herbs and then the two attendants withdrew. Alone, she rocked and sang and drank through the long, expectant afternoon until the mountain mists crept down to shroud the tree line and the cloak of darkness began to gather about the village. Wisps of fog twisted above the waters of the lake.

It was then that the One called by the shamans finally came.

She was tall and strongly built; long, black hair fell to her waist and her arms were muscular and bare under the fur pelisse that covered her upper body. The pelisse was caught in at the waist by an iron-studded belt, in which she carried a sheathed knife of stone.

Her features were grim and cold as she stood in the doorway and stared at the slave woman, the village silent behind her. The slave woman rocked, her eyes closed, her brain dulled with drugged wine. For a long while she who had been called by the shamans remained motionless and then she spread her arms wide, exulting.

Her voice came out harsh and croaking and deadly, emulating the eagle.

'I am come,' she cried.

The silence gathered around her. Her thin lips writhed back to display sharp, gleaming teeth in a mockery of a smile.

'I am the Angel of Death!'

CHAPTER ONE

1

The honeymoon was clearly over.

Simon Brent-Ellis was breathing hard as he stared at Karen Stannard but the passion that had raised his blood pressure was anger, not sexual admiration.

'I think,' he said curtly, 'it's time everyone realized just who is director of this department.'

Karen Stannard raised an elegant, innocent eyebrow. 'I can't imagine what you mean by that remark, Director.'

She was at her cool, impossibly beautiful best. Arnold always felt that when she was faced by a male challenge of the kind Brent-Ellis was making, she seemed to glow with increased confidence, assured in her manner and aware that she could outrun any storms and even turn them to her advantage. She sat just across from Arnold in the director's office, with her long, tanned legs carefully crossed and her slim-fingered hands relaxed in her lap. The morning sunlight, slanting across the room, picked out highlights of gold in her russet hair. She was dressed immaculately as usual, white blouse, dark grey, short-skirted suit, black shoes; smart, efficient — and beautiful.

But Brent-Ellis was no longer a captive, it seemed.

For some months now, ever since she had been appointed as his deputy in the Department of Museums and Antiquities, he had, in common with many men in the department, brightened visibly in her presence, straightened when she entered the room, pulled in his stomach when chatting to her. He had always been a preener, in his cream-coloured suits, bright ties and elegant waistcoats. Since Karen Stannard's arrival he had also trimmed his moustache, Arnold had noted. But, just as other men had gradually become aware of the sharpness of her tongue, her self-motivated ambition and her drive to be in control of everything that went on in the department, so, it seemed, Brent-Ellis had also changed his views after the early enslavement.

'You've been talking to Councillor Tremain,' Brent-Ellis accused.

'I talk to several councillors,' she replied demurely. 'Particularly those on the committees I service.'

There was a short silence. Brent-Ellis fiddled with his red, flowered tie and glowered at the third button of his patterned waistcoat. In a peeved tone he said, 'But you talked to him about a decision that had already been made.'

'Did I?' Her eyes were slightly slanted, and there was a hint of malicious amusement in them as she smiled at him. 'I'm sorry, Director, but I'm not quite clear. What decision are we talking about . . . and who can possibly have made it?'

Her irony and contempt were not cloaked by the sweetness of tone. Arnold sat quietly in his chair as he watched the director stoke up the fires of his rage.

Simon Brent-Ellis was normally a man who disliked scenes and walked away from difficulties. He tended to believe his department was best managed in his absence, and to a certain extent that was right: when he was in his office, rather than in the golf club, the course of life in the department was usually less smooth. His interruptions in the flow of work were rarely useful, partly because he seemed addicted to indecision. His intervention never solved a problem; rather it created two more. Consequently, he had been more than happy when Karen Stannard arrived — it was not merely that she provided some much-needed pulchritude to the department, it was that she brought the added bonus of a clear, analytical approach to the work and had been instrumental in sweeping away a number of the cobwebs that had accumulated in the time that Brent-Ellis had been director. He had been happy enough for that to occur, pleased with his new, beautiful broom.

But it was now clear that, as far as he was concerned, she had overstepped the mark.

'The decision,' Simon Brent-Ellis gritted, 'concerned Landon here, and the decision was mine.'

'Ahhh . . .' It was almost a sigh of understanding, but it held a hint of mockery. While Karen Stannard's smile suggested she was now aware of the area of misunderstanding between herself and the director, it also intimated he was in the wrong, but she forgave him. 'Mr Landon . . . I presume you are referring to the invitation that came in last week, regarding service and representation on the Stiles Committee.'

'Exactly.'

'So what's the problem, Director?' Karen Stannard asked sweetly.

'The problem is,' Brent-Ellis snarled, 'that you've been talking to councillors behind my back.'

'About what?' she challenged.

'About the decision I had made and announced in this room. That Landon here would be nominated by the department to serve on the Stiles Committee.'

Karen Stannard's wide, red mouth broke into a warm smile. 'Decision? I hope you'll forgive me when I say that I'm not aware that a *decision* was made. A discussion took place—'

'You were actually in this room,' Brent-Ellis fumed, 'when I took that call from the Cabinet Office.'

'I was indeed. I recollect the conversation you had. You'll remember, Director, that it was I who suggested you made the enquiry in the first place. The letter we received advised us that the Stiles Committee had been established to hold discussions about the best way to protect archaeological sites, and thereafter to propose legislation. It asked for a nomination from this department. We were being offered a seat on the committee. I suggested you contacted them, asked for further particulars.'

'And they phoned back and mentioned Landon by name!'

Karen Stannard glanced at Arnold. Her eyes seemed this morning to be almost midnight blue in colour, deep and unfathomable. But he had never been able to ascertain their true colour. Her glance locked with his. 'Yes, I remember that quite clearly. I recall being rather . . . surprised that they even knew his name.' She smiled vaguely in Brent-Ellis's direction. 'But then many things about Mr Landon continue to surprise me.'

'It was as a consequence of that conversation that I decided Landon should be nominated to the committee,' Brent-Ellis insisted.

Karen Stannard's tone was cool. 'I understood that you were merely considering it. I pointed out that it should be a departmental decision, not one thrust upon us by some minor civil servant in London.'

'The Cabinet Office—'

'Is staffed by civil servants. They glory in the important-sounding title, but they're little men.'

'But I reached a decision,' Brent-Ellis snapped, drawing around himself the last shreds of his courage.

Her eyes were cold. 'I see. I must say, I wasn't aware that a decision had been taken. Normally, before you take a . . . decision, Director, you and I go over the possible ramifications, and staff impacts—'

'Landon had been specifically suggested by the Cabinet Office, and it was obvious that he was the person to serve.'

'From the Cabinet Office point of view that may be so,' she contended, rather more sharply, 'but we do have other work to deal with here in Morpeth. It is my responsibility to ensure that business proceeds smoothly in this department, and bearing in mind the workload carried by Landon it seemed to me inappropriate that he should be released. There was also the other matter . . .'

Brent-Ellis leaned back in his chair. The effort of argument was already tiring him; he did not relish confrontations and when they did arise they quickly wearied him. He was not a fighter. And yet Arnold had the feeling he was going to dig in his heels in this battle.

'I refer, of course, to the matter of seniority,' Karen Stannard was continuing. 'While I'm aware Landon has been fairly wide ranging in his career, not least in this department, and that he has undertaken activities at various levels, he does not, nevertheless, in my opinion, carry sufficient . . . weight to play a proper part in the debates that will go on in the Stiles Committee.'

'I don't think you should serve,' Brent-Ellis said bluntly.

She was momentarily taken aback by his positive tone. 'I . . . I never said that—'

'Councillor Tremain has said it. After you talked to him.'

Her eyes narrowed. Tightly, she asked, 'Are you suggesting, Director, that I lobbied Councillor Tremain to get him to propose my name for the Stiles Committee?'

She wouldn't have had to be so crude, Arnold thought to himself. He knew Tremain — a middle-aged bachelor with a spreading waistline and a reputation for roving eyes and hands. There had been a few minor scandals regarding office secretaries, which had been hushed up. Karen Stannard would have known exactly how to deal with him, playing him on the end of a sexual line, raising his temperature, teasing him indirectly, making him feel a man among men. It would have been very easy for her to edge Tremain into indignation that a departmental minion was to be nominated to serve on a national committee when there were more senior — and beautiful — people available.

Brent-Ellis wriggled in his chair. 'I'm not suggesting that you put your own name forward,' he said weakly. 'But I am saying that Councillor Tremain has approached me — and

I resent being put in a corner, under pressure to change a decision I've already made.'

'I'm sure,' Karen Stannard replied sweetly, 'you don't feel that I'm the one putting pressure on you.'

It wasn't working. Simon Brent-Ellis regarded her highly as a woman and as someone who removed burdens of responsibility from his back, but Arnold now detected an unsuspected stubbornness in the man. Brent-Ellis leaned back in his chair, a dogged expression on his face. 'I'm not suggesting anything of the sort. But there comes a time when everyone has to draw the line. The Cabinet Office want Landon — the reason why escapes me, but there it is. I have decided that he must be released to serve on the committee—'

'It means absence to attend meetings in London . . .' Karen Stannard warned.

'Nevertheless—'

'. . . and we have two appeals coming up which Landon has been handling, as well as a list of planning applications I was considering handing over to him—'

'Well, you'll have to deal with them yourself,' Brent-Ellis interrupted desperately. 'I don't want to know such details. It's for you to sort out, Miss Stannard. My mind is made up. I won't have councillors interfering with professional decisions for motives of their own. Landon serves on the committee.'

He was sweating profusely with the effort of decision. His moustache hung limp and damp, and there was a hunted look in his eyes. Arnold felt sorry for him as he saw Karen Stannard's glacial features.

Her tone was sharp as broken glass. 'If that is your decision, Director, of course I'll implement it, in spite of all the difficulties that it will cause. Had we discussed it all privately . . . but it is your decision and that's the end of it.'

Arnold knew otherwise, as she glanced at him.

There was a short silence. It was broken by the ringing of the phone. The sound made Brent-Ellis jump. He picked up the phone, his hand shaking slightly.

'Yes?'

Arnold heard the voice of Brent-Ellis's secretary, tinny and distorted.

'Your wife is on the line, Director. Councillor Mrs Brent-Ellis.'

'Ah.' Simon Brent-Ellis dragged a large handkerchief from the top pocket of his cream-coloured suit. 'All right, you can put her through.' He mopped his brow and glanced up at Arnold and Karen Stannard. 'Perhaps you'd be kind enough to leave now. And it's decided — Landon's name will go forward for membership of the Stiles Committee.'

Karen Stannard swept out of the room ahead of Arnold, without a word or a backward glance.

* * *

'She won't let it rest, you know.'

Jerry Picton leaned casually against the doorjamb in Arnold's room and picked his teeth with a sharpened matchstick. He was a small, mean-faced man in his mid-fifties, with narrow eyes and badly pitted skin. He was discontented with his career and lack of promotion, which he put down to the machinations of unnamed enemies, and he spent as much time as possible sowing seeds of similar discontent among his colleagues. He was the office gossip, well enough informed, though his retailing of fact was normally marred and discoloured by malicious interpretations. He sniggered now, unpleasantly.

'And the laugh is, that silly old lecher Tremain will get nothing out of it. He's been sniffing around her like an over-excited basset hound for months, and she gives him just enough encouragement, crossing and uncrossing her legs in committee, for him to think she'll eventually jump into some motel bed with him and realize his wildest fantasies. Fat chance of that, her being the way she is. Some say in the office that's what she really needs — a real man. God knows, Tremain's not it. But what are you going to do about it, Landon?'

'About what?'

'She'll be after your blood. Getting on this committee is one thing but how are you going to make sure she won't undermine you?' Picton sneered.

It was only twenty minutes since Arnold had left the director's office, yet Picton already knew about the events that had occurred in the room. He had a rodent nose for gossip. Arnold shook his head. 'I'm sure Miss Stannard has more important things on her mind.'

'I'm not so sure.' Picton picked thoughtfully at his teeth: for all his attention, they were yellowish in colour, and crumbling in texture. 'She doesn't like you, Arnold, sees you as some kind of needle under her fingernails.'

'Colourfully put, but inaccurate,' Arnold replied drily.

'Well, mark my words, this isn't the end of it yet — she'll get her own way when push comes to shove.'

Picton sauntered off, whistling through his yellowed teeth. Arnold hesitated, then swept aside the files in front of him and picked up the letter half concealed beneath them. He opened the envelope and read the contents again. It contained an invitation that he found flattering and interesting, and it stated that the writer would also be approaching the department formally. He had little confidence that the response from the directorate would be positive, however: when Karen Stannard saw the request she would do everything in her power to block the proposal — even more so now that she was smarting under the decision of the director.

The first he had made in years, Arnold thought sourly. And in that, at least, Picton was probably right. It would fuel the dislike that Karen Stannard already held for him.

The phone rang on his desk. He picked it up. 'Landon speaking.'

'Arnold . . .' The tone was honey, the voice Karen Stannard's. 'Would you mind stepping along to my office for a moment?'

It was coming sooner than he had expected. Arnold replaced the phone and headed for the door. As an afterthought, he went back to his desk and picked up the letter, slipped it into his pocket. It would not be beyond Jerry Picton to snoop around his desk in his absence.

He made his way along the corridor to the rooms occupied by the director, his deputy, and their formidable secretary, Miss Sansom. He had always thought Miss Sansom would not have looked out of place at the Nuremberg trials, but he had never mentioned it to her.

'Miss Stannard wants to see me,' Arnold explained. Fierce-visaged, she gave the impression she would regard discipline in the French Foreign Legion as too soft. She nodded towards the door to the deputy's office. She always left Arnold with the feeling she regarded him as a personal affront. Maybe she gave all visitors a similar impression.

Karen Stannard was seated at ease behind her desk. She was leaning forward on one elbow, an elegant finger caressing the soft curve of her cheek, touching the high cheekbones approvingly. She seemed to have recovered her good humour.

'Please sit down. The director will be joining us in a few moments. He's on the phone again. Such a busy man . . .' Her eyes glittered with pleasure as she looked Arnold up and down, calculating. 'So who is it you know in the Cabinet Office then?'

Arnold shrugged. 'No one that I'm aware of.'

'Oh, come now. You're not telling me it's your fame that led to this invitation to join the Stiles Committee?' she mocked.

'I've no idea how the invitation came about,' Arnold replied stiffly.

She smiled. 'I'm not in the least suggesting, of course, that you wouldn't do a good job on the committee. It's merely that it's a high-profile sort of task, where people get noticed . . . and I feel there are others who could do a better job of it, gain more from it. And there is, also, a matter of pride at stake. I mean, we should do our own selecting, not leave it to some piddling junior officer in Whitehall. Don't you agree, Landon?'

'I've no view about the matter.'

'No view,' she sighed, pleasurably. 'That's why you're where you are, and I'm here as deputy director. A position of no little influence,' she added in a satisfied tone. 'However . . .'

There was a tap on the door, and a moment later Simon Brent-Ellis walked in, tall, straight and sheepish. Significantly, he avoided Arnold's eye and stood next to Miss Stannard's desk. She looked up at him, almost fondly, Arnold thought, like a cat admiring a claw-trapped mouse.

'Director,' she purred. 'You wanted to see us?'

'That's right.' Simon Brent-Ellis tugged at his moustache and frowned, injecting determination into his uncertain eyes. 'There's been a change of plan.'

'Yes?' she queried.

'It's been . . . I decided,' he corrected himself, 'that it would not, after all, be sensible to have Landon as our representative on the Stiles Committee.'

'Why ever not?' Karen Stannard asked, in wide-eyed innocence.

Brent-Ellis ducked his head and waggled his jowls. Behind his moustache, his mouth was unhappy. 'I think the case you argued . . . about a more senior person . . . on reflection, it makes more sense. And it's been brought to my attention that the committee . . . well, it's not likely to have a woman in the group.' He breathed heavily and shuffled his feet. 'So, in the circumstances, I think it best to . . . to change the decision that was made earlier.'

His eyes flickered briefly towards Arnold.

'So now I'm not to be the departmental nominee to Stiles?' Arnold asked.

'That's right,' Brent-Ellis's chin came up. 'We . . . I've decided it had better be my deputy, Miss Stannard. More seniority.'

'And a different sex,' Karen Stannard murmured. She flickered a quick, triumphant glance at Arnold and then smiled at the director. 'I imagine you'll have discussed this with Mrs Brent-Ellis? As a councillor, she will have a point of view, I should think.'

The director was pale. 'Mrs Brent-Ellis's responsibilities as a councillor do not impinge on this department,' he insisted unconvincingly. 'That phone call was a domestic matter . . .'

His voice died away and he looked embarrassed.

'I'm sure Mr Landon won't really have any objection to my nomination to work with Lord Stiles,' Karen Stannard said. 'Isn't that so, Landon?'

'Service on the Stiles Committee is a matter of indifference to *me*,' Arnold replied quietly.

He saw that he had hit home. Her nostrils flared slightly, but she kept her anger in check. She managed a thin smile. 'Well, that's settled then.'

Brent-Ellis, relieved, nodded and turned to go. Arnold stopped him. 'Director . . .'

'Yes?'

'Since this matter is settled now, and I have you both together, maybe I could raise another matter.'

Brent-Ellis shrugged, glancing uncertainly at his deputy. 'What is it you want?'

'I've received a letter from Dr Rena Williams.'

Brent-Ellis frowned. 'I seem to recall the name.'

'She's a professor of archaeology at York University.' Karen Stannard reminded him, her watchful eyes on Arnold.

'We worked with her at the Viking Research Centre, you'll recall,' Arnold offered. 'When we found the boat burial.'

'Ah, yes, I remember it now. Are you still on that Trust Committee?'

'Yes, but it meets only four times a year.'

Suspiciously, Karen Stannard leaned forward. Arnold was aware of the admiration she held for Dr Williams, and the regard in which she held her. She had been jealous of Arnold's involvement with Rena Williams last time.

'What does she want?'

'Apparently she's been given a grant of some considerable size to work on a Celtic shrine that was opened some time ago. She has a joint project with a Professor Westwood, which will entail opening up the rest of the field, including a barrow, adjoining the shrine. They think it could well be a Celtic burial site of some importance.'

'And?' Karen Stannard demanded snappishly.

'She's written to me suggesting that I should join the team.'

'You've got a job here.'

'It would be on a part-time basis.'

'The department couldn't afford it,' she responded in a brisk, dismissive tone.

'I understand that my time would be paid for. The grant is a generous one. She tells me she has written formally to the director—'

'I haven't seen the letter,' Karen Stannard said sharply.

'It's on my desk.' Brent-Ellis's moustache seemed dejected. 'I just haven't got around to dealing with it yet. Time, you know—'

'Well, I don't see how we can accommodate Dr Williams,' Karen Stannard announced.

Arnold shrugged. 'In other circumstances, I would have been inclined to agree. My workload is considerable, as you said earlier, but will reduce when we have the new appointment in place — your assistant comes in next week, I believe, Miss Stannard. That will halve my current commitments, and the planning appeals are some months off yet. Of course, three days a week on the Celtic site would have been impossible had I been appointed to the Stiles Committee, and I wouldn't have dreamed of raising Dr Williams's letter with you in such a case, Director. But now you've decided not to nominate me and that Miss Stannard is to take the seat, it seems to me I have time available to assist Dr Williams on this important and *prestigious* investigation.'

Karen Stannard opened her mouth to argue, but Arnold forestalled her. 'Unless, of course, Miss Stannard is expecting me to take over some of her duties during her absences in London, to make up my workload.'

It would have been the last thing she would want and she saw that he knew it.

'Is that what you have in mind?' Brent-Ellis queried, puzzled.

Cornered, Karen Stannard shook her head. 'No. I'll be able to handle my own work, as well as the Stiles Committee.'

Her tone was sharp. She hadn't known about the invitation from Rena Williams and she was caught off balance. It was an invitation she would dearly have loved for herself, and perhaps one she would have seized, but now that she was committed to Stiles, it was impossible for her to suggest she should also step into the Celtic site investigation, rather than Arnold.

'Well, in view of what Landon says about his workload,' Brent-Ellis said, cheering up, and oblivious to the charged atmosphere, 'I see no reason why we shouldn't respond favourably to Dr Williams's request. Bit of kudos for the department, hey? You on the Stiles Committee and Landon helping out on an important archaeological site. And we get paid for his time!'

He left the room smiling.

There was no smile on Karen Stannard's face. She stared at Arnold, and he knew she felt she had been outmanoeuvred. She did not like the feeling.

'Clever,' she said quietly.

'What was?'

'Keeping the letter back.'

Arnold shrugged. 'I wasn't to know you hadn't seen the request to the director.'

'Oh, I think you knew all right.' There was a cold calculation in her eyes as she glared at him. 'But don't think you're winning hands down.'

'I told you — it's of no concern to me whether I'm on the Stiles Committee or not. This is of much more interest to me.'

'I believe it.' she snapped. 'But you're not getting a free hand, Landon. You'll report on this to me directly, you understand? And every chance I get I'll be up there at the site, to keep an eye on you.'

'Somehow, Miss Stannard,' Arnold replied gently, 'I thought that might well be the case.'

2

Jerry Picton was driving into the car park as Arnold was preparing to get into his own vehicle. Picton slid his car in front of Arnold's, preventing his leaving, and wound down his window. 'You screwed her then, in a manner of speaking.'

'What do you mean?'

'The Wicked Witch of the North, the cold but beautiful Ms Stannard. She's mad as hell at you, they reckon, Arnold.'

'She got what she wanted.'

'The Stiles Committee? Oh, yeah, hobnobbing with his lordship is right up her street. But that doesn't mean she's pleased with you getting this secondment. You know how she managed the Stiles thing, do you?'

Arnold shrugged. He wasn't particularly interested.

'It was Mrs Brent-Ellis. Stannard got Tremain to brief her. And Mrs B-E, she grabbed her husband where it hurts most, got hold of his intellectual follicles. Direct testicular attack. Challenged him to stand up to her. Told him she agreed with old Tremain — they needed a woman on the Stiles Committee. She squeezed him so hard it brought tears to his eyes — so he changed his mind.' Picton clucked his tongue. 'But I reckon she had her own motives too, the director's old lady.'

'What do you mean?' Arnold asked, in spite of himself. Picton chuckled lasciviously. 'Well, you and I and the rest of the department know that the stunning Ms Stannard likes ladies, not gentlemen — but I think the whisper hasn't got to Mrs Brent-Ellis yet. Consequently, I think she's got nervous at the thought of her dear hubby spending time in the office in close proximity to said siren Ms Stannard. So, with the lady in question serving on the Stiles Committee and him on the golf course, there'll be less opportunity for canoodling in the office, hey?'

'There'd be little chance of that in any case,' Arnold snorted.

'*You* know that and I know that,' Picton replied, winking slyly, 'but Councillor Mrs Brent-Ellis doesn't know it, does she?'

'If you wouldn't mind moving your car,' Arnold said levelly, 'I'd like to get out of here.'

* * *

Arnold drove south out of Morpeth on the A1 towards Newcastle and then west for Corbridge on the old Roman road towards Vindolanda and Hexham. He was headed along the valley of the South Tyne, over the hill crests the Romans had used for their northern frontier posts. He was making his way towards the old stone dale that lay between the fells of the West Allen and the Vale of Eden, beyond the high shoulders of Cross Fell.

It was a bright morning as he drove over the heather-topped hills to Alston, reckoned to be the highest market town in England, and juddered his way through its narrow, cobbled main street. Beyond Alston he drove on towards Allendale Town and the high land he crossed was a mixture of moorland swamp, cotton grass and heather moor, rolling green and brown and purple on either side of the road.

As he crossed above Coalcleugh he could look back on the line of abandoned smallholdings that dipped down into the valley, the house ruins drawing his eye towards the brown-grey moortop that merged with the faint green of the Northumberland hills. He was alone in the landscape apart from curlew and snipe rising in the crisp air of the fell, and there were no other cars to disturb the occasional grouse breaking cover and warning him he was heading for the end of the world — 'Go-back, go-back, go-back.'

The site that Rena Williams had invited him to investigate with her and her team lay in the old stone dale beyond Nenthead — narrow, with the abandoned railway line slicing past the meandering river that gleamed blue-black in the morning sun, the dale still boasted two roads that wound through the farm fields and crossed the river up towards the fell rim.

Arnold brought a flask of coffee, since it was a beautiful morning and a stop on the fell would be welcome. Two working days and the weekend stretched ahead of him — Dr Williams had told him she'd arranged a room for him at the George and Dragon, beyond Garrigill, so there'd be no problem with accommodation. It seemed the members of the small party she led were all staying there — welcome boost for the isolated inn which normally relied on walkers and backpackers for its clientele.

Arnold stopped for coffee on the fell above Shaw Side.

This was an ancient gold-mining area, he knew, but Shaw and the other gold-diggers had gone long since. Arnold parked the car and climbed the hill until, in the middle distance, he could see a lone chimney, a reminder that he was in the country of the lead men. The old smelt-mill chimney had been used as a flue for the heavy metal toxics and gases created by the burning of the lead.

His father had brought him up here many years ago, on one of their regular wanderings around the dales. The old man had told him about the lead men and their smelters: how they had drawn the fire and its residues away from the smelter, and Arnold could see the consequences even now, a hundred years after the industry had closed down. Beyond the chimney on the slope there was no trace of grass or heather or sphagnum moss. Bare, grey-tinged peat spread across the fell to a small forest of stunted Scots pine.

Planted forty years ago to give the spoil heaps colour and cover they had failed miserably: the lead in the spoil had poisoned them from their roots upwards. They looked like a Scandinavian advertisement against acid rain, he thought, and turned his back on the scene as he unscrewed the top of his flask, to look out over the unspoiled fell he had just crossed.

He sipped his coffee and studied the map Rena Williams had sent him. Although he and his father had tramped these fells, it was many years since, and he was not familiar with the particular site she had invited him to work at. She'd advised him that if he took the main road towards Lovelady Shield he had gone too far west: a left turn at Nenthead itself through Fiddler Street would take him along the winding route of the Dowgang Hush, where the old lead miners had exposed the silver, lead and iron ores that lay like hidden treasure beneath the surface of the steep fellside.

The archaeological site lay beyond Garrigill.

He opened again the letter Rena Williams had sent him.

> *. . . the field site isn't a new discovery — it was opened up first at least fifty years ago but it was never properly excavated, and when the money ran out no more work was done. The university has now received a generous grant from Northern Heritage, however, and since they — the Heritage, that is — bought the land in question about three years ago they were rather keen that I should get a team up here to take a close look at what we have. I won't tell you too much about it — I think preconceptions are to be avoided, but if I tell you that apart from the shrine site we might have the chance to work on the barrows as well, I don't need to tell you what we might find. A Romano-British site maybe, or a Celtic burial — who knows? So, why not come and see? I'm writing separately to your director, to emphasize how important your presence could be . . .*

Arnold guessed that Karen Stannard would certainly not have liked that last particular phrase. Nor the fact that the letter had got Arnold out of the office.

It was one of the several things he enjoyed about working in the Department of Museums and Antiquities. Brent-Ellis he could suffer in silence, for the director, though irritating in his incompetence, impinged but rarely on Arnold's work. Karen Stannard had stamped her personality on the department in the short time she had been there as deputy and she and Arnold had already clashed, but it was a situation Arnold felt he could handle. For the work genuinely interested him — not so much the committee work, but certainly the archaeological activity, for his father had instilled in him a love for the ancient; the timber and the stone that had been worked by long-gone generations of men and women; the marks they had left on the landscape.

And additionally, the job gave him the opportunity from time to time to leave Morpeth and drive up onto the high fells, smell the clean tang of sea breezes from the wild north-eastern coast, and hear the high cry of harriers and red kite circling far above his head. It cleansed him, removed all irritations from his mind, refreshed and renewed him in senses and body.

When he had finished his coffee he walked back to the car, drove into Nenthead and took the left turn into the Dowgang Hush. The road swung left again towards the Ashgill waterfall and then he was on a side track that narrowed, cutting deep between high drystone walls until it seemed to peter out into a private road. He caught sight of a Northern Heritage sign, however, and was encouraged to carry on. A half-mile further and the track divided, a pitted tarmac surface appearing on the right, a stone track continuing straight ahead.

The surfaced road turned through a stone gateway to his right and, as Arnold drove past, he caught sight of a rocky, hummocky area, a tumble of broken stones scattered around the sloping field. It was, he guessed, the foundations of an old house, now overgrown with grass and thistles, and then, as he came around the bend, he saw the splendid hall on the hill, its reddish stone gleaming warm in the morning sun, its numerous windows sending out flashes of light as he drove past. It was hidden again as the high, bold rocks at its eastern side intruded on his line of sight, and he was climbing up through the trees, bumping over the rough stone track until, ahead of him, he saw the clearing, and the tree-shaded car park.

There were four cars already there, and he drew in beside the nearest, parked tidily beneath the protective boughs of an old horse chestnut. He wound down the car window as he killed the engine and looked out across the field to his left.

Near the gateway there was a wooden hut, presumably used for shelter and storage by the field team. The site itself sloped gently upwards away from the gate but at the far edge he could make out what seemed unnatural areas, tumuli or barrows that would be the sites Dr Williams had mentioned. Beyond them was a small area of scrub and then the hill rose abruptly, dark, craggy rock thrusting out starkly below a crown of thin woodland that stretched up and over the skyline. It was an old wood, an ancient wood, Arnold guessed, that overlooked the field until the slope dropped away sharply into a flat, rushy area on the other side of the fence.

Arnold got out and locked the car. He shivered suddenly, as though a chill struck him, but it was momentary only for the sun was warm on his back when he opened the gate and walked through, towards the small group of people that was clustered near the base of the rocky crags.

As he drew near, the tall woman who was standing at the edge of the group looked behind her, and immediately detached herself to walk towards him. She smiled and held out her hand.

'Arnold! So you made it after all.'

'Without too many trials and tribulations,' Arnold replied and shook hands. He liked Rena Williams. She was a tall, handsome, well-built woman of considerable intellect and charm, but she could be direct and positive when it suited her. She had a well-established reputation in the archaeological field, and her department at the university was well funded, largely because of that reputation. He had worked with her before and enjoyed the experience — well known though she might be, she was not averse to listening to other people's views.

'I had a note from Karen Stannard,' Rena Williams said, eyeing him carefully. 'She stressed how difficult it was releasing you . . . and said she too hoped to get up here from time to time.'

'She likes to keep an eye on me,' Arnold grinned.

'She's welcome here, of course. And you . . . I've told the others about you, so you'd better come to meet some of them right now. It's not the strongest team I'd have liked — four research students and another professor, but you, and Miss Stannard if she makes it, will strengthen us considerably. Anyway, come along and be introduced.'

The group had already broken up, the four younger people walking towards the craggy rocks at the edge of the field, but one man remained, hands on hips, staring at Arnold and Dr Williams.

He was about fifty years of age, stockily built, with powerful shoulders and short-cropped, thinning white hair above a tanned, weather-beaten face. His eyebrows were heavy, in black contrast to his hair, his nose prominent and his mouth aggressive. He was clad in a weatherproof jacket, jeans and gumboots. There was a certain pugnacity about his stance and an air of dissatisfaction about him as he watched them approach, as though he felt disturbed by Arnold's arrival.

'Mr Landon — Professor Geoffrey Westwood.'

Westwood's grip was hard and the skin of his hand was rough. He might be an academic, but he clearly spent a large part of his time out of doors. His heavy-lidded eyes looked Arnold over with a curiosity tinged with annoyance. 'I've heard about you, Landon. For an amateur, you seem to possess an inordinate amount of luck.'

'As you seem to possess a disobliging amount of rudeness,' Rena Williams interposed crisply.

His glance was sour as he looked at her. 'If I'm often out of sorts, it's because I have too many dealings with incompetence.'

'Geoffrey regards as incompetent anyone who disagrees with his views,' Dr Williams explained. 'And it's been one of those mornings. You're going back into the shrine, Geoffrey?'

He shook his head grumpily. 'If I do I might be tempted to knock some sense into the heads of those young clowns. No, I'll get some cataloguing work done for the rest of the day.' He eyed Arnold warily. 'You'll be staying for a few days, I gather?'

'I'm booked in at the George and Dragon for four nights.'

'Well, there's plenty of work to get on with here. I suppose we can use another pair of hands.'

'Educated hands,' Rena Williams added.

Westwood scowled. 'As you say. Well, I'll leave you to it. I'll see you back at the hotel.'

For a moment he seemed about to add something but then humphed noncommittally and turned away. Arnold was left with the feeling that the man didn't entirely approve of his presence in the team. He watched him as he stumped away, thrusting his hands deep into the pockets of his jacket, powerful shoulders hunched. Rena Williams sighed.

'I had hoped Fred Galton would be assigned to this project. But . . . Geoffrey Westwood has seniority, and it is his field of research, so the university . . . well, no matter. As long as I can keep the lid on his temper, it'll be all right, I suppose. But I'm afraid the research students, well, they do tend to . . . shall we say, wind him up from time to time?' She gestured towards the crags. 'Come on, I'll show you the cave and the shrine and introduce you to Milady and the Three Musketeers.'

'Who?'

Dr Williams laughed. 'It's my description for them. The young men are called Ainsley, Peter and Alan, and they do tend to stick closely together at university. So, since they remind me of Athos, Porthos and Aramis, the Three Musketeers they are.'

'And Milady?'

Rena Williams grimaced. 'She's called Elfreda. A sort of romantic name, isn't it? She might even have chosen it for herself — I have my suspicions. As for my referring to her as Milady, well, it's not that she gives herself airs or anything.'

'It's to do with the Musketeers?' Arnold queried as they approached the crags.

Rena Williams smiled. 'You could say that. She can be . . . a source of friction from time to time. She is somewhat mischievous. She plays one off against another, you know what I mean? But I shouldn't bias you against her . . . you'll make up your own mind.'

The young woman who came out of the entrance to the crags was about twenty-five years old. She was something less than middle height, with straight blonde hair which was scraped back into a ponytail. Her eyes were hazel in colour and merry: something had amused her and she was smiling. It was a pleasant smile which lit up her face and emphasized the deep dimple that appeared to one side of her mouth. Her face was round, her skin fresh, her appearance wholesome rather than beautiful. But her glance was coquettish as she looked back into the cave and she moved with a certain awareness, a confident sexuality. She walked towards them with a smile; as she moved, her breasts, unconfined beneath the check shirt she wore, swung heavily. She wiped a hand on her jeans as she approached.

'Hi! I guess you're Arnold Landon. I'm surprised.' So was Arnold. He smiled. 'What do you mean?'

'Dr Williams here spoke of a paragon. You look ordinary. Nice . . . but ordinary.'

'Elfreda . . .' Dr Williams warned.

'Yes, I know, first acquaintance and all that. But you don't really mind me being outspoken, do you, Mr Landon?' She linked her arm in his. 'I mean, I *did* say you looked nice, after all.' She looked up at him, wide-eyed. 'Anyway, I'm Elfreda Gale. And you haven't taken offence, have you?'

She was smiling archly and the coquetry in her tone was deliberate. Arnold inclined his head slightly. 'No offence taken since I presume none was intended.'

'How unworldly, but very sweet, nevertheless.' She caught Dr Williams's disapproving glance. 'Ah, all right, I'll behave, Dr Williams, but let me make up by introducing him to the boys.'

Before Rena Williams could protest Elfreda had squeezed Arnold's arm confidentially and towed him towards the opening in the crags.

The formation was mainly natural, Arnold guessed, though the cave might have been further hollowed out in part to make the entrance wider at some ancient time. The cave mouth broadened as they moved inside and the roof rose to perhaps ten feet in height. The floor was dry and sandy and some fifteen feet inside the cave an area had been pegged out and partly excavated to a depth of three feet or more. Three young men were working in the pit, on hands and knees, sifting soil, brushing, probing in the light of strong lamps that supplemented the dim light filtering through from the mouth of the cave. Cables ran through a second, narrow entrance to the left, too small to allow a human body to squeeze through, but wide enough to link up with the generator that throbbed outside.

'Right,' Elfreda called stridently, 'just stop what you're doing for the moment while I effect introductions. This gentleman I'm holding here is Mr Arnold Landon, come to help us out at the behest of Dr Williams, and to bring us luck, Dr Williams says. And here, Mr Landon, is Ainsley Close — he's the good-looking one with the curly hair and designer beard. He plays rugby rather well, or so he says. Personally, I wouldn't fancy scrumming down with him too often. Now he, on the other hand . . .'

The tall young man nearest to them in the pit looked up. 'Shut up, Elfreda.' He nodded at Arnold, smiling slightly. He was perhaps twenty-three years old, broad-shouldered, and decidedly scruffy in appearance. 'Mr Landon — pleased to meet you.'

Elfreda gestured past him with her free hand, as she still clutched at Arnold's arm with the other. 'The spotty one with the ginger hair, he's called Peter. Surname Burns. Clifton School, you know. Terribly polite and parents very well off. I adore him, don't I, Peter? But I can't get him to take me seriously, however much I coax him to take me to bed. I think sometimes he doesn't like girls.'

'Cut it out, Elfreda,' the red-haired man beyond Ainsley complained. 'Do you always have to try to make me look a fool?' He stood up and walked forward, holding out his hand. His voice was cultured, his tone measured. 'Good to meet you, Mr Landon.'

Arnold leaned down to shake hands. Elfreda sniffed, pushed past him and half dragged Arnold towards the back of the cave. 'And this gorgeous hunk is Alan Frith. How tall are you, Alan . . . six feet? See his muscles, Mr Landon? He lifts weights in his spare time: weights, running, boxing . . . but I know what he dreams of, Mr Landon . . . He dreams of getting into my knickers.'

'Getting my hands around your throat, you mean,' Alan Frith replied. But there was a casual acceptance in his tone that suggested to Arnold he was well used to Elfreda's chatter, and able to cope with it. Even so, when he spoke he looked at her and Arnold caught the glint of admiration, before he turned to Arnold and welcomed him. 'We've heard a lot about you from Dr Williams, Mr Landon. And I know we'll appreciate the help you'll bring. Moreover, we do work as a team — when Elfreda keeps her mouth shut, that is.'

'I liven up all your boring lives, that's the truth,' the young woman said.

'Enliven it further,' Dr Williams suggested from the cave entrance, 'by getting the kettle on and making us some tea.'

'That's sexism!' Elfreda complained.

'It's your turn, Elfreda,' all three young men suddenly burst out in a clearly rehearsed singsong, 'and a woman's place is in the home!'

She flounced out of the cave, grinning nevertheless, and when the men stopped laughing and settled back to their work, Rena Williams led Arnold to the back of the cave.

'I'd better tell you a bit about this area — I take it you haven't read too much about it?'

'Nothing,' Arnold confessed.

'Right. Well, the Victorians first recognized the cave as a likely shrine site and about 1860 there was some work done here. Before that, well, there was a certain reluctance among local people even to come here. It had an evil reputation — ghosts, warlocks, bad omens, all that sort of superstitious nonsense.'

'Still gives me the shivers from time to time,' Ainsley Close called out from where he crouched on his knees.

'When the ghouls gather—' Peter Burns said, chattering his teeth.

'—and the wind whistles across the moor,' Alan Frith added with a low moaning sound.

Rena Williams laughed. 'Well, it can get a bit spooky up here when darkness falls, I'll admit — but that's probably because everyone keeps talking about it.' She turned back to Arnold. 'What was established some sixty years ago, when there was a short-term investigation here, was that the cave was probably a shrine of some sort — maybe Romano-British in origin.'

'Military?' Arnold asked.

'At that stage it wasn't mooted. Of course, we know from what's been found at Hadrian's Wall since that there were a wide range of gods worshipped in northern England. Some came over with the Roman soldiery. Others were already here in the local consciousness. And in the Romano-British period it's well recorded that there was a mingling of cults — old pagan gods were merged with Roman deities, pagan sky cults came to be identified with Roman sky gods, a Celtic wheel could be positioned in a symbolic sculpture between two thunderbolts — emblems of the classical Jupiter—'

'As Dr Westwood will explain ad infinitum,' Ainsley Close called out again.

'Come on, Ainsley, you don't take him seriously,' Peter Burns interposed. 'I find his accounts of the juxtaposition of Celtic and Roman imagery . . .'

'And the relation between the seven-spoked wheel and the seven-petalled rosette . . .' added Alan Frith.

'. . . of immense significance,' they all chorused.

'All right, boys, that's enough,' Rena Williams cautioned. 'Go on, get back for your tea break while I talk to Mr Landon.' The young men rose, dusting themselves down and laughing at a private joke. She smiled indulgently. 'Dr Westwood does sometimes get . . . carried away.'

Arnold nodded. After the others had gone he leaned forward, inspecting the wall closely. 'I get the impression some of this has been hollowed out with stone axes.'

'That's the theory. At some stage the cave was extended, widened to make the shrine larger. We don't know what the original cult was, because as we're digging down we're finding layers that would suggest a very old usage here. It looks as though it's functioned as a shrine for at least two millennia—'

'But not necessarily relating to the same cult,' Arnold suggested.

'That's so. There's always been a tendency, as we know, for holy places to be commandeered time after time. Even Christian churches were often built on pagan sites because of the perceived holiness of the location. And this cave, it seems, was recognized to be a holy place . . .'

Or an evil one. The thought came unbidden to Arnold's mind.

'Have you found anything here of significance?' he asked.

'Or of *immense significance*, as Dr Westwood would say,' she replied, smiling. 'Well, first of all, I should stress that when the site was excavated — not terribly efficiently — sixty years ago, artefacts were found — evidence of a sky cult, for instance, wheel models and a wheel brooch, a bear-lunar crescent and a double-axe model—'

'The thunderbolt symbol.'

'That's right. And therefore a clear Roman influence. But there were older artefacts too. A small horned figure — a carving of a goose, which I imagine you know is often linked with war in vernacular mythology. A severed-head symbol, a plaque, and a small model of a ram-horned snake . . . they're held in the museum at Newcastle. They would suggest a Romano-British shrine, though Dr Westwood — who is an expert on symbolism — argues that the models could be ascribed to a Romano-Celtic solar cult. Whether that's right or wrong, well, it doesn't matter too much, because we're below that level in the deposits anyway and are looking at older remains. Not that we've found much. There are signs of ritual deposits — we came across a small silver *patera*, a bowl dedicated to the three mother-goddesses of the Celts, a few finger rings . . . but that's about all.' She paused thoughtfully. 'The trouble is, the earlier excavations might have removed most of what was here. I'm greatly tempted to leave the shrine with maybe just one of the team carrying on, so the rest of us can move outside.'

'Into the field?'

She nodded. 'The barrow, and the tumulus. It's a bigger job, of course, but all my instincts . . . you go by instinct, don't you, Arnold?'

'I don't discount it,' he replied.

She smiled. 'Well, maybe your instincts may act in support of mine. The way I followed your ideas at the boat burial last time we worked together. Come on, let's join the others for a tea break and talk further.'

* * *

'My own view,' Elfreda announced, tapping on the wooden table with an insistent teaspoon, 'is that there's enough iconographical evidence, from the artefacts at Newcastle and what we ourselves have found, to suggest the shrine was devoted to the worship of a Romano-Celtic war god. The plaque at Newcastle, for instance, could be a Cocidius dedication, representing a stylized Celtic warrior god.'

'But we don't know its provenance,' Peter Burns argued intensely. 'It came from an earlier dig where they were not as scientific in their location recording.'

'Nevertheless,' she insisted, 'if you think about the natural rock-cut chamber and the shelved area at the back it seems to be pretty obvious that the figurine in the museum could well have rested there. It's the figure of a warrior, naked, but with a close-fitting cap and small circular shield. His face is Celtic—'

'How do you come to that conclusion?' Alan Frith queried testily.

'Jutting brows, elongated eyes — definitely a native warrior,' she replied dismissively. 'I reckon a major local war god, or else an anonymous divinity. Romano-Celtic, military.'

'And where was the nearest military camp around here? We're miles from the wall.' Frith pointed out, almost jeeringly.

Arnold listened, sipping his tea, aware that Rena Williams played no part in the discussion. She listened, like him, and there was a small smile of pride on her lips. The earlier flippancy among the young people had gone, as had Elfreda's coquetry. Now they were arguing passionately about academic matters as Rena Williams had clearly taught them to do — accept nothing, question everything, search for the truth.

'It's obvious,' Elfreda was arguing. 'You don't need a Roman camp nearby to have a military shrine. Soldiers could have come here to —propitiate a native Celtic god — that they had adopted as their own already residing in the place before they came.'

'Theory only,' Ainsley Close scoffed.

Elfreda's eyes flashed. 'I'm prepared to bet you we'll turn up something of interest that will support my theory.'

'Such as what?'

She shook her head. 'Maybe something that befits a predominately military zone. A schematized war figure, horned, nude, ithyphallic . . .'

Peter Burns was amused. 'You can never stray far away from your constant theme, can you, Elfreda? *Ithyphallic*!'

'That's right,' she grinned, unabashed. 'Ithyphallic. You know, bigger and more—'

'That, I think, will do,' Rena Williams said positively, rising to her feet. 'Time you four got back to the trenches.'

3

While Arnold familiarized himself with the layout of the shrine and the work that was going on in the pit he continued to listen to their banter. What he had heard during the tea break had convinced him that the group were not airheaded: they had been well taught by Dr Williams, they were knowledgeable and enthusiastic. Behind the veneer of verbal horseplay and suggestive banter there were keen intellects and although the laughing continued intermittently, they were yet careful in their application to the task in hand, wary in their sifting, precise in their scraping away of the detritus of centuries.

In spite of himself, nevertheless, Arnold watched them, trying to weigh up the relationships that might lie behind the jokes. Peter Burns was the chief butt of Elfreda's jibes, which tended to concentrate on his public-school background, but he took them in good part. Her attempts to rouse Ainsley Close were largely unsuccessful: he merely smiled to himself and ignored her challenges. Alan Frith fired back more easily, occasionally riled — but it was interesting to note that none of them was angry with her for long.

And each of them admired her, for her confidence and her sexuality. Arnold saw it in their eyes, in the way they sometimes looked at her.

At the end of the afternoon, when Rena Williams called a halt to the work, the research students climbed into two cars. Rena Williams had come to the site with the students but now suggested she should drive with Arnold, to show him the way to the George and Dragon, while the others went on ahead. She turned off the generator and did a certain amount of tidying away before she locked the shed.

'So what do you think of the young reprobates?' she asked him as she got into Arnold's car. 'Leaving out Professor Westwood, of course!'

'Bright. Intelligent. Enthusiastic.'

'And a bit over the top?' she asked, smiling slightly.

'They're young. Nothing wrong with exuberance.'

Rena Williams grunted thoughtfully. 'I suppose not. I see it that way myself. On the other hand, there are times when Elfreda goes a bit too far. She's the brightest of the lot, you know — she'll get a doctorate with flying colours. But she can be a bit wearing at times, teases the lads too much in my view.'

'Maybe it's a defence mechanism,' Arnold suggested.

'To play down her intellectual superiority in male company, you mean?' Dr Williams shrugged. 'It's possible. I don't know. But there are times . . . well, there's a bit of a hothouse feeling on occasions.'

'I don't understand.'

'Sexual tension,' Rena Williams was silent for a little while as Arnold directed the car down the bumpy stone track. 'I have a feeling she's . . . involved with one of them and is playing some kind of game with the others.'

'A boyfriend? Which one?' Arnold asked. 'I didn't detect any . . . special relationship, but of course I've only just met them.'

Rena Williams laughed out loud. 'I've known them for almost two years, and I can't tell which one she's interested in. Yet there are times . . .' She paused, eyeing Arnold with a sideways glance, and she smiled slowly. 'We're like a pair of old gossips, aren't we?'

Arnold laughed. 'I suppose so.'

They drove in silence for a little while, down the narrow track until they swung out past the gateway to the big house on the hill.

'Hartshorn House,' she said, nodding towards the building. 'That reminds me. We're all invited out to dinner this evening.'

'How do you mean?'

'You know that the site we're working on is owned by Northern Heritage, and that the grant is partly from them to explore the area and partly from government grant?'

'Uh huh.'

'Well, the property was previously a section of the landholdings attached to Hartshorn House. It was sold to Northern Heritage about three years ago. Stephen Alston is the present owner. I've met him once, briefly, and we chatted about the shrine and so on, because obviously he's interested in what's happening on land previously held in the family. Anyway, he contacted me a couple of days ago and suggested that we might like to join him for dinner at Hartshorn.'

'That wouldn't have included me,' Arnold demurred.

'I don't think he's counting,' she laughed. 'One more for dinner will hardly dent the finances of the owner of Hartshorn. Besides, the invitation was to the team — and you're part of the team. Anyway, we're due there at eight so you've got time to have a good hot shower at the George and Dragon and generally settle in before we're due at the house.'

'Well, if you're sure it's all right.'

'It's all right.'

They were headed towards Garrigill. They splashed their way across a shallow ford flanked by a wooden bridge and then at Dr Williams's direction Arnold headed up a narrow road striking high towards the fell until the isolated hotel they were staying at appeared in front of a small, dark copse. Arnold parked beside the other cars to the left of the hotel and opened the boot to get out his bags.

'Stephen Alston . . .' he murmured thoughtfully.

Rena Williams had keen hearing; at the hotel entrance she looked back to him and nodded. 'You've heard of him?'

Arnold frowned. 'I don't really think so, and yet the name Alston, and Hartshorn . . . it's stirring something in my mind . . .'

'*Henry* Alston. Or Sir Henry Alston of Hartshorn House, I should say. Archaeologist, and collector. Stephen Henry Alston's a descendant of his: that's the connection.'

Arnold followed her into the hotel. Sir Henry Alston, the famous archaeologist who had died in the 1960s . . . At the reception desk Rena Williams smiled at him.

'You still don't recall who he was?'

'I'm not quite sure—'

'Sir Henry was the man who discovered the Fleetham Hoard.'

* * *

Arnold unpacked in his room and took a shower. The accommodation was surprisingly comfortable for such a remote hotel bearing in mind that most of the clients using it would probably be fell walkers. He guessed that the Williams research team had been given the best rooms and he certainly had no complaints: his was large and comfortable, with a double bed, television, and *en suite* bathroom. There was even a minibar, recently installed, he imagined.

While he dressed he thought about the Fleetham Hoard. It had been a sensational find, he recalled, made by Henry Alston about eighty years ago. An Iron Age chariot burial, it had included a vast array of artefacts — jewellery, arms, work boxes, mirrors, dress pins and the usual pig remains, but it was the ornate gold amulets and adornments that had created the greatest sensation. Alston had been able to prove links between Fleetham and burials at Écury-le-Repos in Marne, and the Rhineland, suggesting a widespread burial-cult connection. His work at Fleetham, and the books he had published thereafter, had made him a national, and even international figure. It had also made him a relatively wealthy man, although the Fleetham discovery, achieved when he was only twenty-one years old, was something he never managed to repeat.

His life after Fleetham, Arnold guessed, could never have been quite the same again. There must have been professional frustration at making no further important discoveries during his long life. He had died laden with honours, but he might well have felt dissatisfaction at having experienced the greatest moment in his life so early.

At 7.45 Arnold went downstairs. Fortunately, he had brought a suit with him in case of eventualities and felt appropriately dressed; he entered the bar and ordered himself an orange juice. As he was waiting he felt a tap on the shoulder.

'Don't tell me you're teetotal as well as being a paragon!' It was Elfreda.

She was wearing a simple blue dress that emphasized her figure and she had applied a little light make-up to her eyes and mouth. She had dispensed with the ponytail and her fair hair hung loose about her shoulders. She looked older, more mature, but she had lost none of her sparkle; it was her liveliness that made her particularly attractive, Arnold concluded.

'I'm just thirsty,' he explained. 'It's not a constitutional dislike for alcohol.'

'Well, I won't have the same — if you're offering.'

'I'm offering.'

'Gin and tonic, then. Not that there won't be plenty of booze up at Hartshorn House, I guess, but it's a good idea to get in a base. And I've got ten minutes to sink it before we have to leave. Sit over there?'

'Fine.'

Arnold took the drinks across to the table she had commandeered near the window. She nodded her thanks as he sat down in front of her and took her first sip at her gin. 'That'll do nicely,' she breathed. 'So, have you known Dr Williams long?'

She managed to endow even such a simple question with a certain archness. Arnold shook his head.

'We did some work together on a Viking site last year . . . so we don't really know each other at all well. How long had you been working with her before this project?'

'About eighteen months, really. I took my first degree at Bristol, started research at Reading thereafter but, well, there were a few problems there, man trouble, can't you guess? Some people will insist on taking you seriously. It all got a bit . . . intense, so I transferred up to York when I decided to take my doctorate.'

'You've been working pretty fast to get so far academically.'

'Now don't be so flattering, Mr Landon — I'm older than I look. I can give the lads a couple of years — except for Ainsley, anyway. He's getting ancient mid-twenties, like me.'

'You came together as a group in Dr Williams's department, I imagine.'

'That's right . . . but we sort of hang around together generally anyway. Ainsley and I are older than most of the muffs who wander around the campus, and the other two, well, they string along since we all have much the same interests. Like you.' She eyed him teasingly. 'You ought to come out for a few wild archaeological nights with us some time.'

Arnold laughed. 'I can hardly wait.'

He was aware from the corner of his eye that Dr Williams had entered the room. She observed the pair of them sitting there and walked across to them. She frowned down at Arnold. 'Don't let her lead you into bad habits, my friend,' she warned.

'We were just talking about the possibilities,' Elfreda announced.

'What I've seen of her, Arnold, she'd drink you under the table with no trouble at all.'

Arnold finished his orange juice. 'I think that's a distinct possibility.'

Rena Williams smiled. 'Anyway, time to go. May I suggest, Arnold, that you come in my car with me and Peter

Burns? I'm not a great lover of alcohol so it's no problem for me to abstain this evening.' She glanced at Elfreda. 'And I think Ainsley and Alan are expecting you to go with them. Ainsley's not drinking this evening — by agreement, I gather.'

Elfreda nodded. 'It's his turn. It means each of us can let our hair down from time to time. Bad luck he's hit a good booze night. I mean, Mr Alston's likely to provide us with quality wine, don't you think?' She glanced towards the door and a hint of malice crept into her tone. 'So who's taking the immensely important Professor Westwood?'

'He's making his own way there,' Rena Williams replied crisply, and led the way out of the bar to join the others in the reception area.

They arrived in their two cars at Hartshorn House at 8.15. Stephen Alston was standing in the brightly lit doorway of Hartshorn House as the two cars rasped their way up the gravel drive, and he greeted Rena Williams as she led the party up the steps. He ushered them into the hallway where she made the introductions.

Stephen Alston was about six feet in height and carried himself like a guardsman. He was perhaps forty years old with craggy, tanned features and a warm smile. His eyes were grey and his hair brown, with a frosting of white at the temples. His dark suit was well cut, and he wore a regimental tie. His manner was precise, but friendly, his tone slightly clipped and Arnold gained the impression that he was a man who kept control of himself in all areas: his appearance, his voice, his mannerisms and his lifestyle. It could have been his obvious military training, but it could also have been his natural inclinations. He led them into the library, to the left of the hallway, where drinks had already been placed on a mahogany table just inside the door.

'Please help yourselves, gentlemen, while I look after the ladies,' Alston said. 'I thought it would be more comfortable if we looked after ourselves — apart from which, we're a bit tight on staff at the moment with sickness and what have you, and the ones who've survived are involved in dinner preparations, so I'm sure you won't mind. Dr Williams . . . ?'

She settled for a tomato juice, while Elfreda quickly obtained another gin and tonic. Arnold helped himself to a small brandy after Peter Burns and Alan Frith poured themselves stiff whiskies. Ainsley Close, Arnold noted, accepted a mineral water.

Stephen Alston looked around at the group. 'It's good to see you all here, and I'm pleased you were able to accept the invitation. Is this the whole team? I thought—'

'Professor Westwood is yet to arrive,' Rena Williams interposed briskly. 'He should be here shortly. He . . . he likes to drive himself.'

'Ah, well, we're not due in the dining room for a while yet. And my other guest is not yet downstairs.' He smiled faintly at Rena Williams. 'As you'll discover, it so happens that this evening has turned out to be something of a . . . er . . . celebration.'

'Indeed? May I ask—?'

'All will be revealed,' Alston said. 'Ah, I hear a car in the drive . . . will you excuse me?'

Elfreda shuffled up to Arnold's elbow. 'I thought owners of places like this had them stuffed with servants. Still, I could find myself very comfortable here . . .'

Arnold nodded. He glanced around at the splendidly proportioned room. The walls were lined with books and in the far corner an iron spiral staircase gave access to a small catwalk which ran along two walls, where further books were located, stacked and gleaming red and gold and black in their bindings. It was a handsome library, and a well-provided one, yet there was an air of dustiness and decay about it, as though it were little used. The heavy brocade curtains were badly faded, and the carpets beneath their feet, he noted, were scuffed and somewhat worn. He wondered briefly whether the reason given for lack of attendance at the drinks table was more of an excuse than anything else.

Alston returned with Geoffrey Westwood just behind him. Westwood had taken the invitation seriously and had attired himself in a rather too tightly fitting dinner jacket. When he looked around the gathering he clearly felt that he was the only one who knew how to behave on such occasions and was not the slightest put out that his host was also dressed in a lounge suit rather than formal evening wear.

Alston poured him a large sherry and then excused himself and left the room. While the others chatted, Arnold did a slow tour of the library, glancing at the titles. After a little while he realized that it was a specialized collection — the volumes were mainly historical and archaeological in content, and there were leather-bound runs of several out-of-date Victorian magazines of antiquarian interest. From their appearance and the dates on their spines they would probably have formed part of the collection of Sir Henry Alston himself.

Stephen Alston had returned. 'My guest will be here in just a few minutes. I hope you're all looking after yourselves. Ah, Mr Landon, I see you're admiring the library.'

'Did Sir Henry Alston start it?'

Stephen Alston's craggy features broke into a smile. 'Started, and completed, as far as I know. I don't think his son Christopher was terribly interested. Any more than I was when the house devolved to me three years ago. No, I think the library is more or less as the old man left it, when he died in 1965.'

'So you've only been here three years?'

Alston nodded. 'That's right. I've been all over the place with the Royal Artillery — Cyprus, North Africa, the Med . . . a soldier's life — and a penurious one. But when Christopher died with no descendants, this property came to me and I decided to leave the army. I've had a few doubts since, but . . .' He glanced around at the book-lined walls.

'At least the library will have a future, anyway . . .'

Puzzled, Arnold was about to ask what he meant when Alston suddenly turned with a muffled excuse and headed for the door. As he reached it, his final guest appeared.

She was short, slim and dark haired, roughly Alston's age, Arnold guessed, and somewhat overdressed in a fussy, ankle-length, pink and white concoction of frills and bows. Her eyes were heavy lidded and her features somewhat plain; a sallow complexion presented a startling contrast to the bright red lipstick she affected. Alston took her hand and led her into the room.

'May I present Miss Margaret Eaton? Who is, I may add, my fiancée.'

* * *

The dinner was all that Elfreda could have hoped for: seated next to Arnold she told him so, and added that she heartily approved of the wine, both as to selection and quantity. She ate with gusto and drank with even greater pleasure. She took both white wine and red and gradually her cheeks became flushed, but her conversation was as teasing as ever when she spoke to her friends.

Alston had placed himself between Rena Williams and Margaret Eaton. Arnold noted that he was very attentive to his fiancée, who seemed a little shy and reserved; nevertheless, he was a good host, asking Dr Williams about the progress of the work at the shrine. Eventually, however, she rebelled.

'It's all very well, Mr Alston, talking about the shrine and saying nothing about your projected marriage. How long have you been engaged, may I ask?'

Alston smiled, and glanced at his fiancée. 'I suppose, really, a matter of hours. We'd talked about it in the States, but it was only this week that Margaret finally agreed.'

'So was it in the States you met?' Rena Williams asked. Margaret Eaton's voice displayed a certain nervousness.

She giggled. 'That's so. Stephen was out at the house talking to my father about the Alston Collection and this estate. After that, well, I guess we found we had mutual interests . . . and things sort of went on from there. I have to admit there were certain problems . . . mine is a Mormon family, you see—'

'But no problems we haven't overcome,' Alston interrupted easily.

'So will you live here or in the States?' Arnold asked.

'I'm not sure I could stand your weather.' Margaret Eaton exclaimed.

Alston nodded. 'The house will be sold in due course.'

'Ah, that's what you hinted at about the library, earlier,' Arnold said. 'It's to be sold also?'

'Not exactly. The Eaton family established a trust some years ago. The foundation will take over the Alston Collection and the library. It will all be moved to the States, of course, but at least both collection and library will be kept intact. It will be a relief to me, I can tell you. Things have been somewhat tight of late . . .'

He frowned slightly, as though he felt he had said too much, then smiled at his fiancée. She was already turning to the professor on her left.

'Of course, the work you do must be really exciting here. I mean, the length of your history! We just can't match that in the States!'

Geoffrey Westwood was only too pleased to be able to show off to her and launched into an account of his academic and archaeological victories. As he expounded at length Alston was able to talk to Rena Williams. Since Arnold was unburdened by Elfreda, who rarely stopped talking at all he was able to observe the others quietly.

Perhaps a little unkindly, he felt surprised at Alston's choice for a bride. He was a tall, military man of good appearance and confidence but Margaret Eaton seemed mousy at his side, nervous, aware of her essential dowdiness, which was emphasized by the unsuitable dress, and not endowed with small talk. As the evening wore on she fell more and more silent, suffering Westwood's banalities, smiling at Alston from time to time when he spoke to her, clearly adoring him with her glances, but lacking in the kind of personality that would impose itself upon the gathering.

Elfreda, of course, was quite different. As the wine took effect, her bantering remarks to her colleagues became more numerous, and she baited Peter Burns unmercifully. She gained little from him. He took it all with a certain ironic smile, unwilling to respond aggressively in company. And although Ainsley Close tried to suggest she calmed down from time to time, she paid no attention, drawing the occasional sharp glance from Alan Frith when she directed her barbs at him.

But Arnold had not realized how affected she had become by her alcohol intake until, when coffee was being served, Professor Westwood got onto his favourite subject in his monologue to Margaret Eaton.

'Celtic sacral depiction,' he pronounced loudly, 'frequently exhibits features which transform real imagery into something deliberately less lifelike.'

'I don't quite understand,' Margaret Eaton managed to say.

'The Celtic iconographic tradition displays a high degree of stylistic abstraction or schematism—' he began to explain.

'What the professor *means*,' Elfreda interrupted, 'is that the Celts used a "shorthand" method of representation in their art — just putting in essential lines, not carving the whole figure. It's a view of *immense significance*.'

Alan Frith chortled, and Peter Burns took a quick sip of wine to hide his smile.

Westwood frowned. He had accepted very little wine and clearly took a dim view of the manner in which the younger generation had indulged themselves. He cleared his throat. 'This stylistic abstraction led, of course, to inferior workmanship—'

'Rubbish,' Elfreda interrupted casually.

There was a short silence. Rena Williams leaned forward to say something but Professor Westwood recovered first. 'By modern criteria—'

'Modern criteria are irrelevant,' Elfreda interrupted again. 'You should examine these representations on their own terms of function and context. This "schematized" form, as you put it, was a conscious and successful form of image making.'

'The Graeco-Roman ideal—'

'Was simply rejected, not because Celtic artists couldn't produce faithful copies, but because they regarded its rigidity as unnecessary within the context of their own cult imagery!'

She was flushed and excited. Professor Westwood, on the other hand, was offended. His face was pale and his eyes glittered with anger. For the moment he was controlling himself, but Arnold could see that it would not take much more to goad him to explosion point. In an attempt to ignore Elfreda, the professor turned back to Miss Eaton.

'The problem with the young today,' he suggested, 'is that they are not prepared to learn from the wisdom of their elders. They believe only they have the keys to an understanding of the past; only they are capable of interpreting fact; only they understand the symbolism of—'

'Symbolism?' Elfreda's words were slightly slurred, but her tone was scathing. 'You do talk such crap, Professor Westwood. What the hell do you really know about the symbolism of Celtic art?'

'Unlike you, young woman,' he replied cuttingly, 'I have published on the matter.'

'Published unreadable balderdash!' she replied, rather spoiling the effect with a hiccup.

Ainsley Close leaned across and put his hand on Elfreda's, as though to caution her and calm her down. She flung off his hand: her colour was high and her temper suddenly aflame, heated by the wine.

'Not only unreadable, but ignorant!' she continued. 'You've built your reputation on sand: there's no basis to it, no strength. You've been hung up, all your career, on a view of the stylization of Celtic art — the possible correlation between the ethnic origins of the deities represented and the art forms in which they're depicted. And you balance that against Graeco-Roman art and find the Celtic form wanting! But it isn't really about that at all!'

Rena Williams leaned forward. Her voice was cold. 'Elfreda, I don't think this is the right place, or occasion, to carry on a discussion about Celtic art. Professor Westwood, as the expert on the matter—'

'Expert!' Elfreda leaned back in her chair and struck the heel of her left hand against her forehead, in a dramatic gesture of contempt. 'God save us from pompous . . . pompous experts. I've had to listen to his rubbish for eighteen months now, and he's so blindly wrong! He ignores the reality — the animal emphasis, the potent symbolism, the bristle exaggeration of the boar, the symbol of fertility seen in antlers and horns, the exaggeration of the sexual and generative features of the human body—'

'I see,' Westwood grated, 'that we're back to your favourite subject.'

'Is that what you think? I'll tell you what I think,' Elfreda jeered drunkenly. 'If we were to see a sche— schematic Celtic representation of what you stand for, Professor Westwood, its lines would include an exaggerated head but would certainly not include any ithy— ithyphallic representations. Pompous, opinionated and big-headed, yes; but powerful and significant and important . . . decidedly not!'

For a moment, Arnold thought Professor Westwood was going to throw something at her: his hand was tensed on the knife on the table in front of him. But then he regained control. His eyes grew cold and menacing, his mouth was jagged with vicious fury. But he was in control. He turned his head, to look at his host.

'Mr Alston, I regret this . . . ah . . . academic disagreement. I can only apologize for my young friend there, in her overexuberant expression of her viewpoint. Youth and inexperience are terrible burdens to bear. Fortunately, they are behind me and I can express my opinions with restraint. But I'm sure you will excuse me if I now feel it's time to leave.

It's been a splendid meal and an occasion to remember. I've been delighted to meet your fiancée, but I have work to do in preparation for the morning and I'm sure my absence now will not detract from the evening.'

He had come out of the situation with more dignity than his opponent, Arnold thought as Elfreda slumped back in her chair and Westwood rose to leave. Alston got up with him, somewhat embarrassed, and after a moment Margaret Eaton also rose, to follow them nervously into the hall.

Rena Williams pushed back her chair and came to stand behind Elfreda.

'I think, young woman, it's time we all went home. And in the morning, you'll have some hard apologizing to do!'

Elfreda's eyes were bleary. 'What the hell! That randy old goat had eyed me up ever since I started attending his classes. That was bad enough — but when I've had to listen to his drivel as well . . . it's time I told him what I thought of him!'

'Well, now you have told him,' Rena Williams announced sternly, 'you'd better make sure you calm him down in the morning. If you don't, there'll be no way you can stay on the site team, and almost inevitably you'll have to leave the doctorate programme!'

CHAPTER TWO

1

The next few days saw a decided change of atmosphere at the shrine site. Arnold took no breakfast the morning after the dinner at Hartshorn House, but merely had a coffee in his room. When he arrived at the field the young men were already there but there was no sign of Elfreda, Rena Williams or Professor Westwood. Arnold could guess what was happening: the three would be in session at the George and Dragon, trying to repair the situation that had developed the night before.

There was little bantering in the cave. Rena Williams's Three Musketeers were subdued, their thoughts elsewhere, and as the morning advanced their mood became gloomier.

Professor Westwood came on site just before midday. He displayed a triumphant affability towards Arnold, greeting him with an unusual cordiality that made Arnold suspect he had got his way in the discussions that morning. Rena Williams arrived an hour or so later, with Elfreda in tow. The younger woman looked gloomy; her face was somewhat puffy as though she had been crying, but when she glanced at Arnold there was still a devil dancing in her eyes — subdued, but revengeful. Arnold suspected that Westwood might have got the better of the morning discussion, but Elfreda Gale's spirit had not been entirely broken.

Arnold was across to one side, working alone, sifting some of the earth that had been taken from the shrine floor, when Rena Williams came across to join him. She crouched down beside him, peering at the small mound of sifted earth. 'Anything of interest?'

Arnold shook his head.

She sniffed. 'I'm getting a bit concerned about the shrine site. We're spending a lot of time there and I have a feeling it'll be unproductive in the end.' She was silent for a little while. 'I'm sorry about last night. I should have apologized on the way back, but I was too angry.'

'You've nothing to apologize for.' Arnold hesitated. 'And I imagine Elfreda will have mended some fences this morning.'

Rena Williams sighed. 'Yes, I insisted she came with me up to Hartshorn House to make a personal apology to Mr Alston. He was very good. Dismissed it almost airily. Turned the conversation to discuss our work here — said he'd like to come up and see what was happening. No, he was very good about last night's performance from Elfreda. Not like Professor Westwood.'

'The professor had a confrontation with Elfreda this morning?'

Dr Williams nodded, her face serious. 'He was quite cold about it, but very determined. He wanted to sack Elfreda from this programme and indeed he wanted to make a complaint to the vice-chancellor — which could have ended her hopes of continuing with the doctorate.'

'I would have thought that was an overreaction.'

She shrugged. 'She behaved extremely badly, of course. Westwood is a proud man, and jealous of his . . . reputation. I think Elfreda really struck him on the raw last night, criticizing him in front of strangers. It was, of course, unforgivable.'

'Even so . . .'

'Well, the three of us had a long session in a private room at the George and Dragon before I took her to Hartshorn. I persuaded her privately that her apology to Westwood would have to be a generous one — she was inclined, as you might imagine, to defend her corner and even continue with the argument about symbolism.'

'She did actually talk a certain amount of sense,' Arnold suggested gently.

'Albeit drunkenly expressed.' Dr Williams gave him a tired smile. 'That may be so, but a continuation of it would not have served. So I pressed her to apologize. Profusely. She didn't like doing it. There were a few tears, of temper as much as anything else, but in the end she did what she had to. I'm afraid Professor Westwood . . . well, he milked the situation for all it was worth. He really made her grovel.' She paused. 'There never has been much love lost between that pair.'

Arnold glanced across to the shrine cave, where Geoffrey Westwood was standing in the doorway, hands on hips, watching the work carried on by the young people at the shrine. 'He seems to be pleased with the result.'

Dr Williams shrugged. 'He made her crawl. I just hope it's over now. But there's the danger he'll keep needling her.'

Arnold was sure of it. The triumphalism of Westwood's attitude was apparent, and it would be gall to Elfreda. If it continued there was little doubt in Arnold's mind that she would explode again. It would be better if they were kept well apart for a few days.

'If I may make a suggestion . . .'

'Yes?'

'I'm inclined to go along with your feeling regarding the cave. The Victorian excavations have stripped the place pretty cleanly, and we're down to lower levels now and finding very little. My guess is that there's not much more to find. You did suggest moving away, just leaving one person working in the cave, while the rest started opening up the barrow.'

Her eyes fixed on him as she frowned, nodding. 'I think I can guess what you're going to suggest. Elfreda . . .'

'Let her work in the cave by herself for a few days — or maybe leave one of the lads with her for company. But the rest of us could start working on the barrow and it would keep Westwood and Elfreda away from each other. Until things cool down.'

Rena Williams took a deep breath. 'I'll have to discuss it with Professor Westwood, of course. He'll probably want to keep her close so he can crow over her . . . but if I pressed the case for the barrow without mentioning Elfreda . . .'

'I think it would solve a problem, and I think it's right anyway: the shrine site doesn't have much more to offer us, but the barrow could be interesting.'

Rena Williams smiled at him, warmly. She put her hand on his shoulder to help herself rise from her crouching position, and he felt there was gratitude in the gesture. And perhaps something more.

* * *

Arnold enjoyed the weekend. Dr Williams managed to get Westwood committed to splitting the team before he realized he would not be supervising Elfreda's work, but his own professional interest in opening up the barrow finally overcame his objections to losing the chance to lord it over his enemy.

While Elfreda was instructed to continue in the cave with Peter Burns, the rest of the team started work on the barrow, stripping off the turf and a small amount of topsoil and pegging the whole area with Dr Williams's usual collection of coloured golf tees as markers. Geoffrey Westwood took extensive photographs of the area, carefully aligned with the markers, and Arnold lent a hand in writing up a description of the site. On the Sunday they began to select a section for inspection.

Arnold began to wonder whether he was coming down with a cold. As he worked on the site the initial excitement he had experienced began to fade, and he felt somewhat deflated and shivery. The odd thing was that both Westwood and Dr Williams also fell silent, and while Alan Frith and Ainsley Close continued a desultory conversation while they worked, the general atmosphere was subdued.

It could have been the result of Elfreda's absence, working in the cave: she tended to keep spirits high when she was around. But there was more to it than that: clouds had gathered high above them and the day was dull and grey. There was a physical blanket of coldness that seemed to have descended upon the team, almost an air of foreboding, as they worked quietly and carefully at the friable soil. Arnold felt an uneasiness he was unable to explain to himself, an inability to settle, the feeling that something chill and unpleasant was hovering over the team, watching, waiting.

Working on the barrow was not proving to be as pleasant an experience as Arnold had anticipated.

The agreement he had reached with the Morpeth office was that he would spend Mondays and Tuesdays back at his desk, leaving three days and the weekend to work on site with Dr Williams, so he left the hotel on Sunday evening and made his way back to Morpeth. When he arrived at his bungalow there was a car standing outside. Jane Wilson got out of the driving seat.

'I'd just about given up on you and was about to leave.'

'Come on in for a cup of tea,' Arnold suggested.

'I've been up to Edinburgh to a book fair,' she explained as she followed him into the bungalow, 'and thought it would be a good opportunity to call in to see you. It's a few weeks since we've managed a chat.'

Jane was a good friend who had become closer since her uncle had died and she had had to take over the antiquarian bookshop on the Quayside in Newcastle. She and Arnold had interests in common — as an historical novelist she had a similar passion for the past, and she was keen now to hear how things had been going at the shrine site. When she heard they were opening up the barrow she became excited.

'What are you hoping to find there?'

Arnold looked at her. She was not a beautiful woman, like Karen Stannard, but there was an honesty and directness about her that appealed to him. She had a snub nose, and brown hair cut rather severely; she held strong opinions she was quite prepared to state and although she was short in stature she could be quite dominant on occasions. He liked her, was very fond of her, in fact, though their relationship had remained slightly wary, in spite of being close friends. She did have the capacity, however, to transfer some of her own enthusiasms to him.

'We're hoping it's a burial site, of course. But we don't know quite what to expect.'

'No clues from the shrine?'

Arnold shook his head. 'Not really. There's a possibility the shrine was mainly used for the worship of Cocidius, and it might have drawn military attention, but as we've dug deeper, going back further into the past, there's been little to find. It's as though it served as a shrine from shortly before the Roman occupation, but before that . . .'

'You've no theory?'

He shook his head, then hesitated, eyeing her warily. 'I've often enough accused you of . . . romanticism when we've discussed ancient sites.'

'So?'

Arnold sighed. 'It's just that I sort of get . . . feelings about the area.'

She snorted happily. 'Maybe I've been good for you after all!'

He smiled vaguely in response. 'They're not pleasant feelings. A sort of coldness descends on me when I work there. Rena has suggested the site may have been a place of dread, had an evil reputation locally, until finally the shrine was built. Maybe what Rena said influenced me. But I have to say, the place sort of makes me shiver. Silly, isn't it?'

Jane was silent for a little while. She looked away from him, her face impassive. 'Did you tell Dr Williams about these . . . feelings?' she asked in a cool tone.

Arnold shook his head. 'No. I'd have felt foolish.'

She looked at him again. Her tone was warmer when she said, 'But you told *me* about them . . .'

It was a comment he was still puzzling about vaguely the next morning when he drove into Morpeth. She had asked him more about the site, but she seemed very interested in his views about Rena Williams also, and was slightly dismissive at the same time. It was as though she felt a certain resentment at the fact he had been invited to work at the site, even though she was interested to know what he might discover there. He came to the conclusion, as he parked his car in the headquarters car park, that Jane Wilson, like most women, was a mystery to him.

He had not been in his office for more than an hour on Monday morning before he had a summons from Karen Stannard.

He went to her office to find her standing with her back to the window, the sunlight glinting in her hair, looking impossibly beautiful as usual.

'So, you're refreshed after your days away from the office?'

'It's been an interesting experience,' he replied guardedly.

'So has the first meeting of the Stiles Committee. I'm pleased we decided I should be present; I think issues are coming up which would have been beyond your competence.' She flashed him a smile, pleased with herself. 'What about the shrine site? I expected a report.'

'You'll have it this afternoon. I've almost completed it.'

'Meanwhile, you can tell me.'

Arnold gave her a brief rundown of the work that had been undertaken, omitting any mention of the tensions that had arisen on site as a result of the clash between Professor Westwood and Elfreda Gale. He had told Jane Wilson about it, but it did not seem relevant in his report to Karen Stannard.

'So you've started opening up the barrow?' She frowned. 'That could prove to be interesting.' She moved to her desk to consult her diary. 'I think . . . I think I should call up there in a week or so. Take a look for myself. Make the acquaintance of Dr Williams again.'

'I'm sure you'd be welcome,' Arnold replied blandly.

She shot a sharp glance in his direction, searching for irony. She sniffed. 'Stiles doesn't meet again for three weeks and there's plenty on here, but maybe I can find time. Perhaps you'll warn Dr Williams, and meanwhile . . . I'll expect your written reports.'

'Of course, Deputy Director . . .'

Unlike Jane Wilson, Karen Stannard seemed to hold Rena Williams in high regard.

* * *

Arnold returned to the field site on Wednesday of that week and found they had stripped a large section of the barrow and were busy removing a few further inches of topsoil. Rena Williams took him to the shed to show him some items they had already found. The first was a bronze coin. Arnold inspected it closely. On its obverse side there was a badly eroded inscription which he was unable to transcribe; on the reverse he thought he could make out an armed figure.

Rena Williams agreed. 'I think it's a warrior, and you see the boar standard? And that thing at his feet . . .'

'A severed head.'

'Typically Celtic,' she stated. 'It's noteworthy that in images of divine beings there was often an overemphasis upon the head. It denoted power. I've talked it over with Geoffrey Westwood — he agrees that the frequent occurrence of head representation and severed heads is part of the power concept in an extreme form.'

'I've heard of the existence of a Celtic head cult,' Arnold murmured.

She leaned closer to him, her shoulder touching his as together they peered at the coin. 'It's not just head depictions in stone or metal — there's also ritual head collecting. It's well attested in Graeco-Roman and Irish literary sources.'

Her hair smelled of fresh pine, but there was a muskiness also that he found oddly disturbing.

'Then there's this,' she said, leaning across the trestle table and unwrapping another object. She held it up for him to inspect. It was perhaps six inches high, a wooden carving of a warrior, naked, but with torc, helmet and sword belt.

'Celtic?'

'In the Celtic tradition,' she suggested. 'But we found this too.' Once more she reached across to a small cloth-wrapped object. It was a broken carving, showing just the armed torso of a warrior. 'Can you see what's carved on the breastplate?'

She was breathing quickly and her eyes were shining with enthusiasm. The excitement lit up her face, transforming it; she was a handsome woman, but now she was almost beautiful, Arnold thought. He dragged his attention towards the carving.

'A severed-head symbol.'

'That's right.' She drew back slightly to look at him, lips parted. 'I think it's showing us what we might find in the barrow.'

'How do you mean?'

'We discussed it among the group when we found it. Geoffrey, of course, went on about symbolism, but it was Elfreda, to be fair, who came up with the hypothesis.'

'I don't imagine Westwood enjoyed that too much.'

'He didn't,' she agreed emphatically. 'But even he was forced to concede she had a point. She suggested that maybe the torso breastplate with the severed-head carving was part of a depiction that possibly served the dual function of apotropaic — protective — power to shield the fighter with an image of victory, and at the same time terrifying his enemies with the image of their defeat. It's a good analysis, we believe.'

'And the other carved warrior image?'

She took a deep breath. 'A representation of the man himself . . . the man who was laid to rest in the barrow. We conclude, Arnold, we're on a site of—'

'Immense significance,' he interposed and was rewarded by her laugh.

* * *

When Arnold continued the work with them on the site he was aware of a change in the atmosphere. To begin with, Elfreda and Peter Burns had been invited back out of the shrine so that the whole team was working at the barrow. For her it was partly a rehabilitation, partly a recognition that the more important opportunities lay outside the shrine cave. It was also a reward for her cogent analysis of the finds. The excitement generated by the coin and the carvings had affected them all: they worked swiftly and keenly, sifting everything carefully, and though Westwood still took the opportunity to display his dislike of Elfreda with occasional sharp comments, generally the group was working well together.

Over the next two days the project went on apace. They had opened up the eastern end of the barrow and had decided to sink a small exploratory shaft. They quickly found results — an amulet with a wheel motif; a small collection of ritually bent spear models — that convinced both academics that they were on the right track.

Westwood, Dr Williams and Arnold discussed it over a drink in the bar, after dinner at the George and Dragon on the Saturday evening.

'It's my opinion,' Geoffrey Westwood announced portentously, 'that we have come across a discovery of immense significance. Who knows, it might even be as important as the Fleetham Hoard, exposed in 1911.'

'I think that's going a bit too far,' Rena demurred.

'Maybe so, maybe so,' he conceded. 'But the early figurines we have unearthed will have been placed in the barrow at some time after the inhumation—'

'If there is one,' Arnold suggested cautiously.

'I'm pretty confident.' Dr Williams said.

'The ritually bent spear models and the warrior carving would suggest evidence of a cult, arising after the inhumation. What we may well be looking at is the burial of a warrior king, which later became a site of veneration. When we uncover more of the area, I'm sure we'll come across evidence that will lead us back in time, to the inhumation itself, but where the artefacts, such as those we've already discovered, will date to periods at some distance from inhumation . . .'

Westwood and Dr Williams continued the discussion for some time, while Arnold listened. The argument sounded convincing, though he was slightly puzzled how the theory fitted with the earlier suggestion that the area had been regarded as one of potent evil and dread. At what point of time would veneration turn to fear?

Geoffrey Westwood finally gave up at 10.30. After he had gone to bed, Rena Williams offered Arnold a nightcap; he was pleasantly weary after the days in the open air, slightly stiff in his joints, but well inclined towards a final brandy. They sat alone in the residents' lounge of the hotel, companionable, each with a brandy glass in hand.

'Professor Westwood seems to be calming down over the Elfreda business,' Arnold suggested.

'Mmmm.' She wriggled comfortably in the deep, winged easy chair. 'He still takes her to task from time to time needles her unnecessarily. It's a bit of a power game with him, I think.' She smiled. 'But most of the time he's concentrating so much on the dig he forgets all about her. That's good news.'

'Makes your job easier.'

'My job?'

'Site gauleiter.'

She laughed. 'Is that how you see me? Militaristic official in charge of a recalcitrant squad?'

He liked the sound of her laugh. 'No, of course not. But you do have a few tightropes to walk, in personal terms.'

'I suppose so . . . And I have to admit, it sometimes gets tiresome, feeling I have to assert myself. When women are in charge, tensions can arise. Things can be a bit . . . lonely, then. You help things there, Arnold.'

'Me?'

'You shouldn't be surprised.' She looked at him, smiling, and touched the back of his hand lightly. 'You're an outsider, of course, and that helps people behave to a certain extent. But you also have a calming influence that springs from your own personality. You never seem to get particularly ruffled—'

'That's not true, believe me!'

'—and you seem to bring an air of security to the place, a sanity, a harmonization with the environment, the history . . . It's difficult to explain. For instance . . . well, we discussed it somewhat when you were away. There's an odd . . . atmosphere about the place. Have you noticed it?'

'I'm not sure what you mean,' Arnold replied cautiously.

'How can I put it . . . ?' She stared at the brandy glass in her hand for a little while. 'I told you at the beginning, I felt maybe the site had a history of . . . unpleasantness. Shunned by locals — it would account for the relatively late dating of the shrine. Well, that feeling still persists in some degree, and we've all felt it at some time or another. Haven't you?'

Arnold hesitated. 'I suppose so. Nothing tangible, you understand.'

'That's right.' She glanced at him sideways. 'The odd thing is, when you're on site that feeling disappears. As far as I'm concerned, at least.'

'I can't imagine why.'

'Nor I.' She laughed suddenly, and finished her drink. 'At least . . .'

She stopped short, inclined to say no more on the matter.

'You're off to bed?' Arnold asked as she rose to her feet.

She nodded. 'Might be a big day tomorrow.'

She turned and began to walk towards the door. Then she hesitated, stopped, and came back to where Arnold stood, drink half-finished in his hand.

'Good night, Arnold,' she said, and touched him on the cheek.

Arnold was still in the lounge when he heard Elfreda come into the hotel. The Musketeers had spent the evening in the bar but Elfreda apparently had been down to a pub in Garrigill, meeting a friend. Now, as Arnold heard her come in and collect her key from the unmanned reception desk, he had the feeling she was not alone.

When he finally went upstairs some twenty minutes later he passed Elfreda's door and was aware of low, muffled tones in the room. It seemed that for her, at least, the night was not yet over.

He wondered who was with her, but chided himself. It was none of his business. Later, after he had gone to bed he was disturbed by the sound of a car leaving the car park. Next morning Elfreda appeared sullen, and out of sorts, inclined to snap back at Geoffrey Westwood when he spoke sharply to her.

The following two weeks passed by swiftly. Arnold managed his usual four or five days at the site, but Karen Stannard did not put in an appearance. There were no more nightly visits for Elfreda and no late-evening drinks with Rena Williams — indeed, she was slightly cool with him and tended to retire each evening after dinner, unless the group as a whole were together in the lounge. And the work on the barrow proceeded well.

They uncovered a larger section, heading towards the centre, and a few more small artefacts came to light. Arnold was now inclined towards the hypothesis Westwood had expounded: the iconographic evidence suggested a cult burial, a later veneration of the site for some period of time after inhumation. Late on the Saturday afternoon they made an interesting find. Ainsley Close whooped in surprise and called the others around. They watched while he carefully detached from the loose soil a simple boat model. In the shed they cleaned it quickly. It contained five pinewood figures of nude warriors. They were perfectly formed, with quartz-pebble eyes, detachable phalli and round shields.

They discussed the objects at great length but could come up with no hypothesis. In Geoffrey Westwood's view the boat model and its inhabitants would not be precisely datable, but he thought they would be at least as early as the Iron Age.

The find stirred their senses and they worked late that day, almost feverishly, Westwood continuing even when he had to use light from the generator. They were all at the site again early next morning. It was as though they all felt they were close to something: the atmosphere was tense. An electric hostility began to spark between Elfreda and Westwood and there were a few snappish exchanges. The air was crisp and cold and Arnold felt shivery, aware of the hill at their back and the long fall of the field to the rushy meadow below. A cool breeze began to blow, and there was a soughing sound among the trees on the hill as they worked with an odd desperation through the afternoon, edgy, uncertain, strangely ill at ease with each other.

In the late afternoon the sky grew heavier, dark clouds piling up in the west and they heard the occasional roll of distant thunder. With the heaviness, the field grew silent; the trees were still and no birds sang, no rabbits rustled in the undergrowth. It was as though the world was waiting, expectant, and perspiration stung Arnold's eyes as he knelt in the trenched area, sifting, inspecting, scraping.

At five o'clock Peter Burns stood up mutely.

Arnold caught the movement out of the corner of his eye and glanced towards him. The man's red hair was damp, curling around his forehead as he stood staring down at his feet, speechlessly. His stillness drew the attention of the others; each of them slowly turned to look at him.

'Peter!' Rena Williams said sharply. 'What's the matter?'

For a moment it was as though he had not heard her.

Then he turned his head to look at her; a nervous tongue flickered over his dry lips. He pointed down at his feet.

When they drew near they saw what he had found. A single skull, grinning up at them across the gulf of centuries.

A severed head.

2

During the next ten days they uncovered three severed-head skeletons and it caused a minor sensation in the local press. Both Karen Stannard and the director, Brent-Ellis, managed to find time to visit the site, briefly, when the photographers were present; the local police called to be satisfied that there was no question of a criminal act having been committed; and Arnold himself was given the freedom to stay on site for the next three weeks without having to return to the office.

'My assistant is now in place,' Karen Stannard said to him quietly, with a malicious glint in her eye. 'Who knows, we might not even need you back at the office at all!'

She was happy enough, nevertheless, to feed off the media interest in the exhumation. So was Simon Brent-Ellis, who issued a statement at the next council meeting, drawing attention to his department's presence — through Arnold Landon — at the time of the discovery, and almost suggesting it was his own foresightedness that had led directly to the discovery of the burial.

But it was only after some of the brouhaha had calmed down that Stephen Alston visited the site. He had said he was interested in seeing the work, that evening at Hartshorn

House, but Arnold guessed he had been put off by the recent rush of reporters and photographers. He turned up one morning when the site was quieter.

Dr Williams and Arnold stood with him in the tented area, looking down at the cleared area at the edge of which Elfreda and Ainsley Close were working under the supervision of Professor Westwood.

They were silent for a little while.

The skeletons had not been moved yet: Dr Williams wanted to be certain nothing was disturbed too quickly. They lay, all three of them in roughly the same position, on the left side, arms extended, knees raised as though crouching. Each had been decapitated, and the head placed just below the left hand. Beside the right hand of the centrally placed skeleton was a scattered pile of bones, which Professor Westwood declared to be pig bones, and a small jug.

'We've also found some clay Venus figures,' Dr Williams explained, 'which were lying beside the left-hand skeleton. We believe they signify an attempt to protect the dead in the underworld.'

Stephen Alston leaned forward to inspect the remains more closely.

'Are these men or women?' he asked.

'Probably men — difficult to say at this stage.'

'And were they natural deaths — or murder?'

'They are possibly ritual killings but we don't know — it's too early to tell.'

'So what's the significance of the pig bones and the jug?'

She hesitated and glanced towards her colleague. 'Perhaps Geoffrey would like to explain.'

There had been tension at the site all day. Arnold guessed Rena's suggestion was an attempt to mollify Professor Westwood, who had been snapping and snarling at Elfreda Gale for the last three hours. Now, as he heard her suggestion, he straightened, moving sideways. Elfreda was working close to his feet and he stepped on her hand. She let fly at him verbally, with an obscenity, and wrung her hand. 'You did that deliberately!' she shouted as she stepped away from him, nursing her fingers.

He glared coldly at her. 'Don't be absurd! That was your clumsiness, not mine! For God's sake, woman, be careful where you're walking now.' you've been handling that trowel like a spade all day and now you're trampling the edge of the trench! Women are supposed to be deft — but you have the touch of a bull in a china shop!' He turned away from her and shook his head. 'I'm sorry, Dr Williams . . . you were saying?'

She looked at him expressionlessly, but her mouth was tight, as Elfreda stood wringing her hand and Ainsley Close glowered up at the professor. Dr Williams's tone was cool. 'I was suggesting you might like to explain our theories about this burial to Mr Alston.'

Westwood climbed out of the trenched area, red-faced and puffing slightly. Elfreda Gale said nothing but she watched him, still nursing her hand, and Arnold detected the glint of suppressed fury in her eyes. Ainsley touched her shoulder, drawing her away.

Brushing his hands on his jeans, Westwood nodded pompously at Stephen Alston. It was the second time the owner of Hartshorn House had witnessed a quarrel between the professor and the student but Westwood seemed in no way put out. 'Of course, of course,' he said airily. 'We still have only theories, but it's already clear as far as I'm concerned that this was a ritual burial. The presence of pig bones is typical in Celtic inhumations — meat would have been left in the grave for the deceased's journey to the underworld, or for the infernal feast, with wine, or beer, in the jug. The clay figurines, well, it's not unusual for a warrior to be buried with such protective devices as the Venus figures.'

He folded his arms and looked wise.

'As to how they died . . . certainly they might have died naturally, and there are no signs of damaged bones from axe wounds, or spears . . . On the other hand, if you look closely at the right-hand skeleton, there's a ligature lying to one side . . . you see it?'

'You mean that one could have been strangled?' Westwood shrugged.

'There's no way of telling now, of course, not least since all three were decapitated.'

'But doesn't the decapitation mean that they died violent deaths?' Alston asked.

'Not at all.' Westwood shook his head. 'It's more likely to denote a cult inhumation. Skull burials are quite common in Celtic graves — a practice probably apotropaic, protective, a tradition which links closely with the head-collecting customs that one comes across in the literature. It would have been part of the cult, to decapitate, and place the severed head under the left hand. That one,' he pointed out with a bony finger, 'was the first we came across.'

'The one Peter Burns found,' Arnold offered.

Westwood scowled. 'A matter of chance, of course. However, I have now formed my own hypothesis as to what we have here. The inhumation on the left — with the ligature — could have been a captive sacrifice, interred with the chieftain.'

'The one in the centre?' Alston asked.

'Quite probably,' Westwood agreed. 'The central figure is probably the main burial — the chief, perhaps, or a local king. These two will have been interred after the death of the chief, probably by way of sacrifice. Strangled, with the ligature. All three were decapitated before burial in accordance with their cult beliefs.'

'There's also the stones,' Arnold offered.

Westwood did not care for the interruption. He nodded gracelessly. 'I was coming to that. Each skeleton was weighted down with a stone — we removed them; you can see them stacked over there at the side of the trench. It would seem to have been common practice in some cults to dismember skeletons in a ritual body exposure after death, to allow the spirits to depart easily. Here, weighting down the corpses with stones might have been an alternative cult belief — the stones were placed on top of the corpses to prevent the spirits rising. But we can't be certain. That . . .' he hesitated. 'That was a suggestion made by Mr Landon.'

Rena Williams smiled slightly. She was still angry at the way Westwood had been treating Elfreda all morning. 'I don't think Mr Landon actually agrees with all of Professor Westwood's suggestions, in any case.'

Stephen Alston turned to look at Arnold. 'Is that so?'

Arnold hesitated. He had no wish to offend Westwood, particularly in front of a stranger to the team. 'I . . . I just think it's a bit early for hypotheses. The stones, for instance. I'm surprised all three would have been placed under stones — two sacrifices, maybe, but if the central figure is the chief, I would have thought his spirit would have been allowed freedom.' He shook his head doubtfully. 'But in any case, I think we have only a small part of the picture. I believe there's more to find yet in this barrow. At a deeper, older level.'

Westwood snorted. 'By my calculation, these will be fifth-century burials!'

'I'm not inclined to disagree,' Arnold replied mildly. 'But we are still at the edge of the barrow. I have a . . . feeling that there's more to be found yet.'

Stephen Alston folded his arms. He looked tall, and imposing, and militaristic in his bearing. 'There's a great deal here, I would have said. Ritual murder, locking in the spirits, severed heads — it would all have fascinated Sir Henry Alston. And to think this was actually on land that he purchased in the forties! But you think there's more to be discovered?'

'I would guess there are more heads to be found,' Arnold suggested.

'Why do you think that?'

Arnold shrugged. 'Human sacrifice and head collection at burial sites are well attested. Both Irish and Welsh sources support the Celtic reverence for the human head — it had magical properties, was sometimes carried as a talisman. In particular, battle victims of consequence, whether killed in warfare or after capture, were decapitated and their heads enshrined. Maybe these three were warriors.'

'With Venus figures?' Westwood snorted derisively.

'Maybe they were placed there to protect the three warriors in support of their king, buried elsewhere.'

There was a short silence. Westwood clearly did not support Arnold's argument.

'Do we know why the Celts venerated heads in this manner?' Alston asked.

'The theory is that the head was recognized as the power centre for human action,' Rena Williams suggested. 'It led to a head-hunting cult, and the stress on the head in Celtic art is incontestable . . . Anyway, now you've seen what we're up to, perhaps you'd like a closer look at the items we've found. And maybe have a cup of coffee at the same time?'

'That would be splendid,' Alston replied, smiling. 'Thank you, Professor Westwood. I'm most grateful.'

Rather pointedly, Dr Williams suggested Arnold should join them for coffee, ignoring Geoffrey Westwood. He scowled at the snub but said nothing. Arnold had little doubt that he would try to take out his bad temper on Elfreda during the course of the afternoon. The two made no secret of their dislike for each other, and though Westwood held the whip hand as a result of his position and status, Elfreda still managed to get a rise out of him with whispered comments to her companions, and pointed jokes at his expense, often just out of his hearing.

Arnold followed Dr Williams and Stephen Alston across to the shed where they kept the artefacts, and the kettle. Rena Williams made some coffee while Arnold dragged out a couple of stools and set them beside the table. Rena showed Alston the items they had found so far and explained some of the significance normally attached to such items. 'Of course, it's nothing like the Fleetham Hoard,' she said deprecatingly.

Stephen Alston wrinkled his nose. 'Oh, come on, that was a find in a million, as I understand it! And in any case, it's surely rather early to say this site won't match it. I mean, you've only just started work on the barrow really. If Mr

Landon is correct in his guesswork, there's more to find. It might well finally even surpass what Sir Henry discovered in 1911.'

Rena Williams smiled doubtfully. 'So, I agree with you Fleetham was an exceptional find. And Sir Henry was quite a young man at the time, wasn't he?'

Alston sipped his coffee and nodded. 'It made his name, of course. I sometimes think, however, that it came too soon for him, you know what I mean? To make such a major discovery when one is only twenty-one . . . how can one top that?'

'He made a grand reputation for himself,' Arnold demurred. 'He was well known, well respected—'

'Yes, I agree, but from what I've heard in family gossip — his son Christopher, mainly — the old man was still expecting to turn something up again. Even after he was knighted in 1938 he still sought glory. It never came his way again, not the way Fleetham did, so to some extent he died a disappointed man.'

'One discovery of that importance would be enough for me,' Rena Williams said fervently.

'I suppose so,' Alston mused. 'And yet he also built up his Romano-Celtic collection and gained fame from that too. Yet it was never enough . . . it couldn't match the thrill, and the publicity, of that first magnificent find.' He smiled ruefully. 'He was a very vain man, apparently, obsessed with his own importance — and could be like a tiger if his views were ever questioned, or his reputation impugned.'

Arnold laughed. 'Aren't all academics like that?' Rena Williams made a face at him.

'The irony is, of course,' Alston continued, 'that this burial site — which looks as though it could be important — lay right under his nose.'

Arnold nodded. 'He bought Hartshorn in . . . ?'

'In 1947. The field was part of the property then, and it's surprising he did no excavation here. The shrine was well known, and the barrow was there . . . But perhaps he'd lost his old drive, and was spending more time on committees and trusts — it's what happens to famous people, isn't it?'

And people who want to be famous, Arnold thought, with Karen Stannard in mind. 'It's odd, I agree, because he must have realized that there were distinct possibilities in the barrow — even if the cave shrine had already been investigated. And his son, Christopher, did he have no thoughts about it?'

Stephen Alston shook his head. He frowned disapprovingly. 'No. Christopher was no archaeologist, and after his mother died — she left him some money — he went a little wild. He didn't see much of his father in the intervening years. The old man finally left the Alston Collection and Hartshorn House to his son, but Christopher never really had any interest in either.'

He paused reflectively.

'Christopher was a queer fish, really. Never married, rarely came to Hartshorn, stuck the Alston Collection in a bank and never looked at it, spent most of his time — and money — in New York.' His smile was rueful. 'When he died childless in 1990, and the estate fell to me, I thought it was a great windfall. The reality was less than the dream. The house itself was in a bad state of repair, I was not independently wealthy, and I was very quickly forced to make some unpleasant decisions. The first thing I had to do was sell some of the holdings, as a stopgap, like the field here to Northern Heritage. It wasn't enough. In the end, I decided the house had to go. And that's where the Eatons came in.'

'They were interested in buying the estate and the collection?' Dr Williams asked.

'Primarily, the collection. The house . . .' Alston hesitated. 'Well, that sort of emerged when Mr Eaton began to realize I had fallen in love with his daughter Margaret. We're still not quite clear what we'll do with it, but certainly the collection, and the supporting library, will in due course be removed to the States.'

'In due course . . . ?' Rena Williams asked thoughtfully.

Alston nodded. 'The library in six weeks or so. The collection is a bit trickier . . . licences need to be obtained, though I'm assured it's not a real problem. But my prospective father-in-law is very excited about acquiring it. He may be a Mormon banker, and have strict moral views, but he sees this acquisition as the crowning point of his life, and he has, of course, always been a fan of Sir Henry Alston and his work. He's . . . as he says . . . tickled at the thought his daughter's marrying an Alston.'

Dr Williams was silent for a little while, as Stephen Alston inspected the boat model with its pinewood figures.

'I wonder whether I could ask a favour of you?' she said al last, hesitantly.

'Ask away.'

'Sir Henry was justly famous for his discovery of the Fleetham Hoard. It brought to scientific study a vast array of artefacts that enabled us to make positive links with cross-cultural centres in northern France, the Marne, and Ireland. But his library has also been recognized as an extremely important one . . .'

'John Eaton's thirsting to get his hands on it,' Alston replied with a smile.

'I can understand that.' She glanced at the boat model he was holding carefully. 'I have a feeling there's a reference to objects similar to the one in your hands in some Victorian treatises in the British Museum. I'm pretty sure that Sir Henry's library will have a copy of them. Also . . .'

'Yes?'

'I'm fairly confident there will be numerous other volumes which would be of immense interest to us here at this site if we could have the use of them while we're working here.'

Alston looked doubtful. 'I hardly believe John Eaton would be prepared to break up the collection . . .'

'That's not what I mean,' she said hastily. 'No. It's just that . . . until the library is dispatched to the States — that time is short I gather . . .'

'In about six weeks we'll start packing it up,' Alston agreed.

'Well, until then, I wonder whether we could have access to it?' she said with a rush. 'It could make our work here a deal easier, if we were able to reference items as they emerge — and if Arnold is right, there could be material of some significance yet to come.'

Alston considered the matter thoughtfully. 'I don't really see any harm. I'm sure John Eaton couldn't object . . . I should add he's already made a down payment to me on the library.'

'He might even be pleased to think that Sir Henry's library was being put to practical use on a site that Sir Henry used to own,' Arnold suggested.

'He might at that.' Alston nodded. 'I'll fax him tomorrow with the thought . . . But in any case, in the meantime, if your team want to use the library . . .' He looked warningly at Rena Williams. 'Time could be short.'

'What I had in mind,' she replied, 'was for one of the team to spend, say, the next few weeks virtually full time at the library, doing some cataloguing of the holdings for reference purposes and following up on specific items we find on site. It could shorten our work tremendously if we had that sort of off-site support.'

He shrugged. 'I see no major objection. Who do you have in mind?'

She hesitated. 'Elfreda Gale.'

He stared at her, dubiously, no doubt considering the scene at his house and again at the burial site.

'She's bright, intelligent and hard-working.' Dr Williams pressed hurriedly. 'And committed. Her research work is the Celtic period and she's well used to library work — her doctorate will in fact be on Celtic literary sources. She could work faster than any of the other research students. She'd miss the dig, of course . . .'

A slight smile came to Alston's handsome, craggy features 'Well, if you think she's the right person . . .'

'Definitely.'

He nodded. 'All right. I'll check with John Eaton by fax to see if he has any objections. If it's fine with him, when would you want Miss Gale to start?'

'As soon as possible.'

He finished his coffee and nodded. 'All right, then. I'll be in touch — probably in the next couple of days. Well, you must excuse me now — Margaret will be returning to the States today and I must see her off.'

He shook hands with Dr Williams and Arnold and they accompanied him as he made his way to his Land Rover, parked in the roadway.

After he had gone, they walked back towards the tented burial area. Arnold glanced sideways at Rena Williams and snorted.

'You're a devious woman.'

'I can't imagine what you mean!'

'Elfreda, at Hartshorn House library.'

'It's as I told Mr Alston. She's the best person for the job — and we need to use that library before it's packed up and sent to the States. There's a lot of useful reference material there—'

'And it's just coincidence that by sending Elfreda to work in the library you avoid any further confrontations between her and Geoffrey Westwood.'

'Mr Landon,' she said sweetly, 'now you draw my attention to it, well, I suppose that is rather a bonus, isn't it? It means we'll be able to get our work done in a more friendly atmosphere at the burial site. What a happy thought!'

Arnold laughed. 'I'm not sure Professor Westwood will take it kindly. I get the impression he rather likes stamping on Elfreda. Verbally, I mean.'

Rena Williams clucked her tongue. 'I think you're right. But I'll tell him the suggestion came from Alston.'

'As I said . . . devious.'

She smiled. 'Come on. Let's get back to the battle area.'

3

The weather broke the following weekend and heavy rain lashed the fells. For several days the cloud and mist covered the hills with a cold, soaking blanket and the canvas that shielded the burial site proved to be a blessing, for they were still able to work under its cover. The dash from their cars, or the shed, to the tent meant they arrived steaming and wet but at least they were able to continue with the careful work of scraping away at the soil, sifting, brushing, clearing away and moving towards the centre of the barrow.

For Elfreda the invitation to visit Hartshorn House to work in the library, when it came, was a boon. She enjoyed working at the dig; baiting Ainsley, Alan and Peter — especially Peter — was fun, but her battles with Professor Westwood had soured things for her. She detested him heartily and thought him a pompous, hypocritical ass. She was not averse to male admiration — indeed, she admitted freely to herself that she encouraged it — sometimes outrageously. It had got her into trouble more than once, not least at Reading.

But Professor Westwood was something else.

When she had arrived at York and he had conducted private seminars with her as her tutor she had soon realized from the sexual tension in the air just what he had in mind: as she sat in the easy chair with the glass of sherry he had provided, he had prowled the small room, talking, expounding, but managing to lean over her, eyeing he, brushing against her breasts, breathing against her hair. Then there was the occasional comment he made about the morals of the younger generation of students, and the prurient way he asked her about sexual life on the campus . . .

She had brought it all to a head one afternoon in his room. She had made it clear she was certainly not prepared to sleep her way to a doctorate. She had put it baldly.

'Is it that you want to screw me, Professor?'

Westwood had turned three shades of purple.

'I may look and seem easy,' she'd continued, 'but I'm also fussy. And I keep work and sex separate. I didn't pick up my first degree on my back; my master's wasn't earned in the sack; and my choice of partners doesn't include mental geriatrics.'

Since the comment had touched upon his academic ability as well as his physical unattractiveness, maybe it hadn't been too wise, or too gentle, a put-down. Certainly, his embarrassment had flared into anger. And after that he had been gunning for her.

But she reckoned she could give as good as she got. Since the outspoken encounter in his rooms she had been allocated Dr Williams as a tutor, at Westwood's suggestion. Thereafter, he had been studiously, punctiliously correct in his physical behaviour towards her, had kept their relationship on coldly professional terms, but had made no secret of his dislike of her. Even so, it was a dislike founded on frustration — she was sure of that. He hated her for the rejection, but he still wanted her — she could see it in occasional, unguarded glances. But she had embarrassed him at York and damaged his self-esteem, albeit privately; he had taken his revenge in petty ways, with sneering, slighting remarks. The culminating watershed had come at the dinner in Hartshorn House. She knew now she'd gone too far.

She regretted her outburst to some extent — she'd had too much to drink and he had finally got to her with his asinine theories and his pompous delivery of them to the glazed-eyed Margaret Eaton.

Elfreda had lost her cool.

She did not, however, regret her views. Westwood regarded himself as an expert on Celtic symbolism but in her estimation he was purblind: he was out of date, stubborn, disinclined to accept new theories, and unwilling to concede that there could be any correct point of view other than his own. For her, he was all that was spurious in academic life — narrow lines of thought, a self-belief that had turned to arrogance, a myopic view of what was happening around him in the archaeological field, and a dismissal of legitimate lines of enquiry.

The trouble was, he was in a position to affect her future.

Dr Williams was sympathetic, she knew, and would do what she could to help, but Westwood wanted nothing more than to ruin her career. She was certain of that. He was playing a cat and mouse game at the moment — seemingly satisfied to dismiss the scene at Hartshorn House, and the importance it had to his self-regard, coolly accepting her apology. It had cost her blood and sweat to make that apology, and he knew it, but she was not fooled by his acceptance.

She knew what Professor Westwood wanted: public capitulation. He took a sadistic delight in having her work under his supervision and guidance; it gave him the chance to sneer and deride her in front of the lads; it gave a boost to his need to hold the reins of power over her. But she could guess what the end of it would be. All the hard, dry-mouthed work would go for nothing. The subservience, the tongue-biting, the capitulation would have no effect at all.

Professor Westwood would do his damnedest to make sure she was not awarded her doctorate.

But she had little choice if she was not to throw away her ambitions. All she could do was knuckle down for the moment, keep plugging away, and hope that Dr Williams would have a powerful enough voice at the end of the programme to prevent Westwood's vendetta achieving its objective. And she was grateful now for Dr Williams's effort in taking her away from the site.

Elfreda knew she would miss the dig: the excitement, the back-breaking activity that could at any moment turn up something to make the pulses surge, the long, careful paring away of the dust of history to see the slow emergence of a line, a trace, a darker earth, an implement . . . or a skull.

Her spine still tingled at the thought she might have been the one to turn up that first severed head, rather than Peter. She'd have screamed in excitement, she knew — unlike Peter, who had stood there dumbly, unable to say a word. Public-school control, she had snorted to herself at the time. But he had found the skull . . . and now such opportunities would be banned to her during the next two weeks as she worked at Hartshorn House.

Nevertheless, she was grateful to Dr Williams. And she knew she would enjoy the work. The library was a magnificent one, and she would be able to make a selection of the texts that would be useful to them, before carrying out the closer inspection that would support the finds they were making in the barrow.

Moreover, it got her out of the rain — snug, dry and safe from Westwood's bitter tongue.

* * *

Stephen Alston met her the first morning she arrived. His handshake was friendly, his manners polished. He showed her around the main rooms of the house, commenting upon the shortage of servants — before she did — but assuring her that if she wished to stay to lunch each day that could be arranged, and she could always make a cup of coffee for herself in the kitchen when the part-time cook wasn't available. The cook would be leaving at the end of the week but Elfreda could then make coffee for herself in the morning room, which had a pleasant view over the admittedly overgrown gardens. Then he took her on a brief tour of the library, apologizing for the lack of a decent cataloguing system and explaining that after Sir Henry Alston had died the library had been used very little.

But she saw that as a certain challenge: it was somehow skin prickling to feel that she could come into a library that hadn't really been used for thirty years, and maybe put her own imprint on it before it was shipped off to the States, maybe to moulder for another half-century.

She began work that afternoon.

It was a voyage of discovery to begin with: she soon determined that there was a certain idiosyncratic nature to the layout of the books — she doubted whether a professional librarian had ever worked there. So she spent hours scanning the shelves on the ground floor, attempting to reach some idea of the method of classification, making notes as she went along. After three days she had walked the ground floor and the first-floor shelves, up the spiral staircase, and felt she understood the general layout. She also discovered that the holdings were both esoteric and wide ranging, not only in the field of archaeology but also the occult, the history of religious thought, and the development of Romano-Celtic cults. She appreciated even more how wise Dr Williams had been to suggest she should work here in Hartshorn House.

And Stephen Alston was really rather pleasant.

In fact, once or twice, when he wandered into the morning room to join her for a cup of coffee she thought he was in fact quite attractive.

He was too old for her tastes, of course. She didn't mind teasing older men, but really she preferred men of her own generation. Stephen Alston was a good fifteen years older than she was: he was well preserved, had a nice smile, and the army, she guessed, had given him his easy confidence.

She asked him, one afternoon, about his army career.

He shrugged diffidently. 'I can't say it was a glorious success. I made the rank of major but then, who doesn't?'

'I always thought majors were quite important.'

'Not in career terms: he disagreed. 'It's a sort of sidelining rank — a way of telling you you won't get on if you hold it too long. And for me, it was an office job — whereas I rather enjoyed the tearing around bit — Cyprus, the Med generally . . .'

'Don't tell me you did anything really exciting like SAS training!'

He smiled and extended his two hands. 'Not exactly, but I did get shown how to crack necks like rotten twigs!'

The first week flew past. The weather continued to be poor but she barely noticed as she carried on in the library. A large part of the time was spent in working her way through the various sets of Victorian periodical runs that Sir Henry Alston had acquired over the years: some of them dated back to the 1850s and all had antiquarian interest. It fascinated Elfreda to read about long-discarded theories and she was amused by some of the wayward, evangelically orientated arguments that were raised in letters to the journals, squabbling over interpretations of ancient sites and artefacts.

She prepared a catalogue of useful articles, bearing on Romano-Celtic burials, and made careful notes of drawings and sketches of artefacts that had been found at some of the sites listed. In the fifth volume of one of the learned journals she found some yellowed newspaper cuttings about the British Museum, and she flipped through them. They seemed to carry little of interest, since they were general in tone, concentrating upon the contribution made by certain leading lights in the Antiquarian Society — Sir Henry Alston was included. There was also a handwritten list of artefacts; the handwriting was spidery and hurriedly formed. She wondered whether it had actually been Sir Henry Alston who made the list, and then she turned up an old photograph of the trustees of some worthy body taken in the 1930s.

She was looking at it on the afternoon that Arnold Landon came to call, to see how she was getting on and, she suspected, to have his own prowl around the library. She liked Mr Landon: he had a calm, unhurried attitude towards things; a quiet, pleasant way of getting on with people. He also displayed a cool appreciation of her sense of humour.

'That,' she said, pointing with her little finger at the central figure in the group, 'was Sir Henry Alston in all his pomp and prime.'

'Chairman of the Trust,' Landon said. 'And those his minions . . .' He began to read from the list printed below the photograph. 'Charles Liversedge of Stenton Iron and Coal, Norman Caley of the London Scientific Society, Pelham Price-Kennedy, Secretary to the Trust . . . all worthy and eminent gentlemen, I'm sure . . .' He smiled at her. 'And all stalwart supporters and worshippers at the shrine of Sir Henry Alston. In whose library we find ourselves. You don't mind if I have a look around myself? It won't disturb you?'

'Not at all. Glad of the company.'

He spent a couple of hours wandering around the shelves while she carried on with the cataloguing. After a while he came across to her with a thick leather-bound volume. 'I hadn't realized Sir Henry Alston had edited his own antiquarian journal,' he said.

'Neither did I.'

He flicked open the pages and pointed to a head-and-shoulders sepia photograph; it showed a heavy, dark-browed man in a wing collar; his mouth was set and stern, his eyes glaring with a fierce pride. It was captioned: *Sir Henry Alston — The Discoverer of the Fleetham Hoard.*

'The items found in the Fleetham Hoard are listed in the first article,' Landon said. 'Along with several mentions of Sir Henry.'

She giggled. 'He wasn't averse to self-publicity, was he?'

'Oh, to be fair, he also included pictures of the other people involved with the journal. His assistant editor, Pelham Price-Kennedy, for instance.'

He showed her the photograph. A thin-faced man with intense eyes and a stubborn mouth stared at her challengingly. It was a head-and-shoulders photograph, one hand supporting his meagre chin in a thoughtful pose. His tie was discreet, his coat dark. He looked like a man who would believe in eternal certainties, of which compromise would not be one.

'A sober-looking gentleman,' Elfreda suggested.

'Of unforgiving mien. Yet with a rather flamboyant locket ring on his finger, you know, the kind used by popes to hold perfume or poison, depending on their predilections. I wonder what his were.'

'Is this the only volume of the journal?'

He nodded. 'Looks like. It seems as though it wasn't a financial success. I had a look at the editorial board names: after three issues, Price-Kennedy was no longer assistant editor, and the journal folded.'

'Maybe he was supporting the journal financially,' Elfreda suggested.

'Could be. Or maybe he got fed up working with Alston. By all accounts Alston was a fractious, proud, self-centred man.'

'Normal, you mean,' she countered. 'For a man, that is.'

He laughed and went back to his shelf-prowling.

But most of the time Elfreda was working in the library alone.

It was for that reason, later that week, that she began to enjoy Alston's habit of joining her for coffee. It was fine working in the library, but when she needed a break it was pleasant to have company. He could be entertaining, and he regaled her with stories of his days in the army, the childish pranks that he and his younger brother officers had got up to, life under canvas on manoeuvres . . .

'All behind you now,' she suggested, 'with you about to become a married man at long last.' She had a sudden vision in her mind's eye of the rather dowdy Miss Eaton. 'I'm surprised you left it so late.'

He smiled, having got used to her directness. 'Never seemed to have time before . . . or money. If you're going to marry you need stability financially. Can't say I've ever enjoyed that.'

'But coming into your inheritance must have changed things,' she protested.

'Hartshorn House?' There was a weary edge to his smile. 'Hardly. My cousin Chris was somewhat feckless — he mortgaged this house up to the hilt. I had to sell land to pay some immediate debts the day I took over. The only real assets were this library, and the Alston Collection.'

'You don't keep the collection here?'

He shook his head. 'Too valuable. Country houses have a habit of getting burgled if anything expensive is left lying around. No, Chris kept the collection vaulted away in a bank in London. I saw no reason to change that when I took over the estate.'

'So you've never even seen it?'

'I'm no archaeologist — it wouldn't really mean a great deal to me.'

'But the money does,' she said flatly.

He was silent for a while, staring at her. 'You're a very direct young woman. I like that. And I presume you're referring to my projected sale of house, library and collection to the Eatons.'

'It's none of my business,' she replied primly.

'But you mention the financial motive . . .' He sighed. 'Yes, I might as well admit it. I would have liked to keep Hartshorn House and live in style, but that's not the way things worked out. I decided I would need to sell the collection — I had an offer from the States and went out to see John Eaton. That was when I learned he would be interested in buying the house and library as well as the collection. He was a Sir Henry fan.'

'But as it turns out,' Elfreda said coolly, 'you'll end up getting everything back anyway, won't you?' Slowly, he asked, 'How do you mean?'

'You're marrying into the family.'

He finished his coffee, saying nothing. Outside it was raining heavily, drumming on the tall windows, sending long streamers of water down the panes. The rhythmic thunder of the rain was lulling, emphasizing the warmth and comfort of the room. She sat silently, but aware that he was watching her.

'What about you?' he asked at last. 'Me?'

'Not married. No boyfriends?'

'Oh, I tend to play the field,' she announced carelessly.

He smiled. 'Widely?'

'You could say that.'

'You like men, then?'

'Of course. Not the men at university. They tend to be a bit callow.' She held his glance, unable to resist the opportunity. 'I prefer my men a little older.'

His gaze was steady; his tongue flickered nervously over his lips and he smiled slightly. 'How little?'

'Oh, I don't know. Someone who's been around a bit . . . seen the world,' she teased. 'The men at university, they tend to be limited in that respect. The only life they know is their books. It can be a bit . . . boring.'

'But you spend your life in academic matters.'

'Maybe so,' she smiled. 'But don't be misled by the image of me poring over books in this library.'

'Or over archaeological sites?'

She shook her head. 'I think people have a mistaken impression about archaeology.'

She rose, walked away from the table and stood in front of the window, staring out at the rain. 'There's no doubt people think it's all dry as dust and uninteresting, but that's because they don't think about the reality of it all. When I see an artefact I see the person who made it. I imagine the hands that carved it, and the mind that endowed it with the reality of the time. The people who lived those centuries ago, they were closer to the life around them than we are: we've become distanced by our own, spurious, commercially orientated, manufactured needs. Thousands of years ago people lived with the boar and the eagle and the stag: they lived among them in the woods, used them for their daily needs, understood them and appreciated their power, and endowed them with magical properties. When I work and read I'm not seeing just the brittle remains in front of me — I'm seeing people and history and life.'

'And death,' he added. He too had left the table; he was standing just behind her, close.

She turned to look up at him. There was passion in her look, and her cheeks were flushed. 'But it's all part of the one, isn't it? Life, death, sex, children, the promulgation of the species. That's what I find and feel when I bury myself in this work. It's discovering about people, what motivated them, how they lived their lives, how they died, what they believed in.'

'What do you believe in, Elfreda?' he asked huskily.

She was suddenly aware of him in a different way and, recognizing the message in his eyes, she was curious. 'I believe in enjoying myself. I believe in the present. I believe in taking chances.'

'Even with an older man?'

'Especially with an older man,' she teased.

He reached for her; she did not resist. He smelled of cologne and tobacco and his arms were tightly locked around her as he kissed her. For a moment she felt a responsive surge of desire, a sudden, unreasoning passion and she pressed her body against his. The arms tightened around her and she responded.

Behind her the rain hammered at the window and after a little while the sound broke through to her, cooling her, calming, rationalizing the instinctive rush of sexual desire that had swept through her, merely because he was a man, and he had kissed her passionately. She pulled back her head and looked at him.

He did not recognize her change of mood. There was a certainty in his eyes that brought a flicker of annoyance into her mind.

'Now just what are you up to, Mr Alston?' she asked coolly.

'Taking you at your word,' he replied, grinning confidently.

'And what word would that be?'

His grin widened and he slipped his hands down over her waist. 'You like experienced, older men. Well, here we are, alone in the house—'

'And I have work to do.'

'It can wait. This is more . . . urgent.'

She grabbed one hand firmly, pulling it away from her body. 'Urgent for you, maybe . . . not for me. I told you my passion was archaeology. Having sex with a man who's just about to get married is not a priority with me.'

He was breathing hard, and she was aware of a heavy pounding in his chest. He pulled back, nevertheless, a frown appearing on his face. 'I thought—'

'When exactly are you going to get married?' Elfreda asked, taking advantage of the moment as he relaxed, uncertain.

'That's got nothing to do with—'

'With screwing me?' Elfreda smiled cynically. 'I suppose not. But it has some relevance to my screwing you. It's not that I'm against going to bed with someone else's fiancé, or even a married man — I've done a bit of that in my time — but I've got to really fancy him, you know?'

He stepped back, still with one hand on her waist, but his grip relaxing. She was aware of his frustration and recognized the bitterness in his tone. 'There's a word for women like you.'

'In the army? I'm certain of it.' She felt a sudden stab of anger — she had heard this kind of thing too recently from men who became petulant when they didn't get their own way with her sexually. 'But then, there's a word for men like you too, isn't there? Men who marry for money, perhaps, without really caring for the person they marry. And who are only too happy to screw around both before and during the marriage? I've met men like that before now. Maybe you're in that category, Mr Alston.'

He released her and stepped away. He stared at her, weighing her up with a calculating, disappointed glance. 'You really can switch it on and off, can't you?'

'One learns,' she replied casually.

'Learns what? To send out signals—'

'Ah, yes. But of curiosity, mainly. If they're misinterpreted, it's a pity, but a girl has to be able to say no, doesn't she?'

He managed a smile, but it was hard at the edges. 'And that's the answer.'

'Quite certainly, Mr Alston. Now I really must get back to my work.'

'Of course.' He stepped away from her, his grey eyes cold.

He bowed slightly, mockingly. 'Priorities, isn't it? I'll leave you to it.'

At the door, he paused, and looked back at her. 'We're alone in the house at the moment.'

'I guessed that was the case,' she replied with deliberation.

'I have to leave for Manchester early this afternoon — a matter of business. Rather than leave you here alone, maybe I'd better give you a lift back to the field site. So I can lock up behind you.'

'I could make sure—'

'I'd prefer to lock up.'

Somewhat put out, Elfreda said, 'I can walk back to the site.'

'It's raining hard,' he said sharply. 'Don't be foolish. I'll call into the library at three. If you're ready then, I'll drive you back to the field.'

He left her with the disagreeable feeling that she had not behaved too well.

The deflation did not last. As she sat in the library, working, her mind drifted to the situation in the morning room. If anyone had behaved out of line, surely it was Stephen Alston. A man should be able to tell the difference between flirting and a real come-on.

Just as a man should be able to tell when ardour had cooled, and a long-term relationship was not intended. But she didn't want to think about Reading. Or Stephen Alston, for that matter.

She was a free agent. If grown-up men couldn't behave like adults, in an adult relationship, that was their problem. And if Stephen Alston felt annoyed, he had brought it on himself.

* * *

He came to the library promptly at three. She was ready, anorak buttoned up to the throat, and they went out to the car without speaking. There was a certain tension between them, and Alston was clearly annoyed — perhaps as much by his own behaviour as hers, she guessed. As the car windows fogged up, and the rain beat heavily on the windscreen, the silence inside the car made her edgy. She felt constrained, and claustrophobic.

'Don't bother taking me to the field itself. The end of the lane will do.'

'It's raining like hell,' he said sharply.

'I'll be all right.'

'Please yourself,' he replied in a curt tone.

He stopped the car just beyond the gateway to the lane and she got out. She nodded her thanks but he made no reply. She slammed the car door and he pulled away, mud spurting up from his rear wheels and staining her jeans. She stared after him angrily, but most of the anger was directed at herself and her own stupidity. She trudged along the lane in the pouring rain, head lowered, feeling the water trickle down inside the neck of her anorak.

She entered the field. The lower end was awash. There was no one in sight: they would all be working under cover, in the shed or under canvas. The path across the field was inundated, a torrent of water racing along the worn area, stripping away soil and tumbling small stones down the slope. She looked around her: the heavy rain of the past week had caused a cascade from the rocks above the tented site, rivulets carving their way down the hill and the slope of the field, cutting away at the wet soil with several small streams running across the field to the marshy area below. It was waterlogged already, and she had a sudden, swift vision of how it might have been centuries ago, when there would have been a lake down there, below the crags and the slope of the field.

The day was dark and the clouds low. She walked at the edge of the bank above the ancient marsh. She shivered, feeling cold, as she trudged along; the wind seemed to howl as it dashed rain into her face, a strange, high call. She plodded on, avoiding the rivulets where they cut into the earth, collapsing parts of the bank some distance past the lower end of the barrow. She made her way, head down against the driving rain, towards an old tree that the storms of the night before had pushed sideways, tearing its ancient roots from the earth of the bank, exposing the soil. Something caught her eye as it glinted in the mud at the roots of the tree. She hesitated, peering down at the object, and then she crouched, picked it up, examined it.

She felt a movement in her chest, a flutter of excitement.

She stared at the ground about her, putting her find in her pocket. She reached down, scraped away urgently with her hands, fingers covered in mud, and then she straightened in excitement, heart pounding crazily.

She began to run, splashing carelessly through the rivulets, slipping in the wet, muddy grass, sliding and falling as she crossed the barrow and stumbling into the entrance to the tented, protected grave-site area.

They were all there, staring at her in surprise: Ainsley, Peter and Alan in the trench, Professor Westwood glaring at her in disdain, Dr Williams turning aside from her conversation with Arnold Landon.

Elfreda stood in the entrance, gasping, incoherent, unable to get the words out.

'Elfreda!' Rena Williams said in a concerned tone. 'What on earth's the matter? What's happened?'

'The field—' she gasped. 'Down in the field!'

'Pull yourself together, woman: Geoffrey Westwood snarled. 'Stop this hysteria!'

'There's another one!' she cried out.

'Another what?'

'A skull! Another grave! Peter found the first . . . but now I've found another! Down beyond the barrow—' She stopped, gulping in air in her excitement. 'I've found another burial!'

CHAPTER THREE

1

Detective Chief Inspector Garrett had been given the nickname 'Pat' by school friends who had played out on innumerable occasions the killing of Billy the Kid by his erstwhile friend, but later, fatally for Bill Bonney, lawman, Sheriff Garrett. The name had stuck in later life and had quickly been taken up by colleagues in the police force in Cumbria. As far as he could tell he bore little resemblance to the long-dead Western outlaw-killer, being tall, lean, hook-nosed, clean-shaven and hollow-cheeked and suffering from an unfortunate tendency to flatulence, heartburn and bad temper. The last was possibly induced by the others. He had taken no medical advice on the matter.

He did not particularly care for the sobriquet given to him, but on the other hand it did provide a certain glamour to his rather dull personality. He considered himself to be in the wrong job: an erroneous career decision in his late teens had led him into the police force and a location in the North Pennines. He quite liked the countryside but found the people dour, the Saturday night drunks unimaginative in their activities and language, and the opportunity to indulge in his own personal leisure pursuit — amateur opera — non-existent.

He had spent a period in Yorkshire, which proved little better, though it did provide the occasional opportunity to visit Manchester for provincial musical events of some quality, and it was certainly better when he transferred back north to Penrith. He wasn't far from Carlisle, where there was a degree of sophistication — in Cumbrian terms — and live theatre. But generally speaking he felt himself hard done by, as far as life was concerned. A bachelor without a wide circle of friends, he felt he could have done better for himself had he gone to London as a young man and found employment in the theatre. His rank helped his ego somewhat, but when serious crime raised its head and he found it necessary to travel back into the hinterland of the fells, he bemoaned his fate all over again.

Privately.

His inherent dissatisfaction with his job found expression, but in other directions: his colleagues assumed he was naturally short-tempered and were not aware that his aspirations and ambitions had always lain elsewhere, in the direction of the stage.

The visit to Garrigill sharpened his general discontent; the necessity for the journey annoyed him and made his stomach rumble in protest.

Right from the start he had thought it was going to be a wild-goose chase and a waste of his time, which could be better spent doing crosswords in his warm office in Penrith. The discovery of a skeleton on the site of an archaeological dig was always going to raise peculiar problems, and when he finally reached the windswept, godforsaken field high on the fells and met the curious group of enthusiasts gathered at the site his depression deepened.

Young men, he disliked — he had seen too many of them in city centres on Saturday nights tanked up with draught bitter. Young men from university were even worse: they swore at you in cultured accents and used long, unusual, sociologically orientated words when you locked them in the cells overnight to cool off.

They also often had rich, noisy fathers who claimed personal acquaintance with people of quality.

Smart-mouthed young women he liked even less: this one on the Garrigill fell was too lively by half and needed her arse smacked, in his view. Clever, with a quick tongue, and knowing, suggestive eyes, she was aware of her own sexuality and, he guessed, used that knowledge to effect whenever she could. She was no better than she should be and she'd come to a sticky end one of these days, he had no doubt.

Then there were the ones in charge: a woman academic who had cool eyes, considerable confidence, a mind like a razor and a tongue with a similar edge, when unsheathed; her colleague was a self-regarding, empty-voiced man who used his professorial status like a crutch and who believed himself immensely superior to any mere policeman, especially one with a name like Garrett; and then there was the character called Landon.

Pat Garrett didn't know what to make of him. He didn't seem to be of the same academic ilk as the others; he was employed in Morpeth by the local authority, and he had a watchful, wary eye. Garrett suspected an analytical brain behind the self-deprecating manner, and when he felt he could not accurately sum up a man his suspicions were aroused, and dyspepsia intervened.

After he had looked over the site generally, and the position in which the bones had been found under the shattered tree, Garrett left the scene-of-crime unit to it and decided to meet the archaeological group as a whole, at the George and Dragon rather than in the field, where forensic had already started to work around the tree on the rain-damaged bank.

They all met in the residents' lounge. Garrett stood with his back to the fireplace, flanked by the latest disaster wished upon him — the fresh-faced, lumpish and decidedly wooden Detective Constable Clamp.

He was from a farming family out Barnard Castle way; he had three brothers, apparently, all hefty, broad-shouldered and solid-brained. His brothers looked after the farm — he had struck out for a more glamorous life in the Cumbria police force. He occasioned despair in Garrett's breast. The only pleasure Garrett received from his presence was the knowledge that colleagues referred to the constable as 'Spud'. It was one step down from his own nickname. Young Clamp seemed unaware of the off-centre humour that had visited the sobriquet upon him. That also was a source of some satisfaction to Garrett.

'Now then,' Garrett intoned portentously, as he faced the silent group of archaeologists, 'who was it actually found the remains, in the first instance?'

'It was me,' Elfreda Gale announced ungrammatically.

Garrett was pleased to hear slipshod grammar from a so-called academic.

'The circumstances?'

She explained briefly, a little flare of annoyance in her eyes at the brusqueness. She told him she had been making her way across the field; the rain had washed away part of the bank beneath the damaged tree; she had seen the bones of a hand, a shoulder blade, part of a skull; she had run to scream the news to the others.

'You screamed because you were scared?'

She clearly considered the question not only stupid but impertinent. 'Of course not,' she snapped. 'I was excited, not frightened. We'd already found three skeletons — I thought I'd found a new grave site.'

Garrett glowered at her. 'And what happened then?'

Dr Williams spoke up. 'We all went down to take a look, naturally. But there wasn't much we could do just then — it was raining so hard we couldn't work out there.'

'Work?'

'Investigate the remains.' She stared at him, slightly puzzled as he seemed to be waiting for something. 'We — like Elfreda — assumed the bones would be part of an ancient burial.'

'Now why would you assume that?'

'For obvious reasons,' Professor Westwood intervened testily. 'We've been working on a site which has strong suggestions of Romano-Celtic culture. We'd already found three skeletons in the barrow which were clearly fifth-century inhumations. When this . . . this young lady came screaming hysterically that she'd found another burial, we naturally assumed it was another Iron Age discovery. So, when the weather slackened . . .'

'We started work on it,' Dr Williams finished.

'You actually began digging around there?' Garrett asked in an incredulous tone.

'It was not exactly digging,' Dr Williams replied, flushing slightly in annoyance. 'I asked Ainsley, Peter and Alan here to begin clearing the site. It was done with care — picking away the wet mud, trying not to disturb the bones as they lay—'

'Why so careful?' Garrett interrupted.

'Because it's important that as little disturbance as possible is occasioned in the first instance. We need to mark the site, photograph it, ensure we've picked up all traces—'

'And?'

'And that was the first problem. There was very little there, except for the skeleton. No artefacts, no clothing—'

'And then I noticed the teeth,' Elfreda Gale chipped in.

'What about them?' Garrett asked.

'Dental work. Definitely not fifth century,' she added defiantly.

He gave her a sour glance to tell her he was aware that dentistry was not widely practised fifteen hundred years ago. 'So you . . . scraped away with the young men here?'

She shook her head. 'Not immediately. I found the bones when I was making my way back from Hartshorn House — I'd been working in the library there. I went back there for a couple of days—'

'Before access to the library was stopped, by Stephen Alston withdrawing his permission,' Professor Westwood interrupted nastily. 'I should explain, Chief Inspector, Miss

Gale has an unfortunate capacity for upsetting people, though quite what she said down at Hartshorn I don't know—'

'That's irrelevant,' Dr Williams interrupted as Elfreda shot a furious glance in Westwood's direction. She turned back to Garrett. 'Elfreda worked on the site after the first two days as we gradually uncovered the skeleton.'

'You never thought of contacting the police at that stage?'

She shook her head. 'It didn't cross our minds. Not until Elfreda pointed to the dental work. We assumed it was part of the same burial as the ones we'd already been working on — the site has a very old, continuous history — the shrine cave, the barrow . . .' She hesitated. 'We finally realized there were significant differences between these remains and the bones we had earlier uncovered on site.'

'Such as?'

'To begin with, the head had not been severed.'

Garrett sighed and regarded her owlishly. 'Was that something you were expecting?'

'The other inhumations were ritual burials. They had severed heads. This one did not. The teeth had been attended to by a dentist at some time. There was also damage to the back of the skull, which suggested a mode of death. The skeleton didn't have quite the right feel . . .'

'So they've been doing forensics work for us, hey, Clamp?' Garrett said, glancing ironically at the detective constable.

Clamp started; he had been watching Elfreda Gale. 'Er, looks like, sir.'

Garrett scowled. He turned to Arnold Landon. 'And where do you fit into all this?'

Landon shrugged. 'I work three days a week, plus weekends, on site. I was there when Elfreda found the skeleton. My guess is it's an old skeleton — but not old enough to be the kind of burial we're looking for.'

'You can say that again,' Elfreda Gale said, and shivered.

Garrett rocked on his heels, reflectively. 'All right . . . I'm afraid each of you will be required to make a statement to Detective Constable Clamp here. And then, I'll have to ask you to stay away from the field and the site—'

'But we have important work to do!' Dr Williams protested.

'—stay away from the site,' Garrett continued coldly, 'at least until my own men have had the chance to give it a good looking-over, and until I have the forensic report. Thereafter, I may have to interview you again.'

'You mean we'll have to stop work in the meanwhile?' Professor Westwood queried, shooting an angry glance in Elfreda's direction, as though he regarded her as personally responsible for the delay.

'That's what I said, sir,' Garrett replied stiffly. 'You dug him up, now we have to find out who he is. Or was. If we can. And meanwhile, we can't have you all digging away around him, maybe turning up other corpses, and damaging what evidence there is, can we?'

* * *

Back at his office at Carlton House in Penrith, Detective Chief Inspector Garrett contemplated his fate with distaste. It was clear to him that the group working at the site could hardly have had anything to do, nefariously speaking, with the depositing of the bones in the decaying bank. They'd just found them there.

It was equally clear to him there was a degree of unhappiness in the group — he detected various tensions underlining the relationships established there. The snappish, pompous Westwood was universally disliked, even by his colleague Dr Williams; there was a suspicion that Miss Gale had behaved in an inappropriate way at some point, and he could guess in what way it might be; and he wondered which of the three young men she was sleeping with. Maybe all of them.

As for Landon, he sort of drifted at the edge of the group — part of them, and yet holding himself a little at arm's length. He'd need watching, that one, Garrett concluded.

He dismissed them from his mind. There was nothing to be done immediately, until the forensic report came in. Best to wait and see, rather than worry about something that might never happen.

* * *

The report came in later that week. He read it slowly, and with a sinking heart. He had a vague idea where this might end up. He took the report to the chief constable.

When the chief had read it he raised his grey, short-cropped head and looked at Garrett with tired eyes. 'The kind of problem we hardly want,' he suggested, 'with the Royal visit dragging all our manpower onto the streets next week.'

'No, sir.'

'Your summary?'

Garrett shrugged. 'The report says it's old bones, sir. Probably a middle-aged man, hint of early signs of arthritis in one hip. The dental work alone suggests the skeleton is pretty old — could have had his teeth drilled and filled as much as eighty years ago, they reckon, though they're not committing themselves yet. No clothing to go by, no identification—'

'But a badly damaged skull.'

'Heavy thump on the back of the head, looks like the cause of death, sir.'

'And definitely not really old, like the other old bones on site.'

Garrett had a dragging feeling in his chest. 'They've ruled that out, sir. They reckon it's the remains of a middle-aged male who was knocked on the back of the head, stripped, put in a shallow grave, and would have been there even now if it hadn't been for the heavy rain, a washing away of surface soil, collapse of the bank . . . but to put a date to the interment, well, they can't. All they can say is it could be turn of the century, or maybe twenty or thirty years after that.'

'Somewhat unspecific.'

'Yes, sir.'

'But we have a duty to the public.'

The dragging feeling was even heavier. 'Yes, sir.'

'What do you think of our chances of discovering the identity of the dead man?'

'Pretty slim, sir.'

'But it looks like he died from a blow to the head, it could be murder, and we're expected to come up with answers in situations like that. Even if the crime was committed a long time ago.'

'Yes, sir,' Garrett replied unhappily.

'So you'll put your mind to it, Garrett?'

'Of course, Chief Constable.'

'You'll run a check. Missing Persons files going way back, particularly relating to Cumbria and the Garrigill area. Comb the newspapers for odd incidents, local reports. I'll issue a statement tonight — explain to the press that what we've got here is old bones, and the likelihood of identifying them is slim. But you'll work at it, show the flag of endeavour, Garrett?'

'Yes, sir.'

The chief constable regarded him silently for a little while. 'Just one other thing . . . I want you to give this a certain priority. Get shuffled of it as quickly as possible. I want a thorough job — and I want you to do it personally. I'll see your files when you complete them. But speed is of the essence. We don't want this dragging on. And we don't want the archaeological group kept off the site too long — it would look as though we're being bureaucratic and time-wasting, wouldn't it? They could start niggling to the newspapers. So get on with it — thorough but fast, hey? And let's get the archaeologists back on site.'

Bugger the archaeologists, Pat Garrett thought to himself.

2

Jerry Picton leaned on the doorjamb of Arnold's office and picked his teeth with an old matchstick that he produced from his top pocket. Arnold, busy with some files, tried to ignore him, while wondering how it was that Picton always seemed to have time on his hands, with little to do. He appeared to spend most of his day wandering around the sections in the department, picking up odd bits of gossip, relaying them, and causing as much trouble as he could. There was a streak of malice in the man, and Arnold disliked him. Picton seemed impervious to displays of coolness on Arnold's part, however, and continued to visit him at his desk.

He stood in the doorway quietly for a while, watching Arnold dealing with his files.

'So how does it feel to have a full week back in harness?' he asked.

'Nothing new in it.'

'Yes, but when you had the chance to flounder away in fell mud rather than get your head down here at the office, I bet you thought you had it made.'

'Is there anything you want?' Arnold asked wearily.

'Not really.' Picton managed a yellow-toothed smile. 'Just passing the time of day, thassall. But I did hear from a newspaper friend of mine that all the heat and noise is dying down again now. The coppers have come up with zilch over that body one of your female friends found at the site, and now the Royals are in town, our local plods are concentrating on live issues rather than dead ones. So you could be back up on the fells before you get too settled with those papers. And that'll suit you, won't it?'

It certainly suited Arnold better than being forced to listen to Jerry Picton's aimless chatter.

But it seemed Picton was well informed, nevertheless. The following day Arnold was called into Karen Stannard's office. She gave him a flawless smile, but the glance she gave him from her slightly slanted, grey-green eyes was cool.

'I've just had Dr Williams on the phone.' she announced.

Something in her tone suggested she was not pleased. 'The police have given permission for the team to resume work at Garrigill.'

'That's good news.'

'I thought you'd be pleased,' she replied sourly. She inspected her slim fingers, carefully pressing back her cuticles. 'I've had a word with the director, and there's no reason why you shouldn't return to the site at Garrigill. Dr Williams has specifically requested that you should rejoin as soon as possible.' She smiled again, with an edge of malice. 'She seems to regard you as her sort of lucky charm. I'm sure you can bring no more than that to match her expertise.'

Arnold made no response.

'How much have you got on your desk at the moment?' she asked finally, a little nettled at his self-control.

'There are three files I need to deal with.'

'Get them finished today.' she said peremptorily. 'That means you can get up there tomorrow . . . that's Thursday.' She leaned forward and flicked at the pages of her desk diary. She wore an open-necked blouse underneath a grey jacket, and he could see the line of her cleavage. She would be expecting him to. 'I'll be up on Friday morning, to take a look at the site. Perhaps,' she added with an ironic gleam in her eye, 'you'd care to show me around.'

'It would be a pleasure, Deputy Director,' Arnold lied. He drove to Garrigill early next morning.

The recent torrential rains had carved new and wider banks to the deep burns which gutted the steep slopes above the peaty flanks of the high-fell mining area. The water-courses, known locally as sikes, rushed noisily down the steep hillside: those older established had already provided cover over the years to the development of strong growth of alder, oak, birch and willow, giving sanctuary to a range of wildlife. In the spring, Arnold knew, those gullies would be thick with banks of bluebells and golden primroses. The newly carved sikes were still raw and black but at their edge the springy grass and heather looked fresh and thriving. The wandering sheep looked happier, too — less bedraggled than they had been during the last weeks.

When Arnold crossed the fell and finally reached the Garrigill site, he found that there was water still lying on the lower areas below the field, bringing back the image of the ancient lake that had lain there. As he stared at the half-submerged rushes and the marshy ground, gleaming blackly under the slick, unruffled water, he felt he caught, for a few moments, the echoes of long-vanished people, men and women of the fell and the lake, who had lived out their lives there, died there, been sacrificed there.

A cold breeze touched his back, and he shivered.

He heard a voice calling his name; it brought him back to the present.

'I'm glad to see you, Arnold.' Rena Williams greeted him. 'We're moving fast on the site.'

'The police are gone for good?'

She grimaced. 'It looks like it. I had an interview with Chief Inspector Garrett — such an odd man, perpetually surly . . . he really does seem to have some kind of chip on his shoulder. Or maybe he doesn't like archaeologists. Anyway, as far as I can gather they're just giving up the whole thing as a bad job — for the moment, at least. Garrett told me they've searched old files but have no record of a local person going missing, and there's no clues to be picked up from the bones themselves — they've been too long in the ground. Their theory is that he was killed maybe fifty years ago, but even of that they're not entirely sure. They've made a bit of a mess down there on the bank, as you might imagine, torn up the old tree to check the area for clues to the identity of the dead man, and to see if there are any other burials there, but it doesn't really impinge on what we're doing. It's well away from the barrow area and they haven't touched our site.'

Arnold nodded thoughtfully. He stared down past the barrow to the bank where Elfreda Gale had discovered the more modern bones. 'I wonder what Sir Henry Alston would have thought if he'd discovered that skeleton on site.'

Rena Williams laughed. 'Had a fit, I don't doubt. But he wouldn't have found it anyway — he never did any digging on the site after he bought it. And I imagine the corpse would have been buried in the bank some years before he acquired the land with Hartshorn House.'

'Hmm . . . It's strange, really, that he never took a close look at the barrow after he purchased Hartshorn and this land,' Arnold remarked. 'He did undertake some digs in the area though, I seem to recall.'

Rena Williams turned to walk towards the tented area where the group was still working. 'I believe so . . . He worked for two years at a site over at Hawgill — it's only about three miles from here, closer, as the crow flies. I read somewhere — one of his books, I think — that while he was working at Hawgill, he first became familiar with the existence of Hartshorn House and fell in love with it. He came back here to buy house and land, when he could afford it, some years later.' She stopped suddenly, short of the grave site with its canvas screening. 'I should warn you, by the way — there's been more trouble here.'

'Elfreda?'

Rena Williams sighed. 'How did you guess! Her and Geoffrey Westwood. They're like cat and dog. In some ways, one is as bad as another. But he's been riding her very hard, and she seems to have got to the stage where she doesn't give a damn about her doctorate. She's hanging on, but there have been several flare-ups. And there's been trouble with the Musketeers too.'

'How come? I thought they were a pretty tightly knit group.'

She frowned, puzzled. 'I'm not certain — they won't talk to me about it. But Ainsley Close and Alan Frith have had a few words and Peter Burns has gone very quiet.'

'What's caused it?'

She raised her eyebrows and rolled her eyes expressively. 'I wouldn't be a bit surprised if it's Elfreda again, playing one off against another. She really is a bit of a . . . tease, I suppose the word is. But the major problem is still her relationship — or lack of it — with Geoffrey Westwood.'

'Still arguing about symbolism?'

Dr Williams shrugged and brushed a wayward lock of dark hair from her eyes. 'Not just that. I'm not too clear about the whole story. Just before the police threw us off the site, you'll recall, Stephen Alston rang me at the George and Dragon to say that access to the library was no longer possible. Westwood saw that as an excuse to niggle at Elfreda, and it's continued ever since.'

'But why does Westwood blame her? Was it she who was responsible for denial of access?'

'Westwood is convinced that's the case. He's sure she misbehaved in some way. And he's been on her back ever since. In fact . . . well, I went down to see Stephen Alston yesterday, to clear the matter up. He was a bit . . . cool. When I asked him about the closing of the facility, he said he was going to be away a fair bit over the next few weeks and the house would be empty. He thought it wasn't a good idea to have Elfreda working there in his absence.'

'Does he regard her as untrustworthy?'

She wrinkled her nose thoughtfully. 'It's not that. He sort of changed his ground somewhat as the conversation went on. At first, he said the American purchaser, his prospective father-in-law John Eaton, would be unwilling to have us working there. Later, he appeared to backtrack on that. Suggested there was a security problem.'

'But it would surely be better to have someone working there, than to have the house completely empty!' Arnold argued.

'It was a point I put to him, and one which, eventually, he accepted. However, to cut a long story short, I sort of sweet-talked him round in the end, and got him to agree that provided I took full responsibility for making sure the house was locked up and secure each night, we could continue to use the library. So, I now hold a key.'

'And Elfreda?'

'No mention was made of Elfreda.' She glanced around her uncertainly. 'In fact, he skirted around the possibility of her working there . . . Anyway, the main thing is I've got us access again.'

'And you'll continue to use Elfreda down there?'

'She's a good worker and knows her way around.' Dr Williams stated, almost challengingly. 'And to tell you the truth, I've got so fed up with the bickering between her and Geoffrey Westwood . . . so it still seems a sound solution to the problem. We're better keeping them apart. In fact, she's down there now. Somewhat resentful but . . .'

'Why resentful? When I went down and saw her at Hartshorn I got the impression she enjoyed working there.'

'She did — before she found those bones in the bank,' Rena Williams shook her head. 'It's partly the squabble with Westwood, of course, but she feels she's being victimized for his surly behaviour, and she's missing out on the excitement of the dig. And things are moving on, Arnold. Come, let me show you.'

They entered the tented area. The Three Musketeers were on their hands and knees, Geoffrey Westwood working at the edge of the trench. No one was speaking, and there was an air of truculence among the group. Alan Frith smiled when he saw Arnold, and Ainsley Close raised his hand. Peter Burns nodded: his face was red, and Arnold wondered whether he'd felt the edge of Westwood's tongue in the last few minutes. Rena Williams led Arnold to the far end of the trench and pointed to where the extended work had been carried on.

'You see what's happening? We've come across an area of softer soil and we've picked up a number of objects. Some more clay Venus figures, and over there we've found what looks like the opening to a small pit. It was used to store grain. There's also evidence of animal burials — two dog skeletons in three days!'

'So the site is as extensive as we thought it might be?'

Rena Williams nodded vigorously. 'But changing in character. These inhumations were probably ninth century, but the presence of the dog burials and the grain suggests that maybe we should look anew at the three skeletons we found at the beginning. Maybe they were ritual murders after all.'

'In what context?' Arnold asked.

'If there are layers of grain in small pits, it suggests that the ritual was connected with the digging of those pits. The three skeletons could have been evidence of human sacrifice to appease the gods of the underworld: a gift to placate them for the disturbance to the earth. It takes us one step further from our original hypothesis, but the storage of crops underground suggests a certain trust in chthonic powers — the belief may have been that the gods of the underworld were disturbed by the digging and therefore would require propitiation.'

'You're suggesting a veneration of underworld deities.'

'A plutonic cult. Exactly.'

Arnold was silent for a while, staring at the grain pit she had pointed out. 'Have you dug very deeply there yet?'

'We've run a small inspection bore. A couple of iron implements at the edge, but mainly layers of grain.'

Arnold shook his head doubtfully. 'I don't think it's enough.'

'How do you mean?'

'You could well be right about the plutonic deities, and the human sacrifice by way of propitiation. Yet all this is relatively recent, in the context of the site as a whole — ninth century, you said? But Professor Westwood reckoned the skeletons were fifth century.'

Her eyes warned him, and her voice dropped. 'He's possibly revising his hypothesis.'

Arnold grimaced doubtfully. 'But we're still working at the edge of the barrow. We've still got some thirty feet or more to go — the central area hasn't yet been touched. If those skeletons were placed at the edge of the barrow as human sacrifices to the plutonic deities, fine — but I still have a feeling this barrow is much older than that. I suspect we're still just working at the edge of something — without yet appreciating what lies at its heart.'

Rena Williams took a deep breath. 'You could be right. That's why I'm pleased you're back. I have experience of the kind of luck you can bring to a dig — and of the kind of slightly unorthodox reasoning you provide.'

Professor Westwood had caught the last remark. He straightened, turned to look at them. 'Unorthodox, unacademic reasoning, I would argue,' he suggested unpleasantly. 'I believe we shouldn't dash at anything but proceed slowly and methodically — and not indulge in too much wild theorizing.'

'But that's no reason,' Rena Williams said stubbornly, 'why Arnold shouldn't work with Ainsley towards the centre of the barrow. We can run a shallow trench along here and open up that central area. It could give us some early answers, warn us what we're likely to find elsewhere. And it would also give us the chance to determine whether what we've found so far is merely a layer above a much older, quite different cult centre. We've got the cave shrine, which is mainly Romano-Celtic; we've got the remains here which span fifth to ninth centuries. But I'm inclined to agree with Arnold. What we might find at the centre of the barrow could be much different. And much, much older.'

Arnold gained the impression that he was being caught up in an argument that had begun to spark between Rena Williams and Geoffrey Westwood during their enforced absence from the site. That was their problem: he would merely go along, in the end, with whatever the site director suggested.

And that was Rena Williams.

Karen Stannard turned up on the Friday morning and Arnold was grateful that Dr Williams showed her around the site area, while he and Ainsley Close began to work on a trench running towards the centre of the barrow. The deputy director of the Department of Museums and Antiquities was casually dressed for her foray onto the fells: she wore a light tan jacket, close-fitting jeans and elegant boots of expensive leather; her russet hair was loose and blowing in the breeze and the crisp air of Garrigill brought a sparkle to her eyes, so that Arnold thought he had never seen her look so attractive.

She was clearly in professional awe of Rena Williams but the initial nervousness — which surprised Arnold, who saw her as a confident, ruthless woman — wore off gradually until the pair seemed to be getting on like a house on fire. Arnold left them to it, concentrating on stripping the turf carefully from the centre section and marking out the area for photographic purposes later that afternoon.

Rena Williams took Karen Stannard down to look at the place where the mysterious skeleton had been found by Elfreda and they were down there for almost an hour. Arnold had no idea what they were discussing but was not surprised later when they returned to the tented area to say that Karen Stannard had decided to stay for the weekend and lend a hand at the dig.

'I'm assured there's a room available at the George and Dragon,' she told Arnold. 'I can't imagine my presence here will put your nose out of joint, Landon.'

Arnold ignored the mocking tone. 'You should enjoy it, working here — provided you don't mind getting your boots dirty.'

She smiled thinly. 'I've brought other kit. Always be prepared, don't you know? One never knows what might be around the next bend.'

'In the circumstances,' Rena Williams said, 'I'll knock off early today and show Karen to the hotel, arrange for the room and so on. Would you mind, Arnold, if we had a word . . . ?' She gestured surreptitiously in Geoffrey Westwood's direction. Arnold moved to one side for a quiet conversation with her.

'I'll show Karen to the George and Dragon, so would you mind taking the key and going along to Hartshorn House? I promised Stephen Alston that I'd make sure everything was locked up — Elfreda's there and she's got Peter's car, so it's just a matter of checking, really. Would you mind?'

'Not at all,' Arnold replied.

'I could hardly ask Geoffrey Westwood to do it,' Rena Williams smiled gratefully, and slipped the key into his hand.

Arnold knew what she meant.

It was almost five o'clock when Arnold finished clearing up at the site. He was the last to leave. He drove the short distance to Hartshorn House, not certain whether Elfreda would still be there. She was. Peter Burns's car was parked on the gravel drive in front of the house. Stephen Alston, it seemed, was still away.

Arnold parked his car beside hers and ran up the steps.

The front door was locked — a precaution of Elfreda's — so when he unlocked it and went in he called her name in case she might be startled. She was still in the library, replacing some books on the shelves.

'Oh, hi, Mr Landon! I'm packing away, just getting ready to leave. Something you want?'

'No, no, just standing in for Dr Williams.'

She turned to look at him, her smile a little forced. 'Doing the nanny bit, hey? Making sure I haven't left the gas on or forgotten to put out the cat.'

Arnold thought it best to ignore the sarcasm. He walked across to her working desk. 'Still cataloguing?'

'Uh huh. I've still got two journal runs to work on.' She came across to the desk and began to gather up the papers scattered on its surface, as though unwilling to allow him to see them. 'How are things going at Garrigill?'

'Very well. Ainsley and I are opening up the centre of the barrow. I think we might find something interesting.'

'Really?' She hesitated, staring at some yellowing papers in her hand, then thrust them into a plastic folder and slid them between the leaves of a leather-bound volume of an archaeological journal. 'I wish I was there.'

'Getting fed up down here?'

She hesitated. 'It's not that. I just feel that I've been pushed out just because of Professor Westwood. Dr Williams should stand up to him, sort it out.'

'Or maybe you should be more careful what you say,' Arnold suggested gently.

'Bit late for that now, isn't it?' She laughed. But there was a note of bitterness in her tone. 'No, apart from that, it's interesting enough working down here . . . And I think I've come across something . . .' She hesitated, seemed to check herself for a moment, uncertain whether to confide in him. She shook her head. 'No, it's just that I feel I'm missing out on the dig. That's where all the excitement is . . . but I realize it's impossible at the moment. Dr Williams is right, in view of Professor Westwood's attitude. Even so . . .' Once more she hesitated, staring at him in an odd manner. She put the books down. 'Mr Landon, can I ask your advice?'

'Of course.'

She grimaced. 'I don't quite know how to put this. And I haven't yet got it clear in my own mind . . .'

'What's bothering you?'

She took a deep breath. 'Well . . . you know when I found that . . . that skeleton up at the site? I can't be sure, but I think I know—'

She started suddenly, and looked past him, over his shoulder. Her face paled.

Arnold turned. The windows of the library looked out over the gardens, but the view at the moment was blocked. Standing among the rose bushes, close to the window, was a tall, lean man in windcheater and check shirt, open at the throat. He was about thirty years old, with hair that came down thickly to his shoulders, and he was bearded. He was staring intently through the window at Elfreda, and Arnold heard her swear violently.

'I'll have to go,' she muttered and picked up her bag, half running towards the library door. As she did so, the man in the garden turned away and was lost to sight. Puzzled, Arnold hesitated for a few moments, then walked back into the hallway. Elfreda had left the front door open. She was standing beside her borrowed car, next to Arnold's, but there was a third car in the drive now, a Volkswagen, parked near the rhododendron bushes. The bearded man was standing beside the car Elfreda was using, and they appeared to be arguing, in low, bitter undertones. As Arnold stood in the doorway he saw the man put out his hand to Elfreda — she struck it away angrily and opened her car door.

The stranger leaned over her, talking urgently, then caught sight of Arnold standing in the doorway. He stiffened, glared at Arnold, and then as Elfreda slammed her door shut he turned away abruptly and half ran to his car.

Elfreda swung her car around the drive and roared off towards the gates and the roadway, gravel spurting from her tyres. The stranger had some difficulty starting his own vehicle, but finally managed to turn and follow her. Arnold was in some doubt as to what he should do. But Elfreda, he guessed, could take care of herself.

He went back into the library, carried out the checks that Rena Williams had requested, and locked the front door.

When he got back to the George and Dragon he was relieved to see that Peter Burns's car was safely parked there; there was no sign of the strange Volkswagen. Elfreda herself was standing in the residents' lounge, clearly waiting for him to arrive. Her eyes were still angry, her mouth determined. She came forward to greet him.

'I just wanted to apologize,' she said.

'For what?'

'That scene at Hartshorn House. I . . . I can't tell you about it. It was private business.' She hesitated. 'It won't happen again. I guarantee it!'

For a moment he thought she would say more, but she turned away and headed for the stairs. Arnold made his way to his own room, closed the door behind him and took a whisky out of the minibar.

He felt he needed a drink. He was still not quite certain what he should do.

3

The work advanced well over the weekend. To be fair to Karen Stannard, she threw herself enthusiastically into the task, and Arnold was amused at the way the young men looked at her. She played up to them, teasing them, talking with them, dispensing smiles and sunshine into their lives. She displayed none of the toughness that men in the office saw: she was practising her skills, honing them on an admiring group of inexperienced men, and enjoying herself hugely.

She was even pleasant to Arnold.

She seemed also to be getting on very well with Rena Williams. They spent much of the time working closely together, their conversation animated and clearly amusing, and Arnold wondered whether Ms Stannard was enjoying herself so much that she might be coming up to the site more often in future. It was not a prospect he was particularly enamoured of, but he did not spend too much time dwelling on it. Instead, he concentrated on the work he was doing.

And on the Sunday morning Ainsley Close stood up, scratched his designer beard and called to Arnold. 'You'd better have a look here.'

The others had gone for their coffee break. Arnold and Ainsley were alone under cover. 'What is it?'

Ainsley pointed.

The earth at his feet was darker in colour and more friable in texture than the surrounding area. Ainsley had been scraping away at the edge of what seemed to be a piece of sandstone, curving along towards the centre of the mound. 'It looks as though it's not just one piece,' Ainsley said. 'You see? It's as though there's a joint there.'

Arnold squatted down, and ran his fingers along the edge of the stone. Ainsley was right: there was a second piece of stone, smooth to the touch, jointed to the first. He took a trowel and began to clean away at the edge. It curved away from him regularly; he peered at it closely. It had been worked by man; on the flat surface he picked out chisel marks.

Arnold stood up. 'We'd better tell the others.'

The whole group came back to the site, coffee mugs in hand and stood staring down at the stone edge. Rena Williams inspected it, and looked up at Geoffrey Westwood. 'What do you make of it?'

He shook his head. 'A lintel, maybe . . . or the cover of another grain pit.'

'I'm not so sure,' Arnold demurred. 'The bit we've exposed would suggest it would be a very large grain pit, if we follow the curve of the stone.'

'There's only one way to find out,' Rena Williams said in a determined tone. 'I think we should all work here for the time being — there's only about two inches of soil at the top there.'

They started work immediately.

Arnold found himself working next to Karen Stannard.

She said nothing to him, but she worked quietly and carefully and he realized that she was in her element here — all need for the continuing power struggle gone, the urge to dominate forgotten, it was a return to the early things that had driven her. Like Arnold, she had a passion for the past. The pity was, it had been driven back, submerged by her other desire: to succeed in a man's world, to take part in the power politics of the university and now the local authority department. She caught him glancing at her and she was surprised; then perhaps she guessed at his thoughts and her lips tightened, but she said nothing, applying herself even more determinedly to her work.

In the late afternoon Elfreda arrived. Arnold saw her enter the tented area and she seemed edgy, excited. Then she realized that they were working on a new area and came forward, her eyes lighting up.

'What is it?'

'Have you locked up at the library?' Geoffrey Westwood snapped.

'Yes, of course. I'd come to a stopping point . . . but what is it you've found?'

Arnold stood up and wiped his brow. The stone was now half exposed along its length. It consisted of three large sections, chiselled and cut to form close joints. The whole area was perhaps seven feet across, the stone forming a roughly circular shape. He shook his head in uncertainty. 'We don't know yet.'

'It could be another grain pit,' Ainsley Close suggested.

'Or maybe a shrine.' Peter Burns argued.

'Do you think these stones are like the others we found placed on the three skeletons?' Alan Frith asked. 'You know, keeping spirits locked underground?'

'We don't know,' Rena Williams said wearily, getting to her feet. 'But I think we've done all we can for today. Time we should pack in, make our way back to the hotel, get showered, get a good night's sleep and then return to this in the morning.' She glanced at Karen Stannard. 'It's a pity you and Arnold will be going back to the office. Things could be rather interesting tomorrow.'

Karen Stannard hesitated. There was excitement in her eyes, even a certain longing. She glanced at Arnold with a doubtful expression; the uncertainty softened her beauty, made her appear almost vulnerable and for the first time in his experience she seemed possessed of human weakness. 'I think, in the circumstances, you could use us up here tomorrow. I know

Mr Landon doesn't have much on . . . and what I have to do can wait. I'll ring the director in the morning . . .'

If he's in, Arnold thought to himself. He observed Karen Stannard again, appraisingly. She had the capacity to surprise him, after all: putting personal archaeological interest before the power struggle.

Rena Williams glanced thoughtfully at Elfreda. The girl was staring down at the stone, fascinated. Her eyes were bright — almost too bright. 'Are you all right, Elfreda?'

'Of course.'

'Everything fine at the library?'

Elfreda nodded. 'I . . . I'd just had enough for today.'

'Mr Alston back?'

'He called in this morning — but he's gone off again now.' She hesitated, reluctant. 'I'll get back down there tomorrow,' Rena Williams still watched her carefully. 'I'd better call in on the way back, as I promised Mr Alston. Just to check.' Elfreda stared at her, and seemed about to say something, but then remained silent.

The group packed up, the young men chattering excitedly, telling Elfreda the events of the day. They roared off in their cars, returning to the hotel. Westwood hung back around the stones, staring at them for a long time, chin in hand, contemplating. Then they all left the site.

They met for dinner that evening as a group, and Rena Williams ordered some wine. It was a pleasant occasion with everyone in a good humour — even Geoffrey Westwood left off his usual baiting of Elfreda, in anticipation of what their work in the morning might bring. There was an ease in the party that led to them drifting into the bar afterwards for a late-night drink.

Only Elfreda seemed somewhat subdued: serious and preoccupied, she seemed unable to fit in as easily as she normally did. She left the bar early: Arnold was aware that Rena Williams noticed it, with a slight frown of anxiety.

Arnold stood at the bar with the Three Musketeers: they were somewhat boisterous as was to be expected but he didn't mind that. From time to time he glanced across to where Karen Stannard sat with Rena Williams, one arm thrown casually along the back of the site director's chair. Karen Stannard was leaning forward, talking animatedly in half-whispered tones, taking advantage of the growing intimacy that seemed to have arisen between the two women. They looked very close and very friendly. Arnold finished his drink, said goodnight to the boys, and went to his room.

He was not particularly sleepy. He turned on the television set but there was nothing of interest for him, so he switched it off again and picked up a book he had brought with him — Jane Wilson's latest historical novel. She had based it in part on some work they had done together in North Yorkshire, and he was interested in the manner in which she wove some fairly esoteric information on the suppression of the Knights Templar in the fourteenth century into the flow of the novel.

It was after eleven when his bedside phone rang. 'Arnold? Am I disturbing you?'

It was Rena Williams.

'No, not at all. I'm just sitting here, reading a book.'

'I thought I saw your light on when I passed your room. You haven't gone to bed then?'

'No.'

There was a short silence. Then, hesitantly, she said, 'Do you mind if I call in for a few minutes?'

Surprised, Arnold said, 'No, of course. I'm just sitting here . . .'

A few minutes later there was a tap on the door; he tossed his book on the bed and opened the door. At his invitation Rena Williams slipped into his room.

'Hope no one saw me,' she chuckled nervously. 'Don't know what they'd think. I'm sure I'd never hear the end of it from the Three Musketeers . . : She glanced around the room. 'Bigger than mine,' she commented.

'Take a seat,' Arnold suggested, dragging forward the easy chair he had been using.

'Been working?' she asked, glancing at the book.

'Light reading. By a friend of mine — you've met her, of course. Jane Wilson.'

'Ah, yes . . .'

He perched himself on the edge of the bed. 'So what's the problem?'

She leaned back in the chair, clamped her fingers on the arms and frowned. 'It's overreacting maybe . . . Do you think Elfreda's all right?'

'Why do you ask?'

'I don't know. She's been looking tense, uncharacteristically unsure of herself. I feel sure she came up to the site to see me today, to talk to me — but then it got washed away by the excitement of seeing the stone we'd discovered . . . Have you noticed anything?'

'Why do you ask me?'

'Who else should I ask?' she snorted. 'Geoffrey Westwood? He'd as like as not be pleased that she's upset. But Elfreda . . . is it because I've relegated her to the library at Hartshorn, away from the site? Do you think that's what's upsetting her?'

Arnold shook his head. 'I don't think so. She's been resentful about it, to a certain extent, but I think she's got over that. She'd prefer to be at the site, but she understands your reasons — and she's not holding a grudge.'

'Except towards Westwood. That man . . .' She shook herself angrily. 'He dislikes her intensely, almost unreasonably. Sometimes, I've seen him looking at her—'

'I think maybe there's a problem apart from Westwood,' Arnold said quietly.

There was a short silence. Rena Williams eyed him speculatively. 'So are you going to tell me?'

'I don't really see it as my business,' Arnold explained, 'so I've been reluctant to say anything, even tell you. But . . . well, there's someone she knows — and isn't too happy to see — been hanging around, I suspect.'

'What are you talking about?'

'She was out meeting someone one evening, a little while ago, when the rest of us were in the hotel. I heard her come in later that evening — and I heard voices in her room when I went to bed, and a car leaving in the early hours. Then . . . when I was at the library in Hartshorn House, some character turned up. She was very angry. They had words in the car park before she went off. She told me later it wouldn't happen again — though quite what she meant by that I'm not clear — but I think maybe that's what's been bothering her. An unwelcome suitor, I suspect. I had a feeling at one stage she wanted to talk to me about it, maybe as she wanted to talk to you today . . . but the moment passed.'

'I see,' Rena Williams was silent for a little while. She sighed. 'She got into a bit of trouble at Reading, I understand . . . one of the reasons she came up to York.' She shook her head doubtfully. 'Life can be complicated, can't it? I'd better try to find some way of having a word with her tomorrow . . . get her to open up, if she really is troubled. I suspect it might well be . . . well . . .'

Arnold waited. She did not finish what she was about to say. She frowned introspectively, lost in her own thoughts for a while. Then, when she came to herself again, she smiled briefly, looked around the room with a vague air and seemed oddly unwilling to leave. After a few minutes' silence, awkwardly, Arnold asked if she would like to have a nightcap.

'That would be nice,' she agreed quickly.

He opened the minibar. 'Whisky?'

'With some soda, please.'

Arnold took a brandy himself and they sat there for a while. The conversation was desultory, oddly strained, and a certain tension crept between them. She fiddled with the glass in her hand and avoided his eyes and he began to feel uncomfortable. She talked a little of herself, about her life at university, about her childhood and youth in the West Country, and how she had gained her enthusiasm for archaeology. For a short period, as she discussed professional matters, she relaxed, became animated, and smiled. But then the tension returned, and she once more seemed unable to meet his glance.

Finally, she finished her drink, and with a certain reluctance, stood up.

'I'd better go.'

He nodded and stood with her. She looked at him. She was a tall woman; he had once thought her rather mannish in appearance. But she had handsome features and the bone structure of her face was fine. He had never really noticed how dark her eyes were before. She said nothing for a little while, simply holding his glance. At last, quietly, she said, 'I like you, Arnold.'

He was uneasy, not sure what reply to make.

'I feel generally . . . comfortable in your presence.' She managed a tight little smile. 'But not at the moment.'

'It's an unusual situation. And it's pretty late, I suppose. After all the excitement of today we're both tired.'

'And I'm in your bedroom.'

The silence grew sharp between them. Arnold felt a stirring in his veins. He was uncertain of himself. He was not inexperienced, but though he had thought of Rena Williams with admiration, it had been only as a friend and colleague. Not as a woman.

Her eyes were very bright and her glance direct. Slowly she asked, 'Do you find me attractive, Arnold?'

He had the feeling he had only to reach out his hand and she would come to him. She wanted to be kissed and yet it was more than simple curiosity or even desire — he felt there was more than that. She wanted . . . reassurance.

'I think you're a very attractive woman, Rena,' he said at last.

She held his glance for several seconds and then, when he said no more and made no move towards her, she stepped sideways, moved past him to the door. She opened it, hesitated, then glanced back towards him, frowning.

'So does Karen Stannard,' she said.

* * *

The following day, the whole group — with the exception of Elfreda — continued work at the site. Arnold was a little surprised that Elfreda had not put pressure on Rena Williams to be allowed back now that the excitement was running so high, but she had said little that morning at breakfast. She had sat apart, her preoccupation of the previous evening continuing, and Arnold wondered whether it had anything to do with the young man who had visited Hartshorn, to her clear discomfiture.

He dismissed all thoughts of her shortly after they began work on the site, however. It was an oddly interrupted morning, with first Ainsley Close turning up late, and then both Alan Frith and Peter Burns finding reasons to be away from the site for an hour or so. Nevertheless, the work proceeded and during the course of the day they removed most of the layer of soil that covered the flat, chiselled stones and made a series of small finds — a miniature iron dagger with an ornamental hilt, fashioned in the form of two adjacent wheels, a tiny bronze boar figurine, two safety-pin brooches and a belt fragment with a suspended wheel amulet.

They held a conference after lunch about the finds.

'In my view,' Westwood propounded, 'the presence of a temple is suggested. The sacral function of these models cannot be doubted — they might even have served as a kind of religious currency for devotion to the sun god.'

'I'm not so certain,' Dr Williams demurred. 'We know of the existence of the shrine in the cave, but where's the evidence for a temple here at the barrow? This is a grave site, and I would think these amulets may have been cast here sometime after burial — if there is a burial here.'

'Possibly as talismans for the journey of the dead to the afterlife,' Karen Stannard suggested. Her hair was slightly tousled and there were smudges of dirt on her cheek as she crouched close to Rena Williams. They had worked closely together all morning, Arnold had noted.

Dr Williams now turned to him. 'What do you think, Arnold?'

She had been somewhat reserved with him at the site, possibly because of a slight embarrassment over her visit to his room the previous evening and the remark she had made about Karen Stannard. Her conversations had been brief and cool and confined to the work in hand; now, her tone was businesslike.

He shrugged. 'I think it's a little early to say . . . certainly too early to make assumptions.'

'Julius Caesar wrote that the Germanic tribes counted as gods, the sun, fire and moon,' Westwood snapped peevishly. 'What we have here is clear evidence—'

'Of sky and solar symbolism,' Arnold interrupted. 'I don't doubt it. But some scholars have suggested the wheel motif is almost like a Celtic secret society emblem—'

'Nonsense! It has profound religious significance,' Westwood disagreed. 'And what we have here is without doubt a religious site. Maybe linked with the shrine cave, but this whole damned degenerate art medium . . .'

Arnold was grateful that Elfreda was not present. He could well imagine she would have started another argument about Westwood's views of the degeneracy of Celtic symbolic art forms. He became aware that Karen Stannard was watching him carefully with a frown of displeasure, so he took the warning to heart and did not pursue the dispute.

By mid-afternoon they had uncovered the full run of the edges of the stones to the depth of three inches and were brushing away the light soil on the surface. They had uncovered a few scattered bronze coins and a legionary tile stamp marked with a swastika, which suggested that Roman legionaries had certainly visited the site, probably in connection with the shrine cave. It gave them further food for thought as far as interpretation was concerned.

'Do you suppose the legionaries merely lost the artefact,' Karen Stannard queried, 'or had they actually been worshipping at the site?'

'And did they at any time uncover the barrow?' Rena Williams added. 'We've seen no evidence of a temple location — no pillars, no postholes . . .'

'They could have worshipped at the barrow itself, without raising stones above it,' Westwood muttered. 'In fact, somewhere, I've seen a reference—'

'Dr Williams!'

They were interrupted by the call from Alan Frith. The big, square-shouldered young man was on his knees at the centre of the jointed stones, brushing away the surface dirt. 'What is it?' Rena Williams asked.

'It looks like some sort of carving . . . incisions in the stone.'

'Lettering?'

Frith shook his head. 'I don't think so.' He leaned forward, peering at the marks. The others gathered around, looking over his shoulders.

Arnold frowned. 'No . . . it's a motif. There, you see the legs, and the feet at the end?' He stepped past Alan Frith, crouched down and began to trace an outline with his finger, following the curves of the incisions. Gradually the figure emerged: four long, thin, jointed legs ending in representations of hooves; heavy haunches, a tail and a phallus; an attenuated body where the stomach almost touched the back, represented as two narrow lines leading to a muscular shoulder and a prominent snout jutting fiercely forward, the mask eyeless, sharp-eared, threatening.

'It's a boar motif,' Rena Williams announced quietly. They fell silent. The representation cut in the rock was clear. It was of the kind Professor Westwood criticized, representational but unflamboyant, lacking in detail yet to Arnold's eyes wondrously sharp in its delineation. It was spare of line, almost grotesque in its stylized form, but its vigour and strength was immediate. It spoke to them across millennia, the careful, committed carving of unknown hands, the vision of an artist and a warrior possessed by supernatural beliefs that guided his chisel in his representation of power and war and death.

It silenced them.

Arnold was oddly affected by the carving. As he stared at it his senses blurred and the figure seemed to move, to come alive. There was a light singing in his ears and he seemed to hear a long-dead distant wolf call in his head, superseded by the grunting terror of the boar. But it changed, as the sound of the wind would change — the rustling of dry leaves in an autumn breeze, the soft menacing whisper of an unseen hurt, and the distraught keening of a society that had lost its reason for existence in the dying fall of its beliefs. What he seemed to hear could have been a shaman sound, or the dry, fading scream of a woman, high on the hill, echoing down through untold, dark centuries of folk memory and fear.

He shook himself, glanced at the others. They could not have heard what he had, because the sounds were in his head, the memories in his own imagination, but their faces were cold and closed and uncommunicative, each of them staring at the boar motif and bound up in their own visions of the past.

Rena Williams shivered and the movement seemed to unfreeze the group.

'A boar,' Ainsley Close wondered. 'What's the significance of it?'

'I understand it was a common motif among the Celts,' Karen Stannard offered.

Professor Westwood grunted. 'The boar was endowed with supernatural qualities by the Celts. It represented speed, and pugnacity and danger. The animal was believed to lead men to death and to the underworld — that's why the flesh was often placed in the grave, both as a ritual food appropriate for feasts on earth and in the underworld, and also as a recognition of the beast's talismanic properties.'

'But what significance does it have here?' Alan Frith asked quietly.

Rena Williams shrugged. 'Food, hunting, battle, ferocity, possibly apotropaic . . . We found that boar figurine, of course . . .'

Her voice died away. It had an odd, brittle quality, and there was a hint of nervousness in both in her voice and Frith's which suggested to Arnold that each one of the group had been strangely and personally affected by the carving.

'I don't think we'll be able to make an educated guess until we see what's under the stones,' Arnold suggested quietly. 'And we can't do that until we've cleared the edge of the stones to enough depth to lift them without damage.' Rena Williams looked briskly about her, almost shrugging away the darkness of her thoughts. 'I suggest we get on with it. Let's find out what the stones are resting on, and maybe we can then find a way to lift them and determine their function.'

Professor Westwood hesitated, glanced at his watch. 'I'll leave you to it. This motif puzzles me, as far as this location is concerned. We can't do too much more here today so I think I'll go down to the library at Hartshorn. I have a feeling I've seen something like this boar motif before. I'd like to consider the iconography of it in more detail.' He glanced sardonically at Rena Williams. 'I'm sure you can spare me.'

He would be working in the same room as Elfreda at Hartshorn. Arnold knew the thought had sprung to Rena Williams's mind, and was aware of the protest that sparked in her eyes. She wanted no more quarrels between Westwood and Elfreda. But she said nothing and the protest died. She nodded. 'We'll see you at the hotel later.'

They worked on at the site through the late afternoon, in the absence of the professor and Elfreda.

Arnold half wondered whether she would come up to the site, to get away from her professional enemy, but she put in no appearance. The group brushed and picked away at the edge of the jointed stones until it became apparent that they were at least six inches thick. They worked almost silently, each preoccupied with personal thoughts. For Arnold it was the sweep of a cold, high wind on the fell and distant darkness, the howl of unseen men, the sharp keening of women. It was something he seemed to be unable to dismiss from his subconscious and it made the skin on the back of his neck prickle.

They realized towards the end of the afternoon that they would need tackle to lift the stones, fresh minds and bodies and a great deal of care. By then the area had largely been cleared, and the stones completely exposed to view under the lamps they had lit as the afternoon gloom descended.

They stood staring at the boar motif in the centre of the stones and the air was cold about them.

'I get the impression of evil,' Karen Stannard remarked suddenly. She was stony-faced as she looked around at the group. 'Why should that be?'

Arnold was surprised at her comment: she was not normally so open in her thoughts. But she was clearly affected by the motif, as they all were.

'The boar was always used as a warning device,' Rena Williams suggested.

'It certainly sends warning signals in the direction of my spine,' Karen Stannard replied feelingly. 'Enough to suggest to me that a stiff gin and tonic would go down well right now.'

Dr Williams nodded. 'Time to pack in,' she agreed.

They prepared to leave the site. Somewhat subdued, they gathered their belongings together, locked up the site and made their way to the cars. Arnold was the last to arrive at the hotel, just minutes behind the others. As he walked up the steps and through the doorway Rena Williams was standing at reception signing an account for the receptionist. She glanced at him. 'Karen's gone into the bar. She's invited me for a drink. You want to join us?'

He was inclined to thank her and refuse, but there was something in her eyes that stopped him. He had the feeling she would appreciate his presence, so that she would not be left alone with Miss Stannard. He recalled their conversation the previous evening. Arnold smiled, and nodded. 'I'd be happy to join you.'

Karen Stannard was standing at the lounge bar. She had already ordered a gin and tonic for herself and her brow clouded as Arnold approached; somewhat reluctantly she asked Arnold what he wanted to drink. When Rena Williams joined them they took seats at a small table just inside the door. Karen Stannard raised her glass in salute. Something of the confident sparkle she had momentarily lost at the field site was back in her eyes. 'Well, here's to you, Rena, and what we found today. Let's hope it's the start of something exciting—'

She never managed to complete the toast.

There was a sudden disturbance in the hallway. Next moment Geoffrey Westwood came lurching into the lounge. His clothes were muddy and stained, his glance wild. He headed for the bar, calling for a whisky. Then he swung around, glaring distractedly at the three of them sitting there.

'Geoffrey — what's the matter?' Rena Williams demanded sharply.

'Police . . . phone the police!' he almost shouted.

The barman, unnerved, pushed a glass of whisky towards him, half spilling it. Westwood grabbed at the glass, gulped the liquid down and had a brief fit of coughing.

Rena Williams stood up, scraping her chair and almost knocking over Arnold's drink. 'Geoffrey, what on earth are you talking about? What's happened?'

His eyes were glazing as he stared at her. 'Elfreda Gale. In the lane. She's been raped.'

'What?'

'I saw her, in the ditch. She's been raped . . . murdered!'

CHAPTER FOUR

1

Detective Chief Inspector 'Pat' Garrett scowled happily.

Things had now turned out more to his liking. True, he had been forced to make yet another journey to the desolate fells in the old lead-mining country, but at least it was in connection with something he could get his teeth into. This time it was not old bones.

He had already spoken to the chief constable about it. The old man had agreed that it would be wasteful to spend more time on seeking the identity of the skeleton found at the field site: the chances of turning up any hard information now were long gone. It was necessary to devote manpower to the murder and rape of the girl found in the ditch near Hartshorn House — and at least, for once, the police had a flying start. Garrett had already met several of the people working in the locality — and even the murdered girl herself.

'Do you think there's any connection?' the chief constable had asked him. 'Between her getting killed and her finding the old bones previously, I mean.'

'It's a line we won't lose sight of,' Garrett had replied cautiously, wrinkling his nose to demonstrate deep thought, 'but I doubt there's a connection. We've gone over the ground pretty thoroughly and the unfortunate young lady's body is now with forensics, but I can't imagine a rape has anything to do with a body that's been fifty years in the ground. Or however long it's been,' he added uncertainly.

'They haven't been able to fix a date on those old bones?'

'You know what they're like, sir. Pedants.'

'Well, drop it now, anyway. Concentrate on the girl's death. And Garrett . . .'

'Sir?'

'Let's make it quick. And dean.'

The press. He'd be worried about the press.

But Garrett didn't mind that sort of pressure. When he left the chief constable he'd even been humming a tune from *The Student Prince.*

Now, there was the task of interviewing for a second time the group of oddities with whom the girl had been working. First, and most obviously first, was Professor Geoffrey Westwood, the man who'd found the body. Garrett had read his file carefully. Eminent enough, it seemed, but not popular. Garrett himself had taken an instant dislike to the man. His heavy-lidded eyes were arrogant — and he clearly felt being drawn away from his academic work was a waste of time.

'You wanted to see me again?' he began huffily. 'I can't imagine why. I've nothing to add to the statement I made on the first interview.'

'That surprises me.' Garrett sniffed. 'You were somewhat shaken then — after discovering the body.'

'That was natural,' Westwood bridled, as though annoyed at having his lack of control touched upon. 'Finding a body like that is bound to knock a man out of his stride.'

'Particularly when it's the body of someone you knew.' Westwood blinked, but made no reply. Garrett studied the file in front of him for a little while. 'You knew the girl well, of course.'

'She was a student of mine. Of course I knew her.'

'At one stage you were her tutor, it seems. Then she moved to someone else.' He glanced up at Westwood curiously. 'You didn't get on?'

Westwood's mouth was aggressive. 'It's no secret we didn't see eye to eye. She was an insufferable, arrogant, argumentative—' He stopped suddenly, aware of the glint of disapproval in Garrett's eyes.

'What exactly did you two fall out about?'

'Celtic symbolism,' Westwood grunted, drawing his heavy eyebrows together.

'Esoteric.'

'That's all there was to it,' Westwood added defiantly. 'She disagreed with my views and had the arrogance to dispute with me in public. She was merely a student, while I have a widespread reputation! It was insufferable behaviour, as the others will tell you. I felt it necessary to keep her in check. She didn't care for that. We didn't like each other.'

'What exactly were you doing away from the field site?' Garrett asked.

Westwood shrugged. 'We'd discovered something interesting at the site — what looks like a cover stone, carved — and I wanted to go down to the Hartshorn library to look up some references.'

'Elfreda Gale was working there. Why was that, incidentally?'

Westwood wriggled nervously. 'You must ask Dr Williams. But . . .' He hesitated before making the reluctant concession. 'I imagine it was partly the result of the arguments Miss Gale and I had on site.'

'I see . . . Well, then, you went down to the library . . .'

'She wasn't there. The house was unlocked, and I was angry about that because she had specific instructions not to leave the place open. I went in, called her name, there was no sign of her. And she hadn't even bothered to clear up properly — some of the journals she was working on were still on the table. I put them back. Then I went on with what I wanted to do. I expected her to return in a little while, but there was no sign of her. I didn't know what to do — I had no key to the house, so I decided the best thing was to return to the site at the end of the day and have it out with her.'

He would have enjoyed doing that, Garrett thought to himself. Aloud, he said, 'Did you expect her to be up there?'

'I assumed she had returned to the field site, yes. But then . . .' Garrett waited unhelpfully. Westwood was staring at his hands; they were beginning to shake, as his earlier pugnacity deserted him.

'I saw . . . something, in the ditch as I drove past.'

'Elfreda. You didn't see the body on the way down?'

Westwood shook his head. 'It might have been there. I didn't . . . notice it. But on the way back . . . I saw it, drove past, stopped, got out and went back for a closer look.'

There was a short silence. Garrett stared at the file on the desk in front of him. 'You were rather . . . muddied.'

Westwood took a deep breath and stared at Garrett. His glance was stony but determined. 'She looked just like . . . a bundle of clothes. I reached down, tried to drag her from the ditch . . .'

'Somewhat unwise, and unfortunate,' Garrett murmured. 'It would have been more helpful not to disturb the body.'

'I was shaken, disturbed, didn't think what I was doing. I grabbed at her arm, and then I saw who it was and I suppose I was alarmed, I slipped, I slid into the ditch myself.' He licked his lips nervously. 'I just fell, got muddy.'

'There was mud in your car.'

'Of course. I got back in, drove up to the site.'

'Why not back to Hartshorn, or even to the hotel, to phone for the police? You delayed things further by going up to the field site.'

'I tell you I was shaken! God, man, don't you realize? I knew her. She was dead! She'd been raped! Do you expect me to think straight, behave rationally? There was no one at the site, so I went to the hotel.'

'At what point did you realize she'd been raped?'

Westwood snorted. 'It was obvious! Her clothing was disarranged, torn. Her jeans had been half dragged off, her sweater—' He took a deep breath. 'Look here, I told you all

I had to tell last time. What's the point of going over it all again? Do you really regard me as a suspect, for God's sake?'

'At this stage,' Garrett took pleasure in saying, 'we're ruling out no possibilities.'

His pleasure increased when he saw the consternation rise in Professor Westwood's eyes.

* * *

Dr Rena Williams was a different kettle of fish. After Westwood had blustered his way out of the office, swearing to bring the wrath of the politically powerful down on Garrett's head, he interviewed the site director. She was calm, self-possessed and quiet-voiced, but there was an underlying tone of pain as she answered his questions. She had liked Elfreda Gale, she told him; she had regarded her highly as a research student; she had a good relationship with her and she felt Elfreda had a brilliant mind.

'And her feud with Professor Westwood?'

'Elfreda could be outspoken. And she didn't suffer fools gladly.'

'She saw Westwood as a fool?'

Dr Williams hesitated. 'Not a fool, of course. But . . . pompous, and opinionated. And Elfreda lacked . . . discretion. She spoke up for her views when she might have been better employed staying quiet. There was a dreadful row between her and Geoffrey Westwood at Hartshorn House. It made things worse between them.'

There was something left unsaid. Garrett leaned forward. 'Worse? The feud was merely about Celtic symbolism, he told me. But you suggest there might have been something else . . .'

Rena Williams hesitated. 'I don't think it's important.'

'I think I should know, nevertheless,' Garrett prompted. She sighed. 'It'll come out anyway, I suppose. Elfreda told others about it. He was her tutor. She felt he was . . . too interested in her as a woman.'

'He made a pass at her?'

'Something like that. Maybe he hadn't intended it; maybe she was mistaken. But she spoke her mind to him. After that she transferred to me. The issue rankled with Geoffrey, I suspect — and it made her contemptuous of him to some extent, made her less charitable towards his views. Which she disagreed with anyway.'

'I see.'

The silence lay heavy between them. Rena Williams looked at him keenly. 'It's one thing for a young woman to suggest her tutor made a pass at her . . . it's not uncommon in the hothouse of university life. But it's quite another thing to suggest a respected professor would rape and kill—'

'I've made no comment,' Garrett said, a trifle smugly. 'But do you think it would have been possible?'

She stared at him. She opened her mouth to speak, but no words emerged. Then she shook her head. 'I cannot believe . . .'

'What about the young men on the site?' Garrett asked after an interval. He checked his notes. 'Ainsley Close, Alan Frith, Peter Burns . . .'

'What about them?'

'They were friendly with her?'

'Of course. They were all in my department; they formed a team; they spent a great deal of time together socially at York.'

'Was anyone of them, shall we say, more friendly with her than the others?'

Rena Williams was a handsome woman but her mouth was narrow with distaste. 'I told you . . . they were all close friends. It may well be that she was closer to one than another, but it wasn't apparent.'

'She wasn't having an affair with one of them?'

'I can't say,'

'But if she was . . . would anyone of the others be jealous?' Rena Williams was silent. Her gaze was blank, as though she no longer saw him, turning her gaze inwards to seek for signs, and truth, and the admission of suspicion. At last, she shrugged unhappily. 'I really can't answer that. I didn't see jealousy . . . She was always teasing Peter Burns, but he took it well. The others also, but Peter was the main butt of her sexual teasing. And maybe there have been occasions when I wondered—'

'About which of them?' Garrett asked quickly.

'I can't say. She was not . . . inexperienced. And once or twice I wondered whether she was involved with one of them, and used the teasing of each to cover the relationship, but I can't be sure. I don't know that anyone of them was her lover, not for certain.'

Garrett scratched his cheek thoughtfully. 'Why would she wish to cover up a relationship, Dr Williams?'

Rena Williams shook her head helplessly. 'I don't know that I mean anything by that comment. It's just that . . . well, I understand she had a bad relationship with someone when she was at Reading, before she transferred to York . . . I got the impression she avoided relationships, by playing the field. And yet, from time to time I wondered . . .' She looked puzzled. 'I really can't put these feelings into words. I'm confused. I liked Elfreda. And then to see her there in that ditch . . .'

Garrett liked her. And the tears in her eyes led him to end the interview.

Two hours later he interviewed each of the three young men in turn. He got very little from them. Each seemed harrowed by the experience of death in their midst. Each denied having been Elfreda's lover. All three claimed to have been the butt, in turn, of Elfreda's humour. But all denied they took the attacks personally.

'She used sex like a sword,' Ainsley Close said, stroking his beard nervously, 'but she just nicked you, small sharp snicks that sort of heightened the fun, you know what I mean?'

'She was a very provocative woman,' Alan Frith averred.

Big and powerful, he sat squarely in the chair in front of Garrett, frowning thoughtfully. 'But it was all up front, you know? All talk. She'd try to lead you on, but you knew there was nothing doing. It was just fun — barbed, of course, but there was no harm to it. And certainly no come-on, in a serious fashion.'

'She was one of the lads,' Peter Burns suggested. 'Or she wanted to be — you know, seen as no different from the rest of the group, you understand?' He scratched at his crop of red hair in a helpless gesture. 'If she said outrageous, sexy things, it was to show she was one of us. She was a tease, sure . . . but I never laid her and as far as I'm aware none of the others did. There were several in the union bar at York who thought they were in with a chance, but they found out different. I think she got burned once, and had been playing it carefully ever since. The talk . . . that was just cover.'

But cover for what?

It bothered Garrett. He pressed each of the three on their activities during that day. Each had left the site for a period — Burns to go back to the hotel for a fresh pair of shoes after losing the sole of one of his boots. Close to the pub at Garrigill to get in a supply of sandwiches — he'd left his packed lunch behind at the hotel; and Frith to use the phone, to call his mother on her birthday. All innocent reasons, and as far as Garrett was able to check them out, they stood up. But the fact remained — each of them had left the site at various intervals, and each could have had time to meet Elfreda Gale on her way back up from Hartshorn House.

Just as Geoffrey Westwood had had time.

And then there was the matter of her leaving the house unlocked. Why had she done that? What had caused her to leave? She had left the journals off the shelves and walked away from the house, strictly against instructions, and against her normal practice.

'I've no idea why she would have done that,' Stephen Alston replied, when questioned by Garrett. 'I'd left explicit instructions that she was to lock up — I'm selling the library and the house to my prospective father-in-law — and I understand Dr Williams had reiterated the instruction.'

'Miss Gale's body was found in the ditch on the road leading from Hartshorn House — maybe half a mile distant. She'd been working at the library. You saw her on the day she died?'

Alston nodded. 'I did. I should explain that I have a number of small matters to attend to in Manchester — basically business matters concerned with the estate — and I've been in and out of Hartshorn for the last couple of weeks, since my fiancée went back to the States. There's such a lot to do, small, niggling things . . . Anyway, I'd seen Miss Gale at the house several times, as I went in and out, but she was in the library and, well, we barely spoke to each other. On that particular day, I was at the house about ten in the morning but then left for Preston, where I was due to catch a train to London. I'm afraid,' he added ruefully, 'I never made it. I suffered a blown tyre and had to kick my heels for several hours before I could get it changed.'

'You couldn't change the tyre yourself?' Garrett asked. Alston's grey eyes were amused. 'I'm not exactly a handyman. And the nuts on the wheel proved quite beyond my strength. No, I saw Miss Gale about ten, but left before eleven. I was stuck up on the moor, got myself filthy trying to fix the tyre, then trudged back to Garrigill for assistance. Fred Varney came out eventually, drove me up to the car, and fixed it for me. I didn't get to London then until well after six o'clock.'

'When you did see Miss Gale, how did she strike you?' Garrett asked.

'I don't know . . . I mean, we didn't speak — I just saw her as I passed the library. She had her head down in the journals.'

Garrett was silent for a little while. Alston sat very upright in his chair, shoulders squared back in military fashion but his craggy features were relaxed. Yet Garrett detected a hint of tension in his eyes.

'No servants in the house?' Garrett asked. 'Just Elfreda Gale, working in the library, with instructions to lock up after her. That's a bit . . . unusual, isn't it, Mr Alston?'

A nerve twitched in Alston's cheek. He leaned forward. 'It wasn't my idea, her being there alone. The servants, well, as far as I'm concerned the house is really closed up. I don't stay there; don't have time. I'm getting prepared to sell the estate, the house, the library — and get married in the States. There's a lot to do, but the servants are paid off. It was at Dr Williams's request that I allowed Miss Gale to work there. I did withdraw the permission at one stage, but Dr Williams . . . persuaded me to allow Miss Gale to continue. Now . . .' He hesitated, his mouth working silently. 'Now I wish I'd stuck to my guns. If Dr Williams hadn't persuaded me, maybe Elfreda Gale would still be alive.'

'There are always "ifs", Mr Alston,' Garrett said easily.

'Yes, but . . .' He shook his head, and lapsed into silence. Garrett rose to his feet and looked down at the owner of Hartshorn House. There was some further checking to be done about Alston — the tyre blowout, the assistance from Fred Varney; the timing involved and his visit to London.

Alston looked up at him; there was anxiety in his eyes. 'I suppose it hardly needs saying that, apart from the murderer, it seems as though I may have been the last person to see Elfreda Gale alive.'

Garrett nodded. 'It looks that way, sir.'

'And does that make me a suspect?'

'We're looking at all possibilities, Mr Alston.'

Alston continued to stare at him. He licked his lips nervously, and one hand crept up to smooth the frosting at the side of his temple. He hesitated, then seemed to come to some decision. 'I think there's something else you need to know, Chief Inspector.'

After a moment, Garrett sat down again. 'What would that be?'

'I . . . I told you that Miss Gale and I rarely spoke, when I entered the house.'

'I did wonder about that.'

'There was a reason for it,' Alston announced grimly.

'Yes?'

'It doesn't put me in a good light.' He hesitated, managed a weak smile. 'It might even make you think . . .'

'Think what, Mr Alston?' Garrett asked, inserting a steely edge of impatience into his tone.

Alston was suddenly panicky as the words poured out. 'You've got to understand, I'm making this statement voluntarily, not because I have to. That'll stand me in good stead, surely? But the fact is, there was a reason why we didn't speak. You've got to understand something about Elfreda Gale, Chief Inspector. She was a tease. She was . . . sexually aware; she exuded this . . . aura. And as far as I'm concerned, well, although I'm no roué, I'm not inexperienced either, and I could have sworn . . .' He twitched edgily at his military tie.

'Go on.'

'When she . . . when she started working in the library, and I was still messing around in the house we used to meet for coffee or take tea together in the afternoon . . . if I was around. It was . . . pleasant. But then, one day, she gave me the clear impression . . . Look, I'm about to get married. My fiancée was back in the States. I was foolish, stupid, but I found Elfreda an attractive woman — and she gave me the impression she was . . . available. There was no one in the house; my excitement got the better of me . . .'

'You made advances towards her?'

Alston laughed sharply. 'Not without encouragement, believe me! Or at least, what I saw as encouragement. And then . . . she just stopped me. I felt stupid, humiliated in a way. I was angry too, I admit it. As much with myself as with her. My behaviour had been irrational, and ridiculous. I was much older than her. And if my fiancée had found out . . . I should stress,' he added grimly, 'she comes from a very moral family . . . Anyway, I was so angry that I . . . well, I decided I wanted her out of the house. That's when I told Dr Williams the library was no longer available.'

'And that's also why you told Dr Williams.'

'Yes.' Alston frowned unhappily. 'But, she came back to me, persuaded me, and I relented . . . But I felt embarrassed by the girl's presence. So I tended to avoid her during my infrequent visits to the house thereafter. We nodded, said hello, but that was it. I think it suited us both. I don't think she was embarrassed — she'd just dismissed the occasion, for it was meaningless, after all — but I certainly remained ill at ease. It seemed best to avoid her . . .'

Slowly, Garrett asked, 'You didn't try to overcome that embarrassment, or get even with Elfreda, by attacking her in the lane?'

'I didn't attack her, Chief Inspector. And I didn't rape her. As far as I was concerned, the less I saw of Elfreda Gale the better! And I assure you, though I may well have been the last to see her alive, I certainly didn't kill her!'

2

'Do you believe him?' the chief constable asked.

'It's a bit early, sir, to come to any conclusions.'

'You always were a careful man, Garrett.'

Boring, he meant, Garrett shrugged mentally. The chief constable didn't know Garrett was in the wrong job and always had been. An unbidden vision of a swashbuckling Pat Garrett as a Pirate of Penzance suddenly swam into his consciousness. He thrust it aside.

'The way things stand at the moment, sir, there are several lines of enquiry. The dead woman was, to say the least, somewhat provocative, it would seem. Alston admits to having tried it on with her — and he didn't have to tell me that, because I've not heard a whisper elsewhere—'

'Unless he was afraid she might have told someone, and it could come out later.'

'It's a possibility, I suppose, sir. Then there's the three young men—'

'Close, Burns and Frith.' the chief constable interrupted, to show he had read and memorized the file.

'Precisely, sir. They were all very friendly, but not one of them admits to having had an affair with her. Maybe my view of young people is jaundiced, sir, but I find that hard to credit.'

He read the message in the chief constable's glance — what does an ageing bachelor know about it? He ignored the message and ploughed on doggedly.

'At some stage, one of them surely would have attempted a closer relationship . . . Anyway, each of them left the site that morning, and it checks out, but until we get a clear time of death from forensic it's going to be difficult to pin anyone down.'

'And that brings you around to the man who discovered the body.'

'Professor Westwood. He admits he disliked her; they quarrelled frequently. He actually found the body — and claims he got muddy in slipping into the ditch himself. It's all a bit . . . pat. And though he hasn't admitted it personally, it seems he did make a pass at her when he was her tutor at York. She told him where to go in no uncertain terms. As she did Alston.'

'So you see Westwood as a front runner?'

'He had motive and opportunity, sir. But until forensic—'

'I know. When do you expect a report?'

'The liaison officer tells me maybe tomorrow.'

'Well, let's hope they come up with something positive for us to get our teeth into. Meanwhile, do you have anyone else to see?'

'The two from the Department of Museums and Antiquities. The deputy director, Karen Stannard . . . and Arnold Landon.'

'Ah yes.' the chief constable said thoughtfully. 'The amateur archaeologist.'

* * *

Garrett saw them both that afternoon.

He enjoyed interviewing Karen Stannard. Though he was a bachelor, it did not mean he was unable to appreciate beautiful women, and Karen Stannard was certainly beautiful. Her figure was stunning, her cheekbones fine, her hair russet-tinged and her eyes of an indescribable colour. And she knew it. But she was a formidable lady: quick intelligence, sharp responses, a positive manner and decided opinions. He gained little from her that was useful, other than confirmation of other people's impressions — that Elfreda Gale was provocative but mentally tough and in control of her relationship with all on site, except Professor Westwood, to whom she seemed to have a particular aversion.

'Do you think it had a sexual base?' Garrett asked. Karen Stannard considered the matter with care. 'Possibly. But more likely it was merely intellectual. She saw right through Geoffrey Westwood and was contemptuous. And intellectual contempt can be of the fiercest kind. I know it . . . I can guess how Elfreda felt.'

'And how Professor Westwood felt?'

She smiled. 'Now that's something you must ask him about.'

* * *

Arnold Landon made much the same reply when Garrett asked him the question. He did not know Westwood well enough to be able to comment.

'But Elfreda Gale and Professor Westwood clashed regularly,' Garrett pressed.

Arnold Landon nodded. 'They did. My impression was that Westwood was unable to forgive the outburst that occurred at Hartshorn House that evening. And he took advantage of the . . . power that he had thereafter. Once she apologized, and he accepted the apology, he seemed to quite enjoy their relative positions — Elfreda in the wrong, and himself in the driving seat. He took it out on her, and she had to bite her tongue. That's why Rena Williams arranged for her to go to the library at Hartshorn. It got her out of the way — saved her from a further flare-up with Westwood.'

'It was likely?'

'It was always on the cards.' Landon hesitated, and Garrett watched him carefully. There was a straightforwardness about Landon that he admired, although in his interview with Karen Stannard, when Landon's name came up, he seemed to have detected a flash of resentment in the deputy director's eyes. He suspected she and Landon did not get on too well. But Landon was a cautious man too, and he was clearly ill at ease with the direction of the interview.

'Nothing I've said,' Landon remarked at last, 'should be taken to suggest that Professor Westwood was capable of killing Elfreda.'

'No?'

'Their argument was an intellectual one—'

'But they clearly disliked each other.'

'That's true, but it's a far cry from saying it could lead to rape and murder.'

Garrett was silent for a little while. A snatch from Gilbert and Sullivan came to his mind, about punishment fitting crime, and he pursed his lips. 'Perhaps you feel the rape is . . . out of character. But what if I were to tell you that Professor Westwood . . . admired Elfreda Gale. Sexually, I mean.'

Landon blinked. 'I wouldn't know about that.'

'But I'm told from one source at least that Westwood made a pass at Elfreda Gale when she was tutored by him. She rejected him, of course. That could have led to frustration, don't you think? And allied to the running dispute between them . . .'

Landon shook his head. 'This is merely supposition, Chief Inspector. I certainly can't confirm I saw any signs of . . . that kind of emotion between them.'

'But then, you weren't looking for it,' Garrett suggested stubbornly. 'It could have been covered up by the intellectual battle.'

Landon seemed unconvinced. Moreover, he had something else on his mind. His attention was wandering. There was a certain wariness in his glance when he looked at Garrett.

'The others, they will all have given you a view about Elfreda's personality, Chief Inspector.'

Garrett nodded. 'Sexually provocative, in brief.'

'But controlled,' Landon demurred. 'On the other hand, there was one occasion when it seemed to me she was not in control of a situation.'

'What are you talking about?'

Landon hesitated. 'I don't know what you might have heard . . . For instance, has Dr Williams told you anything about Elfreda's history?'

'Why don't you tell me?' Garrett replied, noncommittally. Landon shrugged. 'I'm not very clear about it all. Dr Williams mentioned to me that Elfreda had left Reading University because of a relationship problem and transferred to York.'

'Where she soon transferred tutors,' Garrett intervened, 'because of another relationship problem. So . . . ?'

'I went down to the library one day, when Elfreda was working there. I walked in on something.'

'How do you mean?'

'Some man — a stranger to me — just appeared there. Elfreda seemed to know him. She was upset. She beat a hasty retreat, away from the house, after what seemed to me to be an altercation of some sort in the driveway. I don't know what it was all about, and it wasn't my business anyway. But Elfreda met me at the hotel later and apologized.'

'About the argument?'

Landon shrugged. 'That . . . and the fact that this man had appeared there at all. I didn't quite understand why she felt she should apologize, but she was certainly upset. Anyway, she told me it wouldn't happen again.'

'Did it?'

'Did he appear again, you mean?' Landon shook his head. 'No, but . . .'

'But what?'

Landon was clearly hesitant, unwilling to dispense gossip. 'I never saw the man again, but on the other hand, Elfreda was certainly seeing someone outside the group. There was one evening — she hadn't joined us at dinner, and she came back into the hotel rather late. I was still in the lounge when I heard her return. Later, when I went to my room, I heard voices in hers.'

'You mean she brought someone back with her?'

'Possibly.'

'And the voices you heard — were they arguing?'

'I couldn't say.'

'You think it was the man you saw at Hartshorn House?'

'I've no idea who she met away from the hotel, and I've no idea who was in her room. I saw the man at Hartshorn only once.'

'Did you tell anyone else about this?'

'Dr Williams.'

'You'd recognize this man again if you saw him?'

Landon nodded.

'Then you'd better let me have a description.' Garrett scowled as he drew his notepad forward. Dr Williams was site director, Elfreda Gale's tutor, and to some extent, he guessed, her friend. He wondered why she had not mentioned Landon's report of what had happened at Hartshorn House.

* * *

Work on the site had closed down for the time being. Rena Williams had gathered the group together and told them that she felt it was impossible to carry on for the moment, and the group agreed. They locked up the field site, covered the trenches with tarpaulins and went their separate ways — Karen Stannard and Arnold back to Morpeth, Rena Williams and her team back to York. There was to be no further communication between them for a week or so, when Dr Williams would review the situation.

Arnold saw very little of Karen Stannard during the week.

He had a considerable amount of work to do, files that had piled up on his desk in his absence, and she, he understood, had a two-day meeting with the Stiles Committee in London. Jerry Picton kept calling in and making a nuisance of himself, trying to wheedle out of Arnold titbits of gossip about the killing near Hartshorn.

Arnold kept his counsel.

He heard nothing more from the police at Penrith. Newspaper reports were relatively subdued, and it was obvious that the investigation was being tightly controlled by Garrett. He was letting nothing out as he plodded along his own careful way. But Arnold himself was overtaken by a strange mood. His sleep pattern was disturbed: he woke several times during the course of the night, and there was a recurring, confused dream — a dark hill, the long drawn out, fading scream of an animal, or a woman, distant and only half heard, the rustling sound of ancient leaves on a forest floor.

Jane Wilson, returning from a few days in Scotland doing research on her new book, called to see him at Morpeth on the Friday and invited him out to dinner. It was not a very happy occasion: he was subdued and thoughtful and eventually she suggested he unburden himself. He found it difficult to talk to her. An immense depression lay over him like a dark cloak, and he knew he was not a good companion. She kissed him goodnight, sympathetically, but, he realized, slightly hurt that he seemed unable to talk to her about his problems.

But he could not, for he was unable to identify them to himself. It was not just the distress occasioned by the death of someone he had got to know, and liked, nor the fact that the group had been forced to break off their work at a point when they seemed to be on the edge of an interesting discovery. It was something else that disturbed him, something inexplicable, unseen, inaudible.

Yet he felt the solution lay back at the site.

The conviction came to him late on Saturday. He had gone for a long, lonely walk on the fells above Allendale towards Wolfcleugh Common. Wolves had been numerous above the Allen valleys in ancient days, when the ice had melted sufficiently to allow a forest of hazel and birch to dominate the upper fells. Below, the passes would have been thick with oak and elm, ideal conditions for cover for wolves who could live well on wild pig, deer, small mammals and birds. There was even a tale of the last Allendale wolf, stalking the Allen passes as late as the winter of 1904. It had come to an ignominious end, killed by a train at Cumwhinton, near Carlisle.

He had been thinking about it as he walked, and suddenly the thought of that great grey beast turned his mind to the Dowgang Hush again, and Garrigill, and the ancient shrine-cave site and the boar carving at the Celtic barrow site.

He found the work exciting, and yet he never felt comfortable up there. There was something about the place that made him edgy, uncertain, and he had gained the impression that the rest of the group felt the same way, though they rarely mentioned it. Perhaps it was too fanciful, but now, as he thought about it, he was drawn back to the high fell and almost automatically he turned back, retraced his steps to his car, and drove on past Carr Shield and Coalcleugh to Nenthead and on towards the fell beyond Hartshorn House.

It was a cold afternoon, with a stiff north-westerly breeze stirring the long sedge grass where the lake had lain, millennia ago. Arnold drove past the field and beyond the hill, then parked his car in a gateway entrance half a mile from the site: he wanted to walk the fell, climb back to it over the hill where an ancient forest had once stood, and where there was still evidence of its existence in scrub and ancient oak and rocky outcrops that could have been hut circles. As he stood on the top of the hill, looking down at the site below him, menacing storm clouds began to tower high in the west and the sky grew darker, pierced beyond the Allen valleys by two sharp golden shafts of light. In a while they were gone and grey fingers of dusk began to creep over the fell.

The wind tugged at his coat sleeves and he felt a vast melancholy touch him. If there were any solutions to his depression they were not to be found here. There was a thin sound in the air, a keening wail that seemed to rise from behind him, and his skin was cold and clammy. He turned and there was only the darkening skyline but it was as though he was surrounded by a physical presence, a weight of evil that was incredibly old but still alive . . .

He shuddered, confused, and looked back down to the site. A car was parked down there, at the edge of the field, and in the gathering gloom he could make out the figure of a man walking towards the locked shed on the site.

Curious, his depression suddenly gone, Arnold walked down from the hill and climbed the fence at the edge of the field. The gloom gathered about him and he caught a flash of light from the shed where they kept their tools. He frowned. Only Dr Williams had a key to the shed, and although the artefacts they had discovered were kept there while they worked at the site, they had been removed when they locked up the area. Puzzled, he walked quickly across the field until he drew near the shed; the torchlight shone through the narrow window and he was aware of someone standing just inside the half-open doorway.

'Who's there?' Arnold called.

There was a pause, something fell to the floor of the hut, and the light danced crazily for a moment. Then the man inside the hut came to the door. He looked out, flashed the torch briefly at Arnold.

'Mr Landon. You startled me.'

'Who is it?' Arnold demanded, partly dazzled by the torchlight.

Next moment it played on the features of the intruder, hollowing his cheeks, marking dark stains under his eyes, making his features saturnine and almost menacing. 'Ainsley! What the hell are you doing up here? The site's closed.'

Arnold stepped forward, entering the hut as Ainsley Close moved back. The young man seemed nervous.

'How did you get in here?' Arnold demanded.

Ainsley Close was silent for a few moments. 'I got the key from Dr Williams.'

His voice was edgy, stained with reluctance. 'But what are you doing here?' Arnold asked.

'It . . . it's not easy to explain.'

Try me.'

There was a long silence. Ainsley Close placed the torch on the table and sat down: he seemed miserable. 'I keep thinking about Elfreda,' he said.

A wave of sympathy swept over Arnold. Slightly unnerved by finding someone at the site, he had momentarily forgotten how upset Ainsley, and the other Musketeers, must have been about Elfreda's death. They had been a close social group. He touched the young man's shoulder lightly, and then sat down opposite him. 'Do you want to talk about it?'

Ainsley Close shook his head. 'What is there to say? She was a friend . . . and now she's gone. But I can't handle the way she's gone. I can't . . . Who would want to kill her? She was so alive . . . she was so much fun . . .'

He fell silent. Arnold allowed the silence to grow around them for a while. 'I'm not sure it's a good idea to come up here alone, to think about it,' he suggested. 'If you'd spoken to Dr Williams—'

'She doesn't know I'm up here. But I needed to come . . . I needed to think.'

'You were close, I know—'

'We all were,' Ainsley interrupted. 'But with me and Elfreda, it was different . . . I . . .' He hesitated. 'I lied to the police. I didn't want to get involved. But, Elfreda and I — we had an affair.'

So Rena Williams's suspicions had been accurate, Arnold thought — but she had not detected the identity of Elfreda's lover.

'I can't say it was obvious,' Arnold said quietly.

Ainsley shrugged. 'It was over before we came up here to the site. It was a mutual decision to end it. I understood her, you see.'

'How do you mean?'

'She was a serious person, in spite of the nonsense she talked. But the way she carried on, it was a kind of defensive shellac, a wall she built between herself and men, so she could control situations. She once told me the best way to handle men was to laugh at them; keep everything on a light basis. It was the way it happened with us. We were attracted; we were at a conference; we had too much to drink one night; we started an affair. It lasted a week . . . but there was no bitterness.' He glared at Arnold, hollow-eyed. 'She was tough, ambitious, but fair. She told me she'd had an earlier relationship that turned sour, and she wanted no more commitments — certainly not long term. He was possessive; couldn't understand she didn't want anything permanent. He kept bothering her — and that's why she came north, to get out of his way.'

'Dr Williams told me something about it.'

'Elfreda had it under control. She told me about it. And I understood when she suggested we cool our own relationship.'

'Did Alan and Peter not know about you and Elfreda?' Arnold asked curiously.

Ainsley Close shrugged. 'They guessed. But they never asked. Peter had a thing about her, of course — but she laughed him out of it most of the time. He took it very well, really. Alan came on a bit strong a few times apparently, so Elfreda told me. But . . . what the hell, it's all over now.'

They were silent for a while. Arnold watched the young man closely: he seemed edgy and uncertain, and his tone was depressed. It was odd that he should come all this way from York to grieve, here at the site. A thought struck Arnold.

'You said Dr Williams didn't know you'd come up here.'

'That's right.'

'But the key to this lock-up—'

'I acquired it,' Ainsley snapped.

Arnold frowned. 'I don't understand . . .'

Ainsley Close took a deep breath. He reached out and fiddled with the torch lying on the table, sending its light dancing along the walls. 'I didn't come up here to . . . to mourn for Elfreda. I came to put something right.'

'How do you mean?'

There was a short silence. At last, Ainsley muttered, 'Elfreda had given me something to hold for her. I felt . . . I felt I should put it back.'

'Back where?'

'You've got to understand,' Ainsley said in a rush. 'Elfreda had been given a rough time up here by that arrogant bastard Westwood. He was forever on her back . . . and all right, she went too far that night at Hartshorn House, but that was only the culmination of a running feud. And he wouldn't let it go — you saw the way he behaved. Then . . . well, we all thought Dr Williams did the right thing, arranging for her to work down at the library, and it was, in a sense. It got her out from under Westwood's feet, and she quite enjoyed the work, really.'

That's the impression I got,' Arnold agreed.

'But after a while she became a bit resentful. She was missing the excitement of the site. And when she came across that skeleton, she believed she'd be called back to the site. It was quite a blow to her when we realized it wasn't an ancient burial. And she resented being sent back to the library when we opened up the site again.' He hesitated, frowning. 'There was something else on her mind as well, though she wouldn't tell me about it. Something was bothering her, and it all added to the resentment, I think.'

Arnold thought back to his visit to the library and the appearance of the stranger. He could guess at what had been bothering Elfreda.

'You mentioned Elfreda had told you all about her earlier relationship, at York.'

'The guy who kept bothering her? Yes, that's right.'

'You know his name?'

'Of course. She told me.'

'I think you should tell the police his name.'

Ainsley Close stared at Arnold, his mouth open. 'You surely don't think—'

'The police need all the information they can get. He may be able to help. That's all I'm suggesting. Get in touch with Chief Inspector Garrett. Tell him the name of Elfreda's former lover.'

'If you think it'll help. But the affair was some time ago . . . though he had been bothering her since. Anyway,' Ainsley Close continued mournfully, 'whatever the reason, the last few days she was pretty bloody-minded.'

'In what way?'

'That skeleton she found — it wasn't the only thing she stumbled across.'

'What do you mean?'

The young man hesitated, then slipped his hand into his pocket. He drew something out and stared at it in the dim light. 'She was coming over the field and she saw something in the mud. She picked it up — and then she saw the bones. She slipped this into her pocket, and in the excitement, thinking she had found another Celtic burial, she forgot about it when she ran up to us, called us out to see the bones. Later, when she remembered about it, things had changed. In spite of her discovery, she was sent back to the library, still denied work on the site because of that bastard Westwood. She felt Dr Williams should have stuck up for her more strongly, instead of which there she was, still cataloguing . . . Anyway, she was seriously pissed off, said nothing and kept the thing to herself. But then, last week, it was clearly on her mind. She told me about it; gave it to me, asked me to find some way of pretending I'd found it at the site. She wanted me to place it somewhere, like a new find.' His tone became more snappish, defensive as he guessed at Arnold's disapproval. 'She was a good archaeologist. She knew the importance of find locations, but this wasn't an ancient piece . . . and, as I said, at the time she'd been fed up, upset, angry with Westwood.'

'What was it she found?' Arnold asked gently.

Ainsley Close opened his hand. Gleaming dully in the faint light was a dark-coloured, large-stoned ring.

3

Detective Chief Inspector Garrett nodded to his colleague and 'Spud' Clamp depressed the switch of the tape recorder. At least all mechanical devices were not beyond him, Garrett thought sourly.

'Interview timed at 16.15, in the presence of Detective Constable Clamp.' He settled forward in his chair, leaning on the table with his elbows, fingers linked, hands clasped. He stared stonily at the man facing him across the table.

He was in his early thirties, with hair that grew thickly and had been uncut for some time. It clustered damply to his shoulders, darker than his slightly peppery-coloured beard. He had quick, intelligent eyes, flickering with a nervous tension that was reflected in his whole demeanour. His hands were clenched on the knees of his jeans, below the table edge, and Garrett knew the knuckles would be white. He was tall and leanly built and he was scared.

'Well, bonny lad, seems you're in a bit of trouble, hey?'

'Don't know what you mean.'

Garrett's thin smile was mirthless. 'Come on, hinny, don't know what I mean? As soon as our lads came around to the house you've been renting a room in, you was out of the door like a shot and legging it down the street! Canny burst of speed you showed, too — if it hadn't been for the fact one of the coppers was the northern sprint champion you'd have mebbe made it out of sight. And you don't know the trouble you're in?' He scowled. 'Brendan Green is your name, yes?'

The man licked dry lips. 'That's right.'

'And you did scarper when you saw us.'

'I was panicked. I didn't know—'

'Didn't recognize the uniform, mebbe?' Garrett sneered.

'I didn't think.'

'Well, Brendan, let's hear what you're thinking now. What are you doing living cheap in Durham?'

The man shrugged. 'Nothing against living in Durham. Nice place.'

'But a fair distance from your usual haunts in Reading. What were you doing up here — apart from signing on the dole?'

'Looking for work.'

'Up on the fells? Not a lot happening up there, though, is there?'

'Looking for work in Durham, not on the fells.'

'But you've been spending time up there, haven't you?' Garrett glowered at the file in front of him. 'I'll tell you what I'll do, bonny lad, I'll tell you what we've got so far and you can fill in. You're from Reading, a dropout from a mature entry degree programme after a spell in the navy from which you were discharged as unfit for service. No particular skills to talk of, few job prospects, and you came north about six months or so ago. Still no job, but you hang on in Durham. Now just why would you do that, hey?'

There was no reply, but the eyes avoided Garrett's. 'All right, then,' Garrett said heavily, 'tell us about your friendship with Elfreda Gale.'

There was a short silence. 'Who told you I knew her?'

Garrett heaved an impatient sigh. 'We have little birds all over the place, telling us things. We were told you met her at university where she was doing a postgraduate programme.

Then another little bird at Reading confirmed to us that there was a bit of bother there, when she made some complaints and left. That's when you dropped out. Enquiries in Durham followed the suggestion you'd come up here. I tell you, I've been hearing all sorts of songs. But one of them tells me loud and clear that you've been hanging around Garrigill from time to time. So, you going to tell me why that was?'

'It's a free country,' Green replied sullenly.

'And can remain so — but not for someone who's involved in a violent death.'

'I had nothing to do with Elfreda's killing,' Green burst out in a panicked tone.

'Convince me.'

'I *loved* her, for God's sake!'

'That's why you followed her up north from Reading?'

'Of course! I left my degree programme when she moved to York. I was . . . distraught. We'd been lovers, and I knew she still loved me—'

'That's why she left Reading? Funny way of showing it.'

Green shook his head. 'We quarrelled. But I knew it was . . . nothing. I knew she loved me, really. I wanted to marry her. I followed her. I knew if I could keep talking to her we could work things out.'

'And when she left York for the field trip to Garrigill . . . ?'

He shrugged miserably. 'I followed her again. That's why I came to Durham. Don't you understand? I loved her, and I knew she'd come back to me—'

'And when she refused, what did you do then, Brendan?'

The coldness in Garrett's tone made the man shake. 'I didn't do anything. I kept . . . trying to see her, plead with her . . . tell her she was the only stable thing in my life . . .'

'You went up to Garrigill to see her.'

'I was desperate. I needed her, don't you see? I was with her one night at Garrigill, and I saw her at Hartshorn House—'

'Where she was killed.'

'I didn't see her that night! If I had, maybe she'd be alive now!'

'Someone saw her. Someone spoke to her, got his hands around her neck, raped her, killed her. But not you, Brendan?'

'Of course not! I loved her, you bloody idiot! How many times do I have to tell you?'

The questioning continued for another hour until Green, his hands shaking badly, demanded that a solicitor be present. Disgusted, Garrett ended the interview and told Detective Constable Clamp to get Green down to the cells. He had hardly got back to his own office when the telephone rang. It was the chief constable.

'Better get in here, Garrett.'

The old man was standing in front of the window, hands locked behind his back when Garrett entered.

'You wanted to see me, sir?'

The chief constable turned and nodded. 'You've got someone in for the Gale killing?'

'Her ex-boyfriend, sir. Brendan Green. He's started to scream for a solicitor.'

'You think you can pin things on him?'

Garrett pursed his lips. 'He's a case for a shrink, sir. Inadequate, scared, weak — I can't imagine what the girl saw in him. But he's clearly obsessed with her. Then, women can be funny, can't they? Maybe she saw something in him I can't. They were lovers, anyway. She'd dumped him, seeing the light, probably, but he couldn't accept it. Insists she still loved him. We have information from at least two sources that he pursued her to York, and then up to Garrigill. He's got a grand obsession, and we all know that obsessions can easily turn to violence when they meet the right kind of resistance.'

'Can you fix him to Garrigill the day she died?'

'Not yet. But I don't doubt we will.'

'You think he's our man?'

'Pretty sure. It all fits. She'd dumped him. He couldn't accept the throwing-over. He followed her, pestered her, and in the end lost his rag entirely. When she gave him a final refusal, maybe after another visit to Hartshorn House — he'd been chasing her there before — he went over the top. Frustrated, he attacked her in the lane, raped her, maybe killed her unintentionally, but nevertheless—'

'One flaw, Garrett.'

'Sir?'

The chief constable walked towards his desk and picked up a file. 'I don't quarrel with your scenario so far, but one thing we'll have to drop. The final report is now in from forensic. If you were hoping we could do a DNA match between the murdered girl and your suspect's sperm, forget it.'

'I don't understand, sir.'

The chief constable handed the file to him. 'She wasn't raped, Garrett.'

Garrett stared at the chief constable in disbelief. 'Her clothing—'

'Was ripped and torn. There was bruising around her thighs and chest. But she wasn't raped.'

Garrett was silent for a few moments. Slowly, he shook his head. 'Even if she wasn't raped, Brendan Green is still in the frame. He could have attacked her but failed actually to complete the rape. His anger boiled over . . . he seems bloody inadequate in other directions, so maybe—'

The chief constable shook his head. 'No. You'll have to play this fish a little more carefully. There's a suggestion in the report that maybe this was an attempt to make it appear a rape was intended.' He stared stonily at Garrett. 'Now can you come up with a theory why Elfreda Gale's ex-boyfriend would want it to appear that she had been attacked by someone with a sexual motive?'

'Maybe he did it deliberately,' Garrett protested. 'An attempt to throw us off the scent, so to speak. Make it look like some sex maniac was on the loose. His own motives—'

The chief constable held up a warning hand. 'All I'm saying is, go carefully. We want this one to stick first time.

You've got Green in the frame, all right, but make sure the story's tight. Pin him to the scene. I don't like this kind of murder on our patch. Go canny, and don't let him wriggle off the hook.'

* * *

'It could be withholding evidence, Arnold,' Jane Wilson suggested.

They were sprawled on the settee in the sitting room of her bungalow at Framwellgate Moor. It was Friday evening and they had been to a restaurant at Sunnybrow. They had eaten well. Arnold had taken very little to drink, but Jane had suggested he stayed at her bungalow overnight — as he had done often enough in the past — and had produced a bottle of wine. They were halfway through it before he finished telling her of the events of the last few days.

'I don't see the ring has any relevance to her death,' he protested.

'You don't know that.'

'It stands to reason, surely. Elfreda came up the field that night, after all the rain, and saw the ring, washed out of the ground, somewhere or other. We don't know exactly when she found it. And it all happened some time before she was murdered in the lane near Hartshorn House.'

'But she did have the ring in her possession,' Jane insisted. 'I would have thought anything connected with her should be handed over to the police, in a murder inquiry like this. It could have some bearing on her death.'

'Hardly. It has more bearing on her reputation, as far as Ainsley is concerned.'

'Because of her behaviour in not immediately handing it over to Dr Williams, after she found it at the site?'

Arnold shrugged, and sipped at his wine. 'Ainsley doesn't want her reputation besmirched, really. They all know the importance of provenance in a burial site of this kind. It's important to mark clearly where items are discovered.

Elfreda behaved foolishly — forgetful in the first instance, but then bloody-minded. She realized herself she should have handed the ring in — but didn't want to own up to retaining it. That's why she gave it to Ainsley — for him to say he'd found it later.'

'Even so—'

'It's not an ancient ring, after all. Rather flamboyant, of course . . .' Arnold held up the locket ring between two fingers. It was made of jadeite, large, deep in colour, with a crested setting. Something stirred muddily in his memory. 'It clearly has nothing to do with any Celtic burials, so no real harm was done by Elfreda keeping it . . .'

'So you've not discussed this with your friend Rena Williams?' Jane asked coolly.

'I'm not quite certain how to handle it,' Arnold admitted reluctantly. 'Ainsley is upset about the thought of criticism of Elfreda, now she's dead. He's taking her loss hard. I think he was more involved with her emotionally than he admits. So I don't quite know whether to tell Rena the full story — or go along with Ainsley's attempt to replace the ring.'

'I thought you talked over everything with Dr Williams.'

'How do you mean?' he asked, somewhat puzzled by her tone.

'Well, you seem to have got rather . . . intimate with her. You've told me about how well you seem to get on with her at the site, and that curious story about her visiting your room—'

'She was just disturbed,' Arnold replied uneasily.

'Because she fancied you?'

'No! Because Karen Stannard found her attractive!'

Jane regarded him with a cynical air. 'There's a lot you don't know about women. You surely must realize that was only an excuse.'

'Excuse for what?'

'To get the pair of you into an appropriate situation.'

'Nothing of the kind.'

She poured the remainder of the bottle into their glasses and slumped back on the settee. She was silent for a little while, eyeing him with a little smile. Arnold felt vaguely uncomfortable, turning the ring in his hand over and over, inspecting the crest, watching the changing colours of the large, flamboyant stone.

'We've known each other a few years now, Arnold,' she murmured at last, in a soft tone.

'That's right.'

'Good friends.'

'I would say so.'

She shifted her position in a languid motion, and then turned her head to stare at him. She took a long pull at her glass. 'Friends, but nothing more.'

He frowned. 'I . . . I place a great deal of importance on our friendship.'

'But while you find Rena Williams attractive—'

'I didn't exactly say that!'

'You see me in a different category.'

He shook his head, glancing at her uncertainly. Her eyes were bright, and the wine had brought a light flush to her cheeks. 'I . . . I'm very fond of you, Jane. And we've been good friends. I didn't want . . . I've never wanted to soil that friendship.'

'I see,' she replied, in a tone that suggested disbelief. 'I'm not certain how to respond to that. Other than to disagree about your basic theory — that a friendship is necessarily destroyed if two people become . . . closer.'

He felt warm. He ducked his head. 'I wasn't suggesting that necessarily—'

'I haven't made up the spare bed tonight.'

He stared at her. 'I can always sleep on the settee. I don't mind—'

'It wasn't quite what I had in mind,' she said firmly. She put her glass down on the table and leaned forward and kissed him on the mouth. It was a long kiss, and he enjoyed it.

'Good friends or not,' she said quietly, 'I think it's time the relationship moved on.' She slipped her arms around his neck. 'Don't you?'

He was suddenly inclined to agree. He leaned towards her dropping the jadeite ring into his pocket and returned her kiss.

'You know,' he said after a little while, 'I have a funny feeling I've seen this ring before.'

'We'll talk about it in the morning,' she replied as she stood up and took him by the hand. 'Right now, we have other things to concentrate on. Other investigations to begin.'

CHAPTER FIVE

1

The morning newspaper was on the floor in the hallway when Arnold went through to the kitchen to make a cup of coffee. It was the local newspaper; he picked it up and placed it on the table while he hunted for the coffee jar. He could hear Jane moving about in the bathroom, so he prepared two cups. While he waited for the kettle to boil, he collected the wine glasses they had used the previous evening and washed them. Then he picked up the newspaper.

The headlines were stark: *SUSPECT HELD IN GARRIGILL SLAYING.*

He wondered why it was that newspapers always used the word *slaying*. Perhaps journalists felt it had a particular ring to it — a *frisson* for the public. He read the account below. It was front-page news but the story was pretty thin. The police at Penrith had issued a statement, merely to say that a suspect was being held in custody, 'helping with enquiries'. There was little more than that but there was something about the confident note of the statement that left Arnold with the suspicion that the police felt they had found the man they were seeking.

Jane came into the kitchen behind him. 'Domesticated, I see.'

He grinned, turned and kissed her lightly on the cheek. 'Result of a long bachelorhood.'

She picked up one of the wine glasses and scrutinized it against the light. She humphed. 'You're good at wine glasses, anyway.'

'Is that all I'm good at?'

She smiled. 'If *you* couldn't tell, I'm sure I'm not going to advise you, Mr Landon! I'm not into inflating male egos.'

'You sound like Karen Stannard.'

'Well, maybe she has a point. So what's the news this morning?'

'It seems the police have arrested — or are close to arresting — someone for the murder of Elfreda Gale.'

She read the story quietly to herself. She looked up at Arnold, frowning slightly. 'Doesn't say much. They're being cagey. Who do you think it might be?'

Arnold shrugged. 'My guess is it'll be her ex-boyfriend.'

'The one you think you saw up at Hartshorn House?'

'That's right. Ainsley Close knew his name. I advised him to tell the police. My guess is they pulled him in and he maybe hasn't been able to clear himself.'

'You think he really could have killed her?'

'I've no idea. But he'd certainly been following her, making a nuisance of himself, and it seems she was trying to get rid of him. She moved from Reading to York, but he still followed her, even to Garrigill. He was obsessed with her, that's clear. But at what point that could turn to violence . . .' He hesitated. 'Would you mind if I rang Rena Williams?'

She widened her eyes in mock horror. 'You really are the limit! You sleep with one woman and then ring another on her phone next morning!'

'I—'

'I really don't mind.' She smiled wickedly at him. 'Not now, at least.'

He made the coffee and handed her a cup. 'OK if I use the phone in the sitting room?'

'It's all yours.'

Dr Williams had given him her phone number in York when they had started work together at the field site in Garrigill. He rang it now, and after a short interval she picked up the phone.

'Rena? Have you heard the news about Elfreda's killing?'

'I have. Ainsley was on the phone first thing this morning.'

'How is he?'

'He's still shaken, I think. He told me all about his conversation with you, and about Elfreda . . . I suppose I should have guessed that they'd been having an affair, but she was capable of hiding things pretty well, really.'

'Including the jadeite ring.'

'Yes . . . Ainsley mentioned it to me. You still have it?'

'Uh huh. I thought I'd hang on to it for a while. There's something about it . . . Anyway, I'll let you have it when we meet. I'm afraid we'll never know precisely where she found it, however. When will I be seeing you next?'

'Ah, well, on that point, there's good news. Chief Inspector Garrett questioned me again about Elfreda's move from Reading to York, presumably before they picked up their "suspect" — whom I guess is this man Brendan Green, the one who'd been bothering her. I took the chance to press Garrett about the site. After all, she was found some distance from the field and there's no real connection . . . anyway, I persuaded him we should be allowed to continue with our work there.'

'Do you think that's wise? For the team, I mean?'

She was silent for a few moments. 'I don't know. But I get the impression they're unsettled, the young men. They're finding difficulty coming to terms with Elfreda's death. So, on balance, I think it better that they face up to a return to the site, concentrate on the work there. I think it will be cathartic for them. Geoffrey Westwood is a different matter, of course. He's anxious to get back as soon as possible. He doesn't seem at all affected by Elfreda's death. There's something . . . cold about him. He makes me shudder sometimes.'

'He'll have no one to rough ride now.'

'I don't know . . . he acts as though she never existed. It's . . . peculiar.'

'So when do you hope to return?' Arnold asked, after a short silence.

'Monday morning,' she replied briskly. 'Will you be able to join us?'

'If I can clear it with the office. I'm not sure what Ms Stannard will have to say. But I'll get there as soon as I can.'

He was slightly ashamed, when he put the phone down, at the surge of excitement he suddenly felt at the thought of returning to Garrigill and lifting the cover stones in the barrow. He walked back through to the kitchen.

Jane was sitting at the table with her coffee and a glass of orange juice. She had poured one for him. She was dressed casually in a blue tracksuit, and she looked comfortable and relaxed. 'One of the problems in a bungalow,' she said, 'is that conversations in the sitting room can be heard in the kitchen.'

He smiled. 'There was nothing private about that call.'

'I heard you mention the jadeite ring. It was just about the last thing you mentioned last night, before you got involved with other things.'

'That's true.'

'So are you able to concentrate upon it again now?'

'Just about.' He hesitated, glancing at her quizzically. 'There's something about it that bothers me. It's familiar in some odd way. So, I was wondering . . . I think I'll go up to Newcastle, do some hunting in the library. Have you got much on today?'

'Apart from this tracksuit,' she said, smiling, 'very little. A session in the Newcastle library with you, Arnold, sounds a most romantic and enchanting proposition.'

They left Framwellgate Moor at 10.30 and drove to Newcastle. They found a parking place in the Cattle Market and walked up the road past the railway station, into Grainger Street and on to the Grey Street Monument, erected in honour of the nineteenth-century politician, but now notable for its central underground station. The library lay just off Blackett Street. Jane was known to the senior librarian there because of her antiquarian bookshop at the Quayside so there was no difficulty in getting access to the stack room, and the stock files.

'What exactly are we looking for?' Jane queried.

'Difficult question. Specialist works on jewellery, to begin with. You can do that. Me . . . I'm going to have a wander. Archaeological stuff.'

'But the ring isn't that old.'

'Even so . . . where have I seen it? Not in jewellery books. And most of the reading I do these days is in the field of archaeology — apart from the odd historical novel by Jane Wilson. I just have a feeling that somewhere . . .'

They spent three hours in the stack room. They found nothing that could assist Arnold in his quest. They left the library and went out to have a sandwich and a beer in the Northumberland Arms. They agreed there seemed little point in going back to the library, where they seemed to have exhausted all possibilities.

'You might like to have a browse in the bookshop,' Jane suggested. 'I really ought to spend an hour on my accounts for last week, so it would suit me if you lost yourself among the shelves. You . . . er . . . you weren't thinking of going back home tonight, were you?'

Arnold smiled. 'It hadn't been my intention.'

'A relaxed evening back at Framwellgate, then,' she said, satisfied. 'And a discussion about why we didn't do this a long time ago!'

They walked down Dog Leap Stairs, to the Quayside.

Behind them was the Swing Bridge, built on the ancient Roman bridge site, the Pons Aelius, named in honour of the emperor Hadrian. Saturday traffic poured across it, heading for Gallowgate and the football match, heedless of the history that lay beneath them and in front of them, with the Roman fort still standing on the north bluff above the river.

Jane unlocked the door to the bookshop her uncle had left her.

'You don't open on Saturday mornings, then?' Arnold asked.

'Not when I sleep in.'

She locked the door behind them. 'I'll be working through there,' she said, pointing to the small back room. 'I've left the closed sign on the door so we won't be disturbed. Browse to your heart's content. I'll be an hour or so.'

Arnold left her to it. He took the jadeite ring from his pocket and stared at it for a long while, puzzling. There was something familiar about it . . . shape, crest . . . but not colour, he suddenly realized. That puzzled him. He frowned, replaced it in his pocket and began to walk among the bookshelves.

It was an eclectic collection, idiosyncratically shelved. Ben Gibson, Jane's uncle, had been an old friend of Arnold's and had indulged personal interests that tallied quite closely with Arnold's. Consequently there was a large section of antiquarian volumes on a whole range of historical themes, medieval building and archaeology. There were several short runs of journals, thick with dust, as well as odd volumes which the old man had picked up in house-clearance sales over the years.

Jane's interests had not been the same as her uncle's. She made her living as a writer of historical romances and saw the bookshop very much as a sideline which she kept running partly out of interest, and partly because she felt her uncle would have wished her to continue with the shop. There was not a great movement of stock, however, and her own buying policies leaned towards history rather than her uncle's antiquarian tastes.

Arnold always enjoyed browsing there, however, and now he once again fell into the trap of wandering haphazardly, picking up volumes that caught his eye, reading sections that interested him, half forgetting the purpose for which he was browsing.

Jane came through to join him at last. 'Sorry I've been so long. Never was much of a bookkeeper. You find anything that helps?'

Arnold was seated on the stepladder, reading a volume on Roman coin finds in Cumbria. He shook his head. 'No, I confess to defeat. I've got this idea fluttering around in my head but I can't grasp it. I know I've seen this damned ring somewhere . . .'

'Trick of the memory. Leave it alone. When you're not thinking of it, it'll come back to you.'

'I suppose so.'

'Anyway, I've a bit of shopping to do so you can wait here until I return, and then we'll make our way back to Framwellgate. Eating in tonight — OK?'

'That's fine. But I'll come with you, give you a hand with the shopping. I'm getting nowhere here.' He turned, stood up and climbed a few steps of the ladder to replace the book he was reading. 'Hello . . . I see you've got a couple of volumes of old Alston's journal.'

'What's that?'

Arnold pulled out a dusty, red leather-bound volume of the antiquarian journal. 'Sir Henry Alston . . . you know, the finder of the Fleetham Hoard, and owner of Hartshorn House and collection. He ran a journal for a few issues. It folded fairly quickly, it seems. He might have been a whizz at finding buried treasure, but he wasn't too bright at running a journal, I guess.' Arnold paused, frowning. The memory danced again in his head, a butterfly just out of reach. Thoughtfully, he began to flick through the pages of the journal. After a few moments he replaced it and took down the second volume.

'Make up your mind,' Jane said with a trace of impatience in her tone. 'I'm happy enough to leave you here but—'

'This is it,' Arnold interrupted tensely. 'It was in Alston's journal.'

'What do you mean?'

'The ring. I remember now. It's where I saw the ring. Not its colour . . . it was a photograph. But where exactly . . .'

Jane came closer, staring up at him. Then he uttered a snort of triumph. 'Damn it, here it is!'

He swung down from the ladder with the dusty volume in his hand. She leaned over his shoulder, to look at the photograph he displayed to her. 'That's Sir Henry Alston,' he said quietly. 'And over the page . . .' He pointed to the photograph of the man with the intense eyes and stubborn mouth. 'That's the assistant editor of the journal.'

Slowly she read out his name. 'Pelham Price-Kennedy.'

'The very same. And you see what he's wearing on his finger?' He grinned at her in triumph. 'I knew I'd seen that damned ring before!'

* * *

'So have you come to any great conclusions?' Jane asked Arnold as they walked back to the Cattle Market car park, each carrying a plastic bag of shopping.

Arnold shook his head. 'It's just such a huge coincidence that I can't get the sequence right in my head.'

'Try it on me.'

'Elfreda found the ring at the Garrigill field site. It's not far from Hartshorn House, which was owned by Sir Henry Alston. The ring belonged at one point to Pelham Price-Kennedy, who used to be assistant editor to Alston's journal, and who presumably was involved with Alston on other ventures, one can assume. How did the ring come to be at the field site?'

'I don't see your problem,' Jane argued. 'If they were friends, they could have been walking on the estate—'

'No, that doesn't fit,' Arnold interrupted. 'As far as I recall, Pelham Price-Kennedy and Sir Henry parted company in 1939. The journal appeared in three issues only. Your copies are in separate volumes but the issues held at Hartshorn library are bound in one. There's a hint, somewhere, that Alston and Price-Kennedy didn't exactly part on the best of terms. So, I don't understand about the ring because Alston didn't buy Hartshorn House — which included the Garrigill field site — until some years later. It was in 1947, or thereabouts, I believe. The magazine folded in 1939.'

'You're assuming Pelham Price-Kennedy and Sir Henry Alston didn't remain friends after they parted company on the journal. Surely they could have met after Alston bought Hartshorn. Maybe Price-Kennedy came up for a weekend visit. Maybe they went for a stroll up to the barrow. It could be that the ring was lost then, in the late 1940s.'

'I suppose so,' Arnold agreed reluctantly. 'But I have a feeling there's something amiss in that . . . reconstruction. I've seen something about Price-Kennedy elsewhere. Footnote stuff.'

They reached Arnold's car. He unlocked it and placed the groceries in the back, then slid in behind the wheel. They pulled out into the traffic to head across the Swing Bridge and drive south to the outskirts of Durham and Pity Me.

'Of course, it's also possible the ring was lost at Garrigill long before that. Alston didn't buy Hartshorn until 1947, but he had done some work in the area earlier than that.'

'A dig, you mean?'

'That's right. It's when he stumbled across Hartshorn, according to Stephen Alston, the present owner. Sir Henry had been working at a site near Hawgill, saw Hartshorn House, fell in love with it and some years later returned to buy the place. It's possible that Price-Kennedy was working with him at Hawgill.'

'And they could have visited the barrow site at Garrigill, and Price-Kennedy could have lost the ring then.'

'It's possible,' Arnold agreed. 'And it makes sense . . . I mean, for Sir Henry to visit the Garrigill barrow site when he was working in the area. As a matter of interest, he would probably have wanted to see the site. The curiosity is, he never seems to have investigated the barrow site after he bought Hartshorn, when it was his own land.'

'There it is: human nature,' Jane suggested. 'We never pay much attention to what's literally under our noses.'

'If he had begun a dig at Garrigill, of course, he might have stumbled across those old bones in the bank, years before Elfreda did.'

'Hypothetical, since he never did dig at Garrigill. Too busy looking elsewhere for another Fleetham Hoard.'

Arnold smiled. 'But isn't that the irony? It may be that, all the time, there was another find of great significance right under his nose. The one we're working on right now. Even so . . . I wonder exactly where Elfreda found that ring.'

'Is it important?'

'Provenance always is.'

She was silent for a little while as they negotiated the roundabouts to enter the motorway section. She took a deep breath. 'You're not going to let this go, are you? Something bothers you about the jadeite ring.'

'I suppose so.' Arnold shook his head. 'I can't be certain what concerns me but you're right. Before I hand the ring over to Rena Williams I'd like to learn a bit more about Pelham Price-Kennedy. Are you very busy next week?'

'Why?'

'I've got to get back to the office, and I'd like to get up to the site for the removal of the cover stones. If the Karen Stannard-Simon Brent-Ellis axis allows me, that is. On the other hand, I'd also like to find out a little bit more about our friend Pelham Price-Kennedy. Just what happened to him after he parted company with Sir Henry and his journal venture?'

'You're suggesting I might be interested in doing a little legwork for you?'

'You might enjoy it.'

'It'll cost you.'

'Name your price.'

'Now that,' she said snuggling down into her seat, 'needs some thinking about after last night.'

2

Karen Stannard was not present in the office at Morpeth on the Monday when Arnold reported in. She was due to attend a meeting of the Stiles Committee which would entail her absence from the office for most of the week. Arnold therefore found it necessary to brave the director's fierce-visaged secretary for an appointment.

'Mr Brent-Ellis is very busy,' she snapped, adopting her best Cerberus role.

Bravely, Arnold replied, 'I need to see him today, Miss Sansom.'

She clearly felt he needed some disciplining rather than an interview. She sniffed and buzzed the intercom. Sourly, she admitted a few moments later that Simon Brent-Ellis was not too busy to see him, after all.

He was ushered into the Presence with ill grace. Brent-Ellis was peering out at the distant hills with a longing expression on his face. It was a bright morning and the fairways would be sparkling with dew, the greens sharp and fast. He shook his head dolefully and turned to face Arnold.

'What can I do for you, Landon?'

'Ms Stannard is away, so I thought I'd better check with you, sir. It's about Garrigill—'

'Damn bad business up there. The boys in blue have laid hands on the perpetrator, though, apparently.'

'It's not that I wanted to see you about. The police have given permission for work to continue at the barrow site. I'd like to rejoin them later this week, if that's all right with you.'

Pleasant memories of the earlier press conference at Garrigill flooded back to Brent-Ellis and he smiled.

'The barrow site. Ah, yes. You close to discovering anything else of interest?'

Arnold nodded. 'We've found what appear to be cover stones of some kind, with a boar motif cut into the stone. We don't know what's underneath, but it's likely to be of considerable interest. If they took the trouble to place those stones—'

'You know who they were?' Brent-Ellis asked.

'I'm afraid not, sir. The boar motif is Celtic, of course: a typical representation. But beyond that . . .'

'Beyond that you feel that if it is of significance' — Brent-Ellis licked his lips — 'the department should surely be represented.'

'I think that would be a good idea.'

'And Ms Stannard is away this week,' he considered. 'Yes . . . I think it's necessary you should get up there, Landon. You can clear your desk?'

'Almost immediately.'

'Then you have my permission to go,' Brent-Ellis hesitated. 'One condition. I'm sure Ms Stannard would agree with me when I say that if anything of . . . real significance is unearthed, you should contact this office immediately. It would be essential that a . . . ah . . . senior presence was available at the unearthing.'

Brent-Ellis was learning quickly from his deputy.

* * *

Arnold arrived at the site by ten in the morning to be greeted by a somewhat harassed Rena Williams. The team had spent the previous day cleaning the edge of the stones thoroughly and had then waited for the block and tackle to be erected for the lifting of the large covers. Unfortunately, the contractors who had been commissioned to erect and use the equipment had failed to turn up; she had rung them again and they were expected to arrive this morning.

'Wednesday,' she fumed, 'and we haven't been able to make a proper start yet.' She glanced at him and grimaced. 'At least you've been able to get some more time off from the office, and you'll be here to see the uncovering.'

The others were working along the edge of the trench, but in a rather desultory manner. It was clear they had been disappointed by the failure of the contractors to appear, and their hearts were not in the drudgery of scraping and brushing away at the trench edges. Professor Westwood was supervising the work in his usual sneering bad temper, and the three young men seemed less inclined than usual to indulge in their banter.

'How are things settling down?' Arnold asked quietly.

Dr Williams knew what he meant. She shrugged. 'Things aren't the same, of course. Elfreda brought life to the party; and even when she wasn't here, working down at the Hartshorn library, she left something of herself behind with these lads. I think she was the cement that bound them together, really — they aren't the same people at all now she's gone.'

'But you think it was a good idea to get them all back up here?'

She nodded. 'I believe I was right. I saw them in York and we had a long talk — they were brooding too much. This way, they can concentrate on the site again, and the thought of the cover stones can still excite them.'

'And Ainsley?'

She passed a hand over her eyes in a tired gesture. 'I'm not sure. I've had some late-night sessions with him, and he seems all right, but he's very subdued. He's very upset.' Arnold decided this was the time to give her the jadeite ring and left her to discuss it further with Ainsley Close. The contractors' lorry arrived at the site about half an hour later.

The man in charge was red-faced, flat-capped, beefy in build and Cumbrian in accent. He waved aside Rena's comments about the failure to turn up the previous day with a breezy nonchalance that annoyed her, but he was not a man to be hurried or browbeaten and, with his two workmen, he strolled over to the tented area and inspected the site. There was some discussion of the proper siting of the block and tackle. Dr Williams was insistent that the equipment should be correctly placed so as not to damage the trench in any way. Arnold could appreciate her concern — they had spent so much time in careful sifting of the site that it would be disastrous if the equipment gouged out the area indiscriminately.

While they set up the block and tackle under the eagle eye of Dr Williams, Arnold walked around the site once more. He looked again at the burial area where they had made their first find of the three skeletons, and then inspected the grain pit at the corner. After a while he was joined by Professor Westwood.

'Big day, Landon.' the professor grunted.

'Raising the cover stones? Yes, I suppose it is.'

'You had any further thoughts about this area?' Westwood enquired.

Somewhat surprised, Arnold shook his head. 'Not really. I was just walking the trench, you know, to get a feel of the place again.'

'Humph! I suppose it's useful. I've been thinking a good deal about it myself. Maybe I've been too . . . dogmatic in my theories. The grain pit . . . the three burials . . . maybe they're not linked. Maybe they're different periods, times when the local inhabitants came to the barrow for different purposes.'

Arnold's surprise grew. It was out of character for Westwood to express doubts about his own interpretative powers. He nodded. 'I think it best to keep an open mind at the moment. We don't know what we're going to find under the stones.'

'That's right. My thoughts exactly.' Westwood raised his head and looked out past the tented area to the rising, cloud-shrouded fell beyond the field. 'Strange place this, don't you agree?'

'In what way?'

Westwood wrinkled his nose. 'I can't explain how it affects me, really. I'm well used to working on ancient sites, as you'll imagine, but it seems to me we've all been affected by a kind of . . . melancholy, here. You know what I mean?'

Cagily, unwilling to expose his own fanciful thoughts of recent weeks, Arnold replied, 'Not exactly.'

Westwood shook his head. 'It's not like me to be airy-fairy about such things, but from time to time as I've worked here, particularly in the late afternoons, I've had a shivery feeling. There's something odd about the field, and I can understand how it is that the site has had a bad reputation for a long time. There's a . . . sourness about the place, you know? A feeling that gets into your bones . . .' He grunted suddenly, as though annoyed with himself for speaking in such a manner. His surliness returned, but tinged with a certain wary inquisitiveness. 'You heard any more about the girl's death?'

'Elfreda, you mean?' Arnold asked, slightly annoyed at Westwood's refusal to use her name. It cloaked her with the anonymity of indifference, and he resented it.

'That's right. I gather they've arrested someone for the killing.'

'They are questioning someone, certainly.'

'She was no better than she should be, that one,' Westwood growled. 'If you ask me, she'll have put herself in a position—'

'Professor Westwood!'

Unnoticed by either man, Rena Williams had approached them. She had heard Westwood's last comments, and she was angry. Her mouth twisted as she glared at him. 'They're about to lift the first stone. I imagine you'd want to be there to see it. It'll help you concentrate on things other than Elfreda's death.'

It was clear to Arnold that Westwood had already transgressed in this direction with Dr Williams, commenting unfavourably on Elfreda's character. Maybe that was what had caused some of the edginess among the Three Musketeers also, Arnold guessed. He followed Westwood as he trudged across to the other end of the trench, behind Rena Williams.

The tackle was in place. Arnold joined the other men as they stood at the edge of the first cover stone, guiding it as it was inched from the ground and moved to one side. The heavy stone was swung slowly across to the edge of the trench and slowly lowered until it rested on the grass near the entrance to the tented area. Arnold looked down at the exposed ground where the stone had previously lain.

'Not a lot to see,' Alan Frith muttered.

The earth was compacted and hard, pressed down by the stone for centuries. It was marked, however, by ridge lines, as though materials had been placed under the earth, and at the edge of the uncovered area pieces of thick bone could be seen protruding slightly from the earth.

'What do you make of it?' Ainsley Close asked.

'Too early to say,' Arnold replied. 'We need to get the other stones removed first.'

They stepped back while the contractors relocated the block and tackle and began work on the lifting of the second stone. There was a short break for coffee and then they returned to raise the stone. It came up more easily than the first, to expose a similar area, a compressed patch of earth, with, at its edges, a few pieces of bone exposed.

'It's a pit,' Geoffrey Westwood announced categorically.

'Grain pit?' Peter Burns asked.

'Unlikely,' Rena Williams responded quickly. 'Remember the boar motif on the stones? No, I think we've hit something very interesting.'

It was cold. A stiff easterly breeze had sprung up, setting the flaps to the tented area snapping, and where it thrust through the scattered trees on the hill above them it produced a moaning sound. The men were working on the third stone now, swinging it sideways to the grassed area, and once again they could see the compressed earth and the bone tips.

'The pit doesn't seem to be circular in shape, even though the cover stones form a rough circle,' Dr Williams mused. 'The stones have rested on that lip. The location of these bone ends would suggest — if they form the edge of the pit — a rectangular shape. What do you think, Geoffrey?'

Westwood was prowling around the edge of the area. He was clearly itching to get started on the earth covering. 'I'm not certain, but it looks to me as though those bone ends could be markers of some kind.'

'Or supports,' Arnold murmured.

'What do you mean, supports?' Westwood snapped.

'There are no post holes,' Arnold replied. 'No signs of dark earth at the edge, rotted wood deposits, anything like that. And those ridges . . . it's almost as though there are more bones, or pieces of wood, deposited across the area formed by the rectangle.'

'Well, we won't be able to get anything done here until we get rid of the block and tackle,' Rena Williams said, frowning at the contractors.

The beefy, flat-capped Cumbrian in charge grinned cheerily at her. 'Won't be long, missus, if that's all you want us to do for now.'

'Quite enough, thank you,' she replied icily.

Arnold smiled. Dr Williams clearly did not appreciate being called 'missus'.

* * *

They broke for lunch while the contractors were removing their equipment and in the early afternoon the team began work on the exposed area. It was soon apparent that the covering of earth was light, no more than an inch deep and as they brushed and scraped it away around the bone ends, the ridges were revealed as cross-pinioned pieces of bone and decayed wood, much of which crumbled away as they worked. From the edges of the trench they were able to reach some distance across the area covered by the stones while kneeling on the stony lip, but the young men finally placed planks across the whole area, allowing them to work without weight or pressure being placed on the central part to be investigated.

The debris they discovered was puzzling. Shards of bone and strips of what appeared to be leather were gradually sifted out of the earth covering. Arnold dislodged a piece of hairy cloth and Peter Burns found dark staining which suggested wooden struts had been placed over part of the area. It was not until three in the afternoon that they made the major discovery, however, and it was Professor Westwood who gave the excited grunt.

'Another one!' he exclaimed.

Rena Williams moved across the planked support to take a closer look at his find. It was a finger joint, sticking upright through a covering of decayed leather that crumbled at the touch.

'Another skeleton?' she wondered.

'That would be my guess,' Westwood replied shortly.

'I think we'd better move some of these planks so that several of us can concentrate on this area,' Rena Williams suggested. 'Arnold, would you like to work across there on the left while Geoffrey and I get rid of some of the debris here?'

Arnold thought for a moment that Westwood was about to object, wanting to work alone on the find, but then he thought better of it and stood aside while the three young men moved the planks and rearranged them so that work could go on, some six inches above the surface of the exposed area.

They worked carefully, but swiftly, brushing aside the compacted earth, lifting shreds of leather and woven cloth until gradually they were able to make out the outline of the skeleton.

It was lying on its side, knees drawn up, arms extended.

The head had been removed and the skull placed face down, beside the right knee. The lower jaw had been detached and was placed beside the left knee. A spindle whorl had also been deposited near the left hand. The only ornament disclosed was a wrist bangle of worked gold.

'Female burial,' Westwood grunted.

'That spindle whorl, I've come across something like it before,' Rena Williams said.

Westwood wrinkled his nose and straightened, easing his aching back. 'I've seen something like it in third — and fourth-century burials. There was one at Kimmeridge — third-century cist burial, decapitation rite performed, and a spindle whorl. There's an article I've read, in the *Archaeological Journal*, suggests there may be a witchcraft connection. You know, the village scold with a reputation for evildoing, she gets buried with her face downwards, so she can't escape the underworld, and her lower jaw removed so she can't raise any curses on the living! It would fit in with the damned cold atmosphere of this place!'

'I've always understood the decapitation rite was connected with ease of entry to the underworld,' Rena Williams doubted.

'That may be so,' Westwood grunted, 'but we're in no position to debate it right here. I need to do some checking, and I should think you too are a bit rusty—'

Rena Williams shot a sharp glance at Westwood and Arnold guessed that she was surprised, as Arnold had earlier been, at Westwood's suddenly discovered propensity to admit his own shortcomings. He was less dogmatic than formerly. Arnold wondered again whether it had anything to do with Elfreda's death.

Behind him the wind snapped at the tent flaps with a sharp, cracking sound.

Arnold moved along the planking to inspect the edge of the rectangular area marked out by the bone ends. He reached down and began to tease with his fingers at one of the splinters. It was solidly locked into the earth. He scraped away round it and saw the ridge running away from it. A little more scraping and he realized that the ridge was formed by another strip of bone, locked into the upright section and extended by a darker earth which suggested decayed wood. Beside it was the end of a wooden stake that had not decayed. Oak. Joints of bone. Perhaps at one time ends of bone-sheathed oak.

He stood up, thoughtfully.

'Arnold! You got something?'

He looked across to Rena Williams. He shook his head. 'I think we'd better start moving a bit more carefully.'

'What?' Westwood gasped irritably. 'We're suspended above the detritus. It's playing havoc with my knees — what the hell do you mean more careful?'

'It's these bone ends,' Arnold explained. 'I think they form the edge of a burial pit.'

'God save me from bloody amateurs!' Westwood moaned, casting a despairing glance in Arnold's direction. 'We've all assumed from the start that we've got a pit here, so what's this sudden revelation that's hit you now?'

'If we dig down—' Rena Williams began.

'That's the point,' Arnold interrupted. 'Digging would be unwise.'

'What are you talking about?' Westwood snapped testily. 'How else can we find what's down there?'

'I don't think we'll have to dig.'

Rena Williams stood up, dusting her hands over her thighs. 'What are you saying, Arnold?'

He hesitated. 'Normally, we'd recognize a pit by discoloured earth, different textures, stone or timber linings and so on. But I think this is different. I don't think this pit was ever filled in.'

Westwood swung his head to gape at Arnold. 'Not filled in?'

'I think there's a burial pit here all right,' Arnold explained. 'But, unusually, it wasn't filled in with earth. You see these regularly placed bone ends? I would guess they are supports, driven deep into the earth surrounding the pit itself, and designed to last. The ridges we see running in a crisscross pattern from these bone ends we know to be made up of decayed wood — oak, possibly birch and elm — but their ends were sheathed with bone, and locked into place at the weakest points, where they met the uprights. These bone ends were drilled, and jointed. Then the area was covered with leather, hides, woven cloth and so on, draped over the decapitated sacrificial corpse. Now why would that be?'

'Just what you said. A covering for the decapitated burial we've found here,' Westwood suggested shortly.

'Of course. But the skeleton is lying on top of these cross-pinioned bones and wooden struts. What does it make you think of?'

They were silent, staring at him. At last, Alan Frith found his voice. 'A bed? A stretcher. Something like that.'

'Or a platform?' Arnold suggested quietly.

There was a moment's silence, then Geoffrey Westwood awkwardly hoisted himself to his feet. 'Hell's flames!'

'Arnold,' Rena Williams said hurriedly, 'if you're right—'

'If he's right,' Westwood announced savagely, 'the moment we put any weight on that central area it could collapse!' He glared at Arnold, hating to say it. 'You could be right — and we can't take any chances. If there's an open pit underneath this platform, any pressure could send the whole thing crumbling in and God knows what that would do to whatever's in the pit!'

He moved off the planks, and the others did the same, wordlessly. They all stared at the skeleton lying half exposed in front of them.

'A platform,' Rena Williams breathed.

'I think so,' Arnold replied. 'You see how the struts run? They're mostly decayed now, but there's enough bone in there to hold it up still. It's held it up for over a thousand years already! It's why it was chosen as a material — it wouldn't rot like wood. Though there are some oak struts there, quite clearly.'

'We thought it would be an important site,' Rena Williams said. 'The boar motif cut into the stone covers . . .'

'But what will be under the platform?' Ainsley Close asked hoarsely.

'Who knows?' Arnold said. 'But I would suggest there's an open pit there. Probably shallow, with another burial. The important burial. But the last thing we want to do is to collapse the whole thing inwards. And my guess is that if we're not very careful, that's exactly what we'll do.'

Rena Williams shook her head ruefully. 'When I think what could have happened if we'd located that damned block and tackle in the wrong place!' She consulted her watch. 'It's getting late. I'm reluctant to do too much more work here now — we have things to think about. I suggest we pack up and get back to the George and Dragon. Our plan of campaign—'

'We need to get some answers from the library, too,' Westwood interposed. 'Platform burials are unusual, but there are some recorded finds made in the Victorian period. They were badly documented because methods were haphazard, but I think we'll find some information at Hartshorn House. I would propose that we set up these young men with a specific task tomorrow, to chase up references in the library, while we three work on up here. The last thing we want is clumsiness . . . They'd be better employed doing the research for us.'

Rena Williams hesitated. 'There's a slight problem there.'

'We're surrounded with problems! What's new?' Westwood expostulated.

'I rang Stephen Alston when we arranged to come back to the site. He told me he was beginning to get the library packed up. He did not think it appropriate that we used it anymore.'

'The hell with him,' Westwood grunted. 'All the more important that we should get quick access while it's still there. Is he in residence?'

'I don't think so.'

'You still got the key?'

'Yes, but I said I'd let him have it this week when we were passing—'

'So we can still get in there.' Westwood's eyes gleamed. 'I vote we send the lads down tomorrow with specific tasks. If Alston catches them and kicks up we can always blame them for over enthusiasm. I'd be reluctant to blaze away at this pit until we have some reference points cleared up. What do you say, Landon?'

Arnold was inclined to agree, although uneasy at Westwood's quick suggestion that they could blame the younger members of the team if Alston turned up.

Reluctantly, Rena Williams acquiesced. 'I think it will have to be a quick raid, then. In a sense, Mr Alston has now withdrawn permission—'

'He's done that before,' Westwood growled.

'And the situation here is critical,' Arnold added. 'I'm sure Professor Westwood is right. If we want to work quickly on this site, we need information about other platform burials before we proceed. We know nothing about the likely depth, what we might find there — and it shouldn't take the lads long to pick up the references that are held in Alston's library. They could be out and away before Alston ever turns up, even if he does at all. He's rarely there, after all.' He hesitated, glancing at the others. 'Otherwise, it means the British Museum, or the British Library.'

'Can you raise the references?' Rena Williams asked doubtfully of her colleague.

'This evening, after dinner,' Westwood replied confidently. 'Then we'll send the lads down in the morning to get to work, while we get up here and pick around the edges!'

3

Jane Wilson rang Arnold at the hotel that evening after dinner when he had returned to his room.

'You alone, Arnold?'

'Of course!'

'Just checking.' She chuckled. 'So, what sort of day have you had?'

'Extremely interesting. We think we've found a platform burial underneath the cover stones marked with the boar motif.'

'Another decapitated skeleton?'

'That's right. But it appears to have been placed on a platform, so before we go any further we think we'd better check on other platform burials. It's fairly unusual. We'll use Hartshorn House library, if we can.' He paused. 'Anyway, how have things been going on with you?'

'Cold at night.'

'Apart from that,' he laughed.

'Well, I started looking into our friend Pelham Price-Kennedy. He's mentioned in a few autobiographical reminiscences, although nothing much was written about him directly. There was a brief obituary in the Daily Telegraph in 1939. It seems he was pretty well tied in with Sir Henry

Alston — a sort of acolyte, you might say. They probably met at Cambridge, where Price-Kennedy read history, and it seems he may well have been involved with Alston when the great man found the Fleetham Hoard. I say seems, because Alston tended to take all the limelight himself. A man very conscious of his status and importance, I guess.'

'Fleetham. That would be in 1911.'

'The summer of 1911, that's right. After that, as far as I can make out, they worked together on a number of digs but whereas Alston took up a professorial post at university, Price-Kennedy was forced to enter the family firm. Coal merchants in Bradford, would you believe!'

'New money, then.'

'Which Price-Kennedy cashed in about 1920. Sold the firm when his father died, and more or less lived off the proceeds thereafter. Spent his time on archaeological activity, a satellite to Sir Henry's sun, and when Alston founded his own archaeological journal in 1936 he agreed to become the assistant editor. But the obituary says they fell out over something or other — no one seems to be sure what it was all about — and he resigned from the journal. It folded shortly after that anyway. There's a hint in the obituary that though Alston founded the journal it was Price-Kennedy who was the driving force behind it, so it collapsed after his withdrawal.'

'So what happened to Price-Kennedy after that?'

There was a short pause. 'Well it's all a bit unsatisfactory. It seems he decided to emigrate, go to the States. He'd been offered a post in Virginia. But according to an interview given by Sir Henry Alston he was invited to cross to France on a private yacht, owned by Lord Cradock, before setting off for America. Alston said he also had been invited but declined — presumably because he and Price-Kennedy weren't on speaking terms. Anyway, Alston was lucky: there was a storm in the Channel, the yacht was lost, bodies never recovered. And Price-Kennedy never took up his post in Virginia. There was a letter in The Times from Sir Henry Alston, recounting the circumstances surrounding the invitation to the yacht, and his sadness at his friend's unfortunate death.'

'So we're no further forward, really, with regard to the jadeite ring.'

'I'm afraid not. There's another photograph I've come across, however, taken about 1936. He's wearing the ring in that photograph — he was clearly proud of it, and wore it habitually.'

'But must have lost it in the field site when he and Alston were working at Hawgill.'

'Oh, yes. I've checked — they were both working at that site together. So they could easily have visited the barrow at that time, and I suppose that's how the ring came to be at the site.'

'So that's it, then. No progress.'

'Not really. And yet . . .' She paused. 'It's odd no one seems to know what the quarrel between Alston and Price-Kennedy was about. There are hints that they fell out over an archaeological matter, but what mention there is of it at the time was very cagey. I think I'll keep on looking for the time being, anyway. I've got sort of hooked on it. I get the feeling there are odd undercurrents to the whole thing.'

'Let me know what you come up with.'

'I'll do that, Arnold. As for you, make sure you don't give Rena Williams any encouragement.'

'You're getting possessive.'

'Certainly not. Sisterly.'

'Hardly that,' Arnold demurred. 'Anyway, I hope to see you in a few days.'

* * *

Next morning, at the field site, Arnold, Rena Williams and Geoffrey Westwood held a discussion about the platform burial and the best way to deal with it. Westwood had been as good as his word and had produced a number of references which he gave to Ainsley Close. The three young men went into the library after Dr Williams opened up the house. Stephen Alston was not in residence and the house was deserted.

They did some photographic work at the edges of the site and sifted away some of the earth to disclose decayed deer hides, but no implements or artefacts of any sort. They agreed that the burial was a sacrificial one, with the head being placed face down as a contact with the chthonic powers, but they came to no conclusion with regard to what possibly lay underneath the platform. Professor Westwood busied himself with writing up his notes, but at lunch time Dr Williams drew Arnold to one side.

'I'm a bit concerned about Ainsley and the other two.'

'Why?'

'We don't really have permission to work in the library at the moment. If Stephen Alston comes back, there could be a scene.'

'You've not tried to contact him?'

She shook her head anxiously. 'I wouldn't know where to get in touch with him. He's rarely at Hartshorn — he seems to be getting ready to leave for the States.'

'And his prospective marriage. So . . .'

'I wonder if you'd mind going down to the library, Arnold? To supervise the work, and also to be on hand just in case Stephen Alston gets back. There's not a lot we can do here at the site until we've looked at the references Geoffrey has produced and worked out how best to approach the problem.'

'I'll go down straight after lunch,' Arnold replied.

He arrived at the library at 1.30. Peter Burns welcomed him with a grimace: it was clear the three of them had been having a real problem. During the team's absence from Garrigill a large number of the shelves had been stripped of books, but they had not been packed, even though the packing cases were stacked in one corner of the room. Arnold was surprised to see they had been piled somewhat haphazardly against the walls, prior to their placing in the cases — which seemed to him to be a waste of time and energy, unless the purpose had been to catalogue them as they came off the shelves. Somehow, he hardly thought Stephen Alston would have bothered to do that.

'Trouble, lads?' he enquired.

'You can say that again,' Alan Frith moaned. 'The books we want are all over the place. Even the journal runs are out of sequence. I've no idea what Mr Alston has been doing, but he certainly hasn't done it logically.'

'We've managed to get the journal runs partly sequenced,' Ainsley Close said, 'and Peter's started work on the first batch of references.'

'Anything useful?' Arnold asked.

'Most of Professor Westwood's references aren't panning out,' Burns said slowly, scratching his thick red thatch with a stubby pencil. 'But I've got two accounts which might be useful. I've been making notes on them. They might have some relevance to the barrow burial.'

'Anything else?'

'I've turned up one description of a Kent barrow,' Alan Frith announced, 'but whether it's relevant . . .'

'I'm still trying to sort order out of chaos,' Ainsley muttered.

'Well, I'll give you a hand with that,' Arnold said.

They spent the next two hours sorting and checking through the piles of books, rearranging them in some sort of sequence. It was a pity Alston had started this way, Arnold concluded: the four of them could have helped by sorting and packing at the same time. He was also puzzled why Alston should have wanted to do it like this: a professional haulage firm would have done the job much more expertly.

In the late afternoon they had more or less sorted out all the references that Westwood had suggested. Arnold had placed the journals that Elfreda had been working on in a small pile: they had still been shelved, in the far corner of the room, where Alston had not yet stripped the shelves, and when he took them down he noticed a plastic file cover that had been slipped between the leaves of one of the journals. He remembered Elfreda putting it there, the last time he had been at the library. He took it out, and pulled out the notes and clippings it contained.

'What have you got there?' Peter Burns asked.

Arnold flicked through the pages. 'Elfreda's notes. And there's a handwritten list of letters and numbers that Elfreda wrote down. I don't know what they're for.'

'Let me see,' Ainsley Close said snappishly. He stared at the list. 'She was bothered about something that she was working on down here.'

'I suppose she told you all about it,' Peter Burns sneered. 'And what if she did? You were never her confidant!'

'Not that you had enough sense to look after her and protect her!'

'And were you any better?' Alan Frith interposed.

Arnold held up a hand, and recovered the plastic file from Ainsley Close. 'Calm down a little, hey? We don't want squabbles over personal relationships here. It's something to sort out in private.'

Alan Frith grunted. There was an unpleasant twist to his mouth. 'Don't worry. It's of no consequence. It's just a kicking up of heels by two unsatisfied stallions.'

Ainsley Close turned on him angrily. 'If there was anyone unsatisfied —'

'I said we should stop this!' Arnold snapped. 'Get your things together. I don't think there's anything more we can usefully do here now.'

He was annoyed that they should have allowed resentments to boil over in this manner. Clearly Elfreda's death had left scars on the emotions of each of them, and from the glances cast among them the earlier close friendships were now dissolving. Elfreda had kept them together, but her death had opened up sores that had been kept concealed previously. There was an air of suspicion and resentment in the room. The fact that Elfreda had spent so much time in this room before she died also had its effect — it was as though her presence hovered over them, charging the atmosphere with tension.

'You'd better put these papers somewhere too.' Peter Burns said sullenly. 'Elfreda had attached a note to them.'

He handed Arnold some yellowed newspaper cuttings.

Elfreda's note was brief. It simply stated: 'Holdings Crosscheck.' Arnold glanced through the cuttings. They were taken from various newspapers, dated between 1933 and 1937, with one further cutting of an article which was undated but appeared to be from a somewhat later period. The photograph of the author, a man called John Brazier, looked as though it had been taken in the fifties. Arnold skipped briefly through the article. It relayed the argument that security at the British Museum left a great deal to be desired in that the trustees of the museum had been unable to account over the years for a significant range of artefacts from various collections. Examples were provided together with reference numbers, and some broad hints given that even the most eminent of researchers were thought to be, on occasion, 'forgetful of their duties and their charges'.

Arnold hesitated, then riffled through the other cuttings.

After a few minutes he realized that the later article had been culled from some of the pieces in the older newspapers. It would appear that in the 1930s a great deal of concern was being expressed about losses from the museum. The odd thing was that no suggestion was being made that the police should be called in, and no explanation was given as to how the breaches of security had taken place. He dismissed the matter mentally, and was slipping the newspaper cuttings into the plastic file when the library door opened.

He turned his head. Standing in the doorway, his features reddening with anger, was Stephen Alston.

'What the hell is going on here?'

Arnold glanced around at his companions. They were rigid, embarrassed.

'I'm sorry,' Arnold said, 'but—'

'I expressly told Dr Williams that the library was now closed to all of you! Everything is being packed up. I've been working in here at odd moments to prepare for the packing, as you can damned well see, and I told her that it was inconvenient to have you lot here. She agreed to let me have the key back, and now I find . . . !'

He was furious; his speech died away in a vague spluttering.

Lamely, Arnold began, 'It's just that we've hit a critical point in our work at the site. It wasn't possible to contact you. We felt if we could only have access again, to pull out a few references—'

'But I told Dr Williams!' His eyes were blazing, his hands shaking with anger. Arnold felt he was overreacting somewhat, but it was his house after all, and his library, and he was entitled to be angry.

Arnold nodded in recognition of Alston's rights. 'I can only apologize. We'll leave at once.'

'And you'll return the house key immediately!' Alston flashed.

Wordlessly, Arnold dug in his pocket and handed over the key. He turned back to the young men. 'You've got all your things together?'

They all nodded.

'And I trust you'll be taking nothing that doesn't belong to you?' Alston said cuttingly.

Arnold stared at him, his own anger beginning to rise, but made no reply. He tucked the plastic folder under his arm and began to lead the way out.

'One moment,' Alston said in a frosty tone. 'What do you have under your arm?'

'Nothing that belongs to the library,' Arnold replied. 'Look, I'm truly sorry we've upset you, Mr Alston, but we certainly wouldn't take anything belonging to you as we leave. These are merely some notes that Elfreda Gale was working on—'

'Let me see them!'

Arnold took a deep breath. 'I can assure you they don't belong to the library. She wrote them when she was down here, and they relate to the site investigation.'

'I'd still like to see them,' Alston insisted harshly. Arnold's own temper was now difficult to check; he already felt guilty that they were here, but he also felt Alston was being unnecessarily unpleasant. It caused a confusion of emotions in him, but anger was foremost. Contemptuously, he flipped open the plastic folder. 'As you can see—'

There was a short silence.

'What are those?' Alston demanded icily.

Arnold had slipped the newspaper cuttings into the folder.

They belonged to the library, not to Elfreda. He extracted them silently and handed them to Alston. 'I'm sorry,' he said quietly.

The man was breathing hard. He glanced quickly at the cuttings and then back to Arnold. 'And the rest?'

'I told you. Elfreda's notes.'

'I want to see them.'

'They relate to the field site!'

'You've already lied to me once. Why should I take your word now?'

Arnold glared at him. Suddenly he had had enough. They were in the wrong, being here, but Alston was going too far.

He turned to the three silent young men. 'Come on. We're going.'

'Landon. Those notes—'

Arnold stared at him coolly and shook his head. 'Mr Alston, you can go to hell.'

'You've trespassed here. I want that folder!'

'So sue me,' Arnold growled and led the way out of the library, through the hallway and down the front steps of the house. He was aware of Alston behind them, following them, clutching the cuttings. He seemed to have realized he had overreacted. 'Look here, Landon . . . It's just . . . it's just that I told Dr Williams . . .'

Arnold ignored him.

He ushered the three young men across the drive to the cars. When he drove into the lane, following the car driven by Ainsley Close, Arnold glanced in his rear mirror — Stephen Alston was standing at the top of the steps in front of the house, staring after them. He was clearly very upset by what had happened.

So was Arnold.

* * *

'I suppose he had every right to be furious,' Rena Williams muttered. 'He had told me, after all, that he was withdrawing permission.'

'Oh, for God's sake,' Geoffrey Westwood interposed irritably. 'You'd have thought we were doing something illegal!'

'Entering someone's house without permission isn't exactly ethical,' Arnold suggested. While he was still smarting at Alston's attitude and rudeness, he felt that he himself had not behaved too well. If Alston wanted to see the notes, where was the harm? Arnold regretted having reacted so childishly himself now — it would have been more dignified to allow Alston sight of Elfreda's scribblings. They were completely unimportant anyway.

'But damn it, why did the man get so uptight about it?' Westwood insisted. 'You'd think we were behaving nefariously. We were only checking on some damn references. That was no reason for him to start bawling about his rights!'

'It's my fault,' Rena Williams said crisply. 'I should not have agreed to the lads going down there to start with.'

'Stuff and rubbish! The man's an irrational idiot!'

Attempting to calm troubled waters, Arnold said mildly, 'Well, at least we managed to check all the references Professor Westwood raised. The lads have made notes — I think we'll need to study them in detail tonight at the hotel, before we go much further.'

Westwood grunted. 'Maybe so. But I think we can make a start. I've been looking closely at the whole area this afternoon. I think it's clear it is a platform, and I've dug away at one corner. There's certainly a void down below, a pit of some sort, but how deep I can't tell. I didn't want to drop anything down to check — it could cause damage. We should have brought in the geophysicists, and to hell with the expense.' He shook his head doubtfully. 'Anyway, if we rearrange the planks now I think we can work on the skeleton. We've taken all the photographs we need — we can probably start moving the skeleton itself. And then, I hope, open up the pit tomorrow morning. What do you think, Dr Williams?'

'I think it's possible,' she agreed doubtfully. 'But I'm not certain how we're going to lift the platform. We'll check the notes the lads have made. But it's going to be delicate work—'

'All the more reason to remove the skeleton. We don't want the thing falling into the pit.'

It was agreed. They arranged the planking and began the awkward work of removing the ancient bones from the platform. It took them well over an hour and the light was fading fast, but they completed the task, and laid out the bones, some of which had become detached in the process of movement, on a plastic sheet on the grass.

'That's enough for me for one day,' Rena Williams suggested. 'I think I'd better pay a brief call at Hartshorn House to make an apology to Alston. Then I'll get back to the hotel. We'll need to have the skeleton locked away in the hut . . .'

'Professor Westwood and I can do that,' Arnold suggested. 'If it's all right with him, the rest of you can knock off.'

'Geoffrey?'

He nodded. 'Better Landon and I do it, rather than have those clumsy fingers messing things up.'

'We'll get it done,' Arnold assured her. 'Professor Westwood and I can move the remains into the hut and lock up if you leave us the key.'

'If you're sure,' Rena Williams said. Arnold could see she was tired, perhaps drained by the guilt she felt at having exposed the team to Stephen Alston's wrath, and not looking forward to her encounter with him, to apologize. He guessed it would be a very brief meeting.

'We're sure,' Arnold said. Westwood was already kneeling beside the pile of bones, starting to rearrange them.

* * *

The work took rather longer than Arnold had expected. They had taken a few final photographs before removal but it was necessary to tag some of the bones in order to log their placing. It was slow, deliberate work, and it was not helped by the fact that dusk was falling. Finally they completed the job and had the skeleton safely stored away in the hut. They had started to collect their personal belongings together when Westwood pointed to the yellow plastic folder on the table.

'What's that?'

'The cause of the final battle,' Arnold replied grimly.

'The girl's notes?'

'That's right.'

Westwood picked up the folder and riffled through the notes. 'Hardly worth the bother, I'd have said. For the time she spent down there she didn't come up with much that's useful to us, as far as I can see.'

'She'd catalogued articles in various texts and journals,' Arnold argued defensively. 'It means we can follow up—'

'But what's the point of this?' Westwood demanded in a sarcastic tone. 'This list of letters and numbers for checking . . . no use to us, if we don't know what they refer to. You might just as well have given Alston the lot and let him get on with it.'

'It was her work. It didn't belong to him. I gave him the cuttings, anyway.'

'Cuttings?'

Arnold shrugged. 'I didn't read them closely. They concerned security at the British Museum.'

'What the hell was the girl doing looking at those?'

'Interest, probably. You know how it is. I often set out to do some research and then get sidetracked.' He paused, looking at Westwood uncertainly. He knew Dr Williams had not told Westwood about the discovery of the jadeite locket ring, because of the bad blood that had existed between the professor and the research student. 'Talking of sidetracks, do you know anything about Pelham Price-Kennedy, the man who worked with Sir Henry Alston on a number of projects?'

'Price-Kennedy?' Westwood wrinkled his nose in thought. 'Yes . . . the name rings bells. He worked with Alston at Fleetham but got no credit for it. Fell out with the old man later. Then got himself drowned, I believe.'

'What was the cause of the quarrel, do you know?'

'All a bit vague, I understand. Although I read a postgraduate thesis once . . . now when was that . . . ? Ten years since, maybe. I had a student who took his master's by thesis, and he argued . . . now what was it? That's right, he suggested the argument was partly about Fleetham, and partly about the Alston Collection.'

'You mean the one Stephen Alston keeps in the bank?'

'And which is going to the States, if a licence can be obtained.' Westwood nodded. 'That's right. My student argued there was the chance that Price-Kennedy suggested the provenance of the collection was not all it should be. But I couldn't agree with his thesis on that point. There was no evidence. Rumours, certainly . . .'

'How do you mean?'

'In academic circles.' He paused, staring at Arnold thoughtfully. 'What did you say those cuttings were about?'

Arnold shrugged. 'Security at the British Museum.'

Westwood smiled thinly. 'Maybe the girl was running down the same doubtful path that was shown to me years ago. Researchers "acquiring" items from museums for their own collections. But where's the proof? And why couldn't she just get on with what she was supposed to do at the library?' He picked up his bag. 'I'm off. You'll lock up?'

Arnold nodded.

He felt ill at ease, oddly disorientated. It was probably due to the outburst he had suffered from Alston but he could not be sure. It was possibly a combination of things: Elfreda's death, the jadeite ring, the uncertainties surrounding the barrow burial.

He was reluctant to go back to the hotel. After a little while he locked up the shed and walked out into the gathering gloom. The evening was still; nothing seemed to move and there was a half-moon, pale and low in the sky, tipping the edge of the fell with a ghostly glow, deepening the shadows that ran down towards the ancient lake site and making everything unfamiliar in shape and form. He looked about him and wondered what it would have been like, millennia ago, when warrior peoples would have lived on these fells, building their stone-walled villages, fighting over land and slaves and women, creating a society that would have been shaman-ridden, violent and mystic in their beliefs, strange in their rituals.

They would have been closely bound to the hills and the forests, would have claimed relationships with the wolf and the bear, and on nights like this they would have huddled around their smoky fires and dozed and dreamed terrifying dreams. In that society, perhaps, the people buried in the barrow had lived out their lives and met their violent ends. Sacrifice and blood-letting would have been common, to bring good harvests, to plead and intercede with the gods of rock and wood, stylized in their art depicting the boar and the eagle and the powerful stag. He shivered, and almost without thinking he turned and headed back towards the tented area.

It was dark under the screen. He stood beside the ancient platform and tried to imagine what it would have been like, the digging of the pit under the flaming torches, the interment of the sacrificial victims, decapitated, placed in their tomb in a shamanic ritual. As he stood there, musing, the ancient whispers came back into his head. A coldness touched his back, and his skin crawled; he imagined he felt icy fingers brush his cheek. He heard a slight movement behind him and an unreasoning panic leapt in his chest.

He turned.

The dark figure was standing there, motionless, silent. His heart thundered, and a faint, shrill wailing in his head seemed to rise to a crescendo as he had a brief, swift vision of a deathly figure from the distant past. Then reason prevailed. He stepped forward. 'Westwood?' he said. 'Is that you? You forget something?'

The blow came swinging at him from the darkness. The heavy wood struck him across the shoulder and he heard his collarbone crack. He staggered backwards under the violence of the blow, a sharp stab of pain striking through his shoulder before another clubbing blow took him at the side of his head. He was aware of the club raised again, swinging at him once more and he leaned forward, in spite of the thrust of pain in his neck and shoulder and grabbed at the man in front of him. They lurched together, straining and locked in their struggle, silent except for their harsh, labouring breathing. But Arnold was weak; the pain from the broken collarbone sent agonizing spears into his chest and he found himself falling backwards. Desperately he wound his fingers into his assailant's jacket and they whirled around. Arnold was forced back, and felt the edge of the trenching under his feet, the earth at the edge of the platform giving way with a cracking, rushing sound. Wildly, he swung his assailant around in a desperate attempt to avoid the fall, but the next moment they were both crashing onto the platform. It was not equal to their weight; he felt it give with a rending sound and then they were both falling, tumbling into the pit below the burial platform. Something hard struck at the side of Arnold's head and he crashed to the floor of the pit, winded, unable to draw breath for a moment in the darkness.

But the flailing hands no longer grabbed at him. He lay there, prone on the floor of the burial pit they had sought to open, but his assailant no longer fought him. Instead, Arnold heard an odd, snoring sound, and slow, tortured breathing, like an animal in pain. He waited, unable to move for the shooting agony in his shoulder, feeling the slow trickle of blood matting his hair, and still dazed by the blow to his head. He lay there and listened until the gurgling sound came, slowly, and in a little while ceased.

It was then that his own senses left him, and the fetid darkness gathered him in.

* * *

There were a thousand whispers in that darkness. There was the sound of small, scurrying feet seeking food in rotting flesh; there was the booming sound of a horn, distant and far off in time, and the clash of steel, the creak of leather, the snarling breath of dying men. He fancied he could smell the oily smoke that came from the flaring torches that lined the pit and yet there was no light. The wind played its part, moaning and whining in dark corners, snapping at cloaks that whirled raggedly in the dimness. There were echoes of ritual chants in his head that drove on and on, a call to the dark heavens and the darker earth, dances of death to a wild, insistent, drug-enhanced rhythm. The voices of crying women were added to the harsh sound of battle, but when they all died away in his confused mind, the night was still and black. Spirits seemed to rise up around him, the ancient dead, and his head filled with visions of fire and smoke and the glaring eyes of the animal gods. They were there all about him, snarling, their fangs black with blood, talons crooked for the tearing of flesh, the great wings beating in the air.

And beyond it all, on the high fell, he seemed to hear, as if in a folk memory, the triumphant cry of a woman, the bringer of death, the shape-shifter.

It was silent in the pit at last. His senses returned and the visions withdrew to the darker recesses of his mind. He reached out a hand, feeling about, scrabbling with his fingers at the floor of the grave pit. He touched a foot: it lay unmoving. He sat back then, hearing nothing, and knew that the man with him in the pit was dead.

He waited silently, thinking of nothing, but weighed down by the darkness. Time passed, and it meant nothing to him. He waited for death in the ancient pit, but it did not come as he drifted in and out of the conscious world.

Instead, hours later, there were faint lights and voices.

They had missed him at the George and Dragon, and come searching. Torchlight stabbed into the pit and he heard someone shout. Then the light slipped sideways and he saw the man with him in the grave. His face was distorted by the shadows, his mouth open, black, dried blood marking his jawline, eyes staring sightlessly. One arm was flung wide, held by the broken shaft of the spear.

It had entered Stephen Alston's armpit and driven straight into his heart. The thrust, Arnold guessed incoherently, would have been swift and deadly; the last killing of the king who had been interred in this tomb.

4

Jane had got him a private room at the hospital where he had been treated for shock, concussion, and a broken collarbone. She had advised him that he needed to take some time off from work. Karen Stannard had agreed when, surprisingly, she called in to see how he was. She could not resist telling him she had also been appointed to a think tank committee by the Secretary of State, as a result of her brilliant contributions to the Stiles Committee, but at least she had expressed concern for his welfare. Even if she'd said it with an obvious degree of insincerity.

A week later, when Arnold was recuperating at Jane's bungalow in Framwellgate — she had insisted he could not look after himself with a broken collarbone — Rena Williams called to see him. Arnold was amused to see the wariness with which Jane allowed her in, stressing that Arnold was still not up to long visits.

'It's only a broken collarbone,' he protested.

'And a bang on the head,' Jane snapped. 'That could have done unseen damage.'

'Not enough to justify my being mollycoddled in this way!'

'Dr Williams?' Jane appealed. 'What do you think?'

Rena Williams caught the slight frostiness in her tone. She ducked her head awkwardly. 'I only called really to see how Arnold was recovering. And maybe to bring him up to date. But I shan't stay long.'

'That's all right then. Sit down, Dr Williams,' Jane herself took a seat: she was not leaving Rena Williams alone with Arnold.

'Have you done any more work in the pit?' Arnold asked. Dr Williams shook her head. 'Not a great deal. The police have been up there, of course, because of Alston, so we've not had the chance to return.'

'Why on earth did Alston attack me like that?' Arnold wondered.

Rena Williams took a deep breath. 'I've spent some time with Chief Inspector Garrett. So has Geoffrey Westwood — in fact, it was Geoffrey who came up with the answer, oddly enough, from Elfreda's notes.'

'Those damn notes! What did *they* have to do with it?'

'Everything. The argument is still largely a theory, it seems, but the police are fairly confident they'll piece it together in time. It all hinges really on Elfreda's notes. It was Geoffrey who first picked up on them: he pointed out that the lists of letters and numbers seem to have been taken from the Brazier article on security at the British Museum. In other words, they refer to items that were stolen from the museum.'

'So?'

'He suggested that Garrett should instigate a check with items in the Alston Collection.'

'Why on earth—?'

'Geoffrey pointed to Elfreda's note about crosschecking holdings. What holdings? She'd been working in Hartshorn House, so it's logical to suggest she was referring to the items held in the Alston Collection. Then there were the newspaper cuttings — they all referred to much the same thing. Losses at the museum, security, rumours about academic researchers who "lifted" items. He suggested Elfreda might have wondered whether there was fire as well as smoke . . . and maybe the smoke related to Sir Henry Alston.'

'You're not serious!'

'Never more so.' She paused reflectively. 'It was interesting to see Geoffrey Westwood second-guessing Elfreda. He'd never given her credit for anything, and yet now . . . I could see he was trying to get inside her head.' She shook herself out of her reverie. 'Anyway, Geoffrey got a commission out of it immediately. The police are paying him to check the Alston Collection. He rang me last night. He's already found two items on the museum list in the collection.'

'You mean Alston stole items over the years?'

Rena Williams inclined her head gravely. 'It seems so. He visited the museum regularly in the twenties and thirties, was well known there, a respected figure, an expert. He took items home with him for study — and, it seems, sometimes never returned them. It would appear that there were suspicions at the time, gossip and rumours, but no one had the courage to come right out and accuse the great man. He was too big a name, with his knighthood and his reputation with the Establishment.'

'It's hardly credible,' Jane suggested.

Rena Williams eyed her quizzically. 'I can believe it. Academics can be cowards. People whispered in corners but did nothing. A few articles like that by Brazier were published later, but with the Alston Collection locked away no one could actually point the finger with any confidence. And then it was all forgotten. Sir Henry died; his son Christopher left the collection locked up. And then Stephen Alston wanted to sell it. But Elfreda, by chance, came across the list, read the articles, began to put two and two together. But she made a mistake.'

'How do you mean?' Jane Wilson asked.

Rena Williams turned to her. 'Looking back, I knew Elfreda was worried about something, but I thought it was just resentment at working in the library.'

'I got the feeling at one stage she wanted to talk to me about something that was bothering her,' Arnold added. 'And Ainsley Close knew she was upset, too . . .'

'Unfortunately she got sidetracked. Instead of talking it over with us, she made the mistake of telling Stephen Alston of her suspicions.'

Arnold could guess what was coming, and a slow crawl of horror touched him. 'Alston killed her . . .'

Rena Williams nodded soberly. 'Garrett tells me the police were already getting suspicious of Alston . . . his alibi didn't really stand up when they looked at it. They were still questioning Brendan Green but they hadn't charged him, and were beginning to look again at Alston . . . Anyway, they now believe that Elfreda told Alston about her suspicions and he panicked, attacked her in the lane, killed her, and then tried to make it appear as though she'd been raped.'

'But why did he panic like that?' Jane asked. 'Surely not because of a long-forgotten, suppressed scandal!'

Arnold frowned thoughtfully. He glanced at Jane. 'Alston was penniless. He was on the point of selling the house and the collection. He'd found a buyer. And he'd arranged to marry Margaret Eaton, the buyer's daughter.'

'And the Eatons are a very upright, moral family, it seems,' Rena Williams added. 'Alston must have realized that if it came out that there were stolen items in the Alston Collection the sale would fall through. And it's likely the marriage would also go west in the resultant hullabaloo. The Eatons would not appreciate publicity of that kind. Moreover, Alston could be bound up in lawsuits for years . . . he saw all his plans going down the drain, and he reacted.'

'So he killed her?' Jane asked incredulously.

'Garrett thinks he may have tried to argue with Elfreda, but she didn't like him, there was already a certain edge between them . . . and she could be sharp-tongued. If he asked her to keep quiet, she'd have told him to get lost. I think it cost her . . . her life.'

Arnold tried to recall the image of the vivacious, laughing Elfreda, but it was overscored by the thought of the way she must have struggled for her life in the lane. 'When I was down at the library the last time,' Arnold said slowly, 'everything was piled haphazardly about the floor. He must have been looking for something . . . the information which had led Elfreda to the truth. But he probably wouldn't even have known what to look for. And Westwood told us he replaced the books she'd been using — he probably shelved them out of sequence. Alston had to start from scratch . . . almost blindly . . .'

'He would have found them, in time,' Rena Williams guessed, 'but you beat him to it.'

'And he realized his problem hadn't gone away. If Elfreda could work it out, maybe I . . .'

Rena Williams nodded. 'I saw him that evening, to apologize. He didn't seem to care — he was in a highly agitated state. He asked about you, and I told him you were still up at the site. To that extent, I feel I'm a little to blame for the subsequent attack . . .'

Arnold shook his head. 'If not then, some other time,' he suggested, 'if Alston was panicked enough to try to get the notes back from me. I understand now why he was so insistent at the library. He didn't know what I had, but he was scared it could lead to the same conclusion Elfreda reached. The irony is, I doubt if I would have made the connection without the cuttings, which I'd already returned to him.'

Dr Williams was silent for a little while. 'There's another thing,' she added.

'Yes?'

'I gave the police the jadeite locket ring.' She hesitated. 'You didn't tell me it had belonged to Pelham Price-Kennedy. It was only when Miss Wilson told the police, after I took the ring to them . . . It's odd in a way: Elfreda was preoccupied with her suspicions about the Alston Collection, and she never made the connection between Price-Kennedy and the ring, even though she'd seen the photograph, as you had.'

Arnold stared at her and waited.

'The police are of the opinion that the ring wasn't lost by accident.'

'Not lost in 1936?' Arnold asked, his mouth dry.

'No. The bones Elfreda found in the bank — they think they could have been the owner's.'

'Pelham Price-Kennedy? But he drowned at sea in 1939,' Arnold protested.

'We have only Sir Henry Alston's word for that. He said that both he and Price-Kennedy had been invited to Lord Cradock's yacht — but there's no independent corroboration of that. There's a theory they are now working on — Price-Kennedy quarrelled with Sir Henry Alston while they were working together at Hawgill, because Price-Kennedy had found out about Sir Henry's thefts. He possibly threatened to expose him, branding him as a thief, purloining items for his personal collection. Garrett thinks maybe they argued, Alston killed him, and buried him in the field at Garrigill. But he would have been worried thereafter that the body might come to light. That's why he jumped at the chance, years later, to buy the site.'

'And that's why Sir Henry never investigated the barrow itself,' Arnold murmured. 'Because if he'd brought an investigation team there, it was always possible they might accidentally disinter the remains of the man he'd buried in 1939.' He shook his head. 'But how much of this is supposition? How much can they prove?'

Rena Williams shrugged. 'It's a working hypothesis at the moment, although Geoffrey has already come up with some evidence of theft, now he's looked at the Alston Collection. The forensic people might link the bones to Pelham Price-Kennedy eventually. But it was all so long ago . . . My guess is they'll never manage to prove everything . . . at least not regarding the death of Pelham Price-Kennedy. But they think that's what happened. Sir Henry killed him to avoid being exposed — and he was a vain man, much concerned by status and position—'

'He'd have stripped the body before he buried it,' Arnold mused. 'But in the darkness, maybe, he missed the ring, and it lay there half buried, until the rains — and Elfreda — came along more than fifty years later.'

They were all silent for a little while, preoccupied with their own thoughts. Dr Williams sighed and rose. 'I'd better be on my way. I'm off up to Garrigill, actually. I want to see when we can get back to the site, and what work we'll have to do.'

'Was much damage done?'

She nodded thoughtfully. 'The pair of you smashing through that platform made a hell of a mess. And the burial, well, as far as I can make out — and it's difficult with the police trampling around in the pit — it was a king burial. An upright interment, with his weapons to hand. The spear must have been placed upright in the ground, and when Alston went crashing in . . .' She glanced at him, frowning. 'It could easily have been you, Arnold.'

He shuddered. He could recall the close darkness again, and the stertorous breathing of the man dying beside him.

'Will you be able to reconstruct the burial itself?'

She shook her head. 'Not satisfactorily. Too much damage — from you, and the police. We have a collection of bones to sift through, and the artefacts, but whether we'll ever be able to piece together the details, and the rituals . . . I'm afraid I'm not very sanguine at the prospect.' She stared at him, her brow clouded. 'But it's an evil place, Arnold . . . I feel it. As to how you felt, down there in the darkness . . .'

Arnold was not sure whether he would ever be able to explain. Not to her, not even to Jane Wilson. But he knew his experience would come back, hauntingly, in his dreams.

5

When the grave pit of Volcas was finally excavated to the proper depth they brought the corpse of their chief out from under the shelter and they clothed it in a tunic with buttons of silver, and armlets of gold, and covered his body with a wide mantle. They brought fruits and onions and sweet-smelling herbs and threw them into the pit, together with the flesh of a pig. Two male slaves were strangled and decapitated, and their bodies placed in the pit, companions in the chief's long sojourn. And at the dawning of that last day the shamans took the slave woman and placed her in a separate hut and each of the six lieutenants of Volcas went in turn to the hut and each entered into her body.

And each man said to her, as they had intercourse, 'Tell your master that I have done this out of love for him.'

In the evening they constructed the platform of oak and bone and deer hide under the incantations of the shamans and they lashed the slave girl to it with thongs of leather, spread-eagled, and they gave her more fermented drink until she cried out in ecstasy, 'Look, I see my master in the green fields and with him are warriors and young men. He calls to me, he calls, and I will go to him . . .' And the warriors about her bayed in sorrow and in triumph.

Then the Angel of Death came to her and took from her ankles the two linked serpent rings she wore. The last cup was filled with the fermented drink and given to the slave woman to drink, and the woman destined for eternity with her lord sang her incoherent songs while the Angel of Death made the final preparations. The warriors gathered around and the torches were lit as the night shadows grew about them and in the smoky, dancing light they began to beat with their wooden staves upon the shields so that the slave woman's shrieks would not be heard, for other girls might become frightened and thus not seek death with their masters.

The six lieutenants returned and again had intercourse with the slave girl, as she was spread-eagled upon the bone and wood frame; then they laid her by the side of her dead master and two took her legs, two took her hands, and the woman called the Angel of Death put a rope around her neck. The two senior lieutenants pulled on the rope in opposite directions and the cries of the slave girl were stifled. Then the Angel of Death knelt above her and took in her hand a dagger with a broad stone blade and she thrust it, time and time again, deep into the breast of the girl, slipping it between her ribs while the two lieutenants pulled on the rope and she choked and she died.

The son of Volcas was naked as he entered the pit.

With two assistants he placed upright the body of his father and lashed it to the oak supports driven and pegged into the wall of the pit. The shield and sword of Volcas were placed near his right hand: the iron-bladed spear was driven haft first into the earth and locked beside his left hand, with its gleaming point raised towards the night sky and the mouth of the pit. The torches flared, playing their smoky light over the dead Volcas and his two slain companions, and the feet of the warriors beat the death stamp on the hard ground.

The Angel of Death stayed with them in the village until the ceremonies were complete. The rim of the pit was lined with stone, and the platform with the body of the slave girl was placed over the open mouth of the grave. The Angel of Death removed the head of the dead woman, and when the flesh had been stripped away and the jawbone detached she placed it face down with ritual incantations, trapping her spirit, to serve wordlessly and to look down upon her master, where he feasted and drank through eternity with the gods of the underworld. Then they covered the platform with hides and skins and earth.

Finally they placed the great stones, carved with the image of the boar god, on a raised stone lip above the platform and as the trees on the hill bent and strained under the rising night wind, the Angel of Death stood above the carved stone with arms spread wide to the darkness. In a high powerful voice she proclaimed her immortality; she called to the gods of the earth and sky, the boar, the stag, the eagle. And the warriors about her groaned as she foretold that this grave pit would forever be a place of worship and of blood, of sacrifice and death, how others would come and place their dead here above the lake and below the hill, and the gods of terror and darkness would watch over it for eternity, just as her own voice would be heard in the heavens and the hills, and in the minds of men, echoing down the centuries, until the end of time . . .

THE END

ALSO BY ROY LEWIS

ERIC WARD MYSTERIES

Book 1: THE SEDLEIGH HALL MURDER
Book 2: THE FARMING MURDER
Book 3: THE QUAYSIDE MURDER
Book 4: THE DIAMOND MURDER
Book 5: THE GEORDIE MURDER
Book 6: THE SHIPPING MURDER
Book 7: THE CITY OF LONDON MURDER
Book 8: THE APARTMENT MURDER
Book 9: THE SPANISH VILLA MURDER
Book 10: THE MARRIAGE MURDER
Book 11: THE WASTEFUL MURDER
Book 12: THE PHANTOM MURDER
Book 13: THE SLAUGHTERHOUSE MURDER
Book 14: THE TATTOO MURDER
Book 15: THE FOOTBALL MURDER
Book 16: THE TUTANKHAMUN MURDER
Book 17: THE ZODIAC MURDER

INSPECTOR JOHN CROW

Book 1: A LOVER TOO MANY
Book 2: ERROR OF JUDGMENT
Book 3: THE WOODS MURDER
Book 4: MURDER FOR MONEY
Book 5: MURDER IN THE MINE
Book 6: A COTSWOLDS MURDER
Book 7: A FOX HUNTING MURDER
Book 8: A DARTMOOR MURDER

ARNOLD LANDON MYSTERIES

Book 1: MURDER IN THE BARN
Book 2: MURDER IN THE MANOR
Book 3: MURDER IN THE FARMHOUSE
Book 4: MURDER IN THE STABLE YARD

Book 5: MURDER IN THE CHURCH
Book 6: MURDER IN THE HOUSE
Book 7: MURDER IN THE TOWER
Book 8: MURDER UNDER THE BRIDGE
Book 9: MURDER BY THE QUAY
Book 10: MURDER AT THE FOLLY
Book 11: MURDER IN THE FIELD

Thank you for reading this book.

If you enjoyed it please leave feedback on Amazon or Goodreads, and if there is anything we missed or you have a question about, then please get in touch. We appreciate you choosing our book.

Founded in 2014 in Shoreditch, London, we at Joffe Books pride ourselves on our history of innovative publishing. We were thrilled to be shortlisted for Independent Publisher of the Year at the British Book Awards.

www.joffebooks.com

We're very grateful to eagle-eyed readers who take the time to contact us. Please send any errors you find to corrections@joffebooks.com. We'll get them fixed ASAP.

Printed in Great Britain
by Amazon

72660541R00137